Return to Zion

I0642434

Return to Zion

The Seventh Art West Adventure

By Ben and Ann Witherington

PICKWICK *Publications* · Eugene, Oregon

RETURN TO ZION
The Seventh Art West Adventure

Pickwick Publications
An Imprint of Wipf and Stock Publishers
199 W. 8th Ave., Suite 3
Eugene, OR 97401

www.wipfandstock.com

ISBN 13: 978–1-62564–414–5

Cataloguing-in-Publication Data

Witherington, Ben, 1951–

    Return to Zion : the seventh Art West adventure / Ben Witherington III and Ann
Witherington

    226 p. ; 23 cm. Includes bibliographical references.

    ISBN 13: 978–1-62564–414–5

    1. Archaeology—Fiction. I. Witherington, Ann. II. Title.

PS3605 W55 2015

Manufactured in the U.S.A.   10/14/2015

A majority of the photos found in the book were provided graciously by Mark Fairchild. The authors and the publisher are grateful.

"This is what the LORD says: 'I will return to Zion and dwell in Jerusalem. Then Jerusalem will be called the city of Truth, and the mountain of the Lord will be called the Holy Mountain'"

—ZECHARIAH 8:3

"Jesus turned to them and said: 'Daughters of Jerusalem do not weep for me, weep for yourselves and your children'"

—LUKE 23:28

"Speak tenderly to Jerusalem and cry to her that her warfare is ended, that her iniquity is pardoned, that she has received from the Lord's hand a double portion for her sins"

—ISAIAH 40:2

CHAPTER ONE

BOXED IN

Now WELL PAST MIDNIGHT, the city was mostly silent on this Friday morning. Chilly gusts of wind blew down the road alongside the concrete wall erected around Bethlehem. The Hizma checkpoint on the north side of Jerusalem was not a beehive of activity at this hour; nevertheless, the guards drank more coffee to keep themselves alert. Besides, it was so cold they could hardly fall asleep. Instead, they turned the kerosene heater higher and warmed their hands vigorously.

The winds blew clouds of dust down the road alongside the concrete wall that ran through the Jerusalem suburb of Hizma. Once a thriving town with an educated workforce and low unemployment, Hizma is now a ghetto. Without an Israeli ID card, its citizens can no longer work in Jerusalem as they have done for generations. Travel back and forth is at the whim of the Israeli guards—sometimes they let people through and sometimes they don't. Rules can change depending on the time of day. Citizens of the Palestinian capital of Ramallah also use this checkpoint to get to Jerusalem. On a good day, the twenty-minute drive from Ramallah to Jerusalem can take up to two hours thanks to the checkpoint. While the Palestinians tended to just wave people coming into the West Bank right through, this was definitely not the modus operandi of the Israeli soldiers with traffic going in the opposite direction.[1]

1. The Israeli West Bank barrier, or separation wall, makes the Berlin Wall look like a backyard fence. When completed it will stretch over four hundred miles and effectively separate the West Bank from the rest of Israel. The majority of Palestinians will be fenced off and traversing the checkpoints is often difficult if not impossible.

Ever vigilant, Israeli guard Tevi Schneider noticed several men congregating near vans at least two hundred yards away from his booth. Pointing to the distant group, he said, "Jacob, let's go for a walk on the dark side." The pair quietly approached, taking advantage of every hiding spot. Finally, they were able to hear several voices speaking rapidly in Arabic, a language Tevi learned in preparation for his border patrol job.

"Move a little faster!" growled one of the four men. "Get this stuff on board!"

"Relax! Who's going to bother us? The Israelis are way over at the checkpoint probably trying to stay awake."

Tevi and Jacob crept closer. On Tevi's signal, they leapt out, their flashlights spotlighting the men and their two vans. "Halt! This is a security check!" cried Tevi.

Startled, one of the men began to run behind the vehicles, but Jacob stopped the man cold by pointing his M14 at him and herded him back to the group. Tevi called for more backup.

A tall man with a black beard and a red and white *keffiyeh* began to walk toward him. "Let me explain," he began with a smile.

"Down on your knees," barked Jacob. By then more guards arrived at a run. As he approached the black van, Tevi could see that the back doors were open. But he was not prepared for what he found inside. There were no less than eleven ossuaries, ancient burial boxes from the biblical period, neatly lined up, apparently ready to be transferred to the other vehicle. Tevi could see that one of them was quite ornate. "We received a memo to be on the lookout for stolen ossuaries," cried Tevi. "I think we've found them!"

"Looks like stolen antiquities to me," agreed Jacob. "I'll call the IAA police. This is out of our jurisdiction."

Tevi blinked and looked closely at the man standing by the empty van. "Say, haven't I seen you somewhere before? Aren't you one of the antiquities dealers in the Cardo?"

The man flinched, but did not answer the question replying instead in a deep raspy voice, "I will not say anything without my lawyer present."

"Whatever! You can all call your lawyers from headquarters, because that's where you're all going tonight. I'm sure they'll be thrilled to hear from you at this hour!" laughed Tevi.

And so it was that eleven ancient ossuaries were intercepted at the point where they were about to become items on the black market.[2] About twenty minutes later, the flashing lights of the IAA police van arrive, sirens blaring. "Just another dark night in Judea," Tevi said with a little laugh. "Never a dull moment!"

2. Recovery of the eleven ossuaries actually occurred Friday morning, March 28, 2014 after extensive detective work by the IAA and Shefet Police Station in Jerusalem. Read more: http://www.antiquities.org.il/Article_eng.aspx?sec_id=25&subj_id=240&id=4050&hist=1

~ ~ ~

Sean walked along the Pool of Siloam and stood near the entrance of Hezekiah's Tunnel in the Old City of David. He could see a man coming up the path—but it was not his intended contact! The man spotted him and began running. Sean also ran into the tunnel—the dark, wet, 1500-foot long tunnel. Somehow he knew he was running for his life. Sean was soon out of breath, completely out of breath, and yet still he continued running through the cold water. When he stopped briefly, he heard someone running toward him also, the splashing sounds echoing against the walls of the tunnel.

"I'm trapped!" he muttered. The phone call had promised money, a lot of money, for the evidence he had—photographic evidence of a crime, a crime so outrageous, so important, that men would kill to get hold of it. The footsteps were getting closer and closer on both sides. A shot rang out and Sean fell headlong into the water. Blood began to stream from the wound in the back of his head. Only seconds later, a dark shadow loomed over the fallen form, frantically searching for the precious evidence he sought. He emptied pockets until finally, zipped inside the man's jacket he found a flash drive. Two gold teeth gleamed in the dark.

"Ensh'allah" said Abdullah as he stepped over the body and walked out the front entrance with his newly-arrived accomplice. With a sinister laugh he remarked, "Just another night in old Jerusalem, another dark and dangerous night!"

CHAPTER TWO

NEWS TRAVELS FAST

IAA DIRECTOR DR. SAMUEL Cohen was very pleased with himself. Months of work had finally led to the interception of eleven stolen ossuaries, albeit, a bit by chance. He called a quick press conference for Friday noon. The *Jerusalem Post* and *Ha'aretz* were the first to arrive, followed by a better than usual showing from the international press. The word was out already.

Sammy, as his friends called him, began by explaining that the boxes were stolen from a cave near Jerusalem with the intent of being sold to collectors. He reported that IAA had been tracking the suspects for some time, and that the exchange involved an Israeli and a Palestinian seller attempting ultimately to make the sale to an Israeli customer. He added that the two most ornate boxes seem to have belonged to a nobleman and his family, and yes, several of the boxes contained bone fragments and pottery items buried with the deceased.

Dr. Ethan Klein, the IAA's Director of the Unit for the Prevention of Antiquities Robbery, rushed into the conference to help out. "We can learn from each ossuary about a different aspect of language, art, and burial practice. And we can learn about the soul of the person."[1] Klein was noted for his enthusiasm and the press was loving it.

When pressed for details, Klein went on to add that two of the ossuaries were inscribed in Hebrew with the names Yoezer and Ralphine. "These ossuaries held the remains primarily of rabbis, businessmen, and aristocrats of the time, in other words the social elite."

---

1. Quoted from IAA deputy director, Eitan Klein. Read more. http://news.national-post.com/2014/03/31/israel-unveils-11-ancient-burial-boxes-or-ossuaries-stolen-from-a-cave-after-midnight-raid-on-antiquities-dealers/

Finally, he reminded the press that the use of ossuaries became popular during the second century BC, influenced by the individualism of Greek and Roman societies. They fell out of fashion after Roman domination of Jerusalem in AD 70, though the practice continued into the second century and was even taken up by the followers of Jesus.

When challenged about the authenticity of the ossuaries by Simon Kalman, famous for being the one reporter who sat through the entire James ossuary trial, Klein added he had no doubts about the authenticity of the latest discovery. "These ossuaries are authentic," he affirmed. "Everything here smells authentic."

Cohen was beaming throughout the short news conference. He was still in damage control after the humiliation of losing the trial of Oded Golan. The judge ruled that Golan was wrongly accused of forging the first-century ossuary bearing the inscription, "James, son of Joseph, brother of Jesus." After years of litigation Cohen rued the fact that Golan would probably never turn it over to the IAA!

Today's recovery of eleven ossuaries would begin the rehabilitation of the reputation of the IAA. What Cohen could not have anticipated was that this story, after being the talk in the coffee shops on Ben Yehuda Street over the weekend, would disappear entirely off the radar after Monday morning.

One reporter from the *Jerusalem Post* asked a surprising question. "Do either of you have any information on the body that was found this morning at the end of Hezekiah's Tunnel? Apparently, the man wasn't carrying any identification."

Cohen and Klein looked at each other in genuine shock, both shaking their heads. "We haven't heard about this yet! That's an active dig and a major tourist site! I guarantee I'll be checking into this right away!"

Sighing loudly, Sammy called Police Commissioner Danino right after the short conference. "Is it true you found a dead man in Hezekiah's Tunnel?"

The Police Chief confirmed it all. "He's not from around here— American I think. We haven't identified him yet. Our internal Intelligence Agency, Mossad, is still checking his prints. Right now the tunnel is closed to tourists of course. It's a crime scene! But I promise to keep you in the loop given I know how much you're involved in the City of David dig!"

"Thanks. I hate getting my news from the news!" groaned Sammy before hanging up.

CHAPTER THREE

PRELUDE TO A REUNION

It was a damp Monday morning, half past eight, and the wind was whipping up the incline of Mount Scopus, 2700 feet above sea level. Grace walked quickly, her collar turned up against the wind, hoping to get to class a few minutes early. Though she was going to give yet another lecture at Hebrew University's main campus, her mind was far from the classroom. Two things predominated her thoughts—her daughter Yelena, and the storm clouds that hovered over the Holy Land. Clashes between Israel and Palestinians, Hezbollah, Iran, Syria and others were endless. Even relations with the US were suffering due primarily to Netanyahu's hard line on Palestinian and Iranian issues. So many distracting ill winds were blowing through Jerusalem and her mind. It seemed like nothing could keep her focused on her scholarly work these days.

The political situation had not been getting better in the past few months, with Israelis shelling Gaza yet again and Palestinians retaliating by blowing up buses in Haifa. The struggle for turf seemed unending and relentless with no peace and quiet in sight anywhere, or by any means. And what did this augur for Yelena if she grew up in Israel? Now officially on the citizen list at fourteen years of age as the adopted child of Manny Cohen and Grace Levine, Yelena had blossomed into a beautiful and bright young lady whose modern Israeli Hebrew was coming along nicely. Just last fall she celebrated her *bas mitzvah*. Even the Wests had flown in from America to be there on the special day. What future was there for Yelena in this volatile country? Maybe she could get some fresh perspectives when her friends arrived soon for a reunion of sorts.

The reunion, as she had dubbed it, was a get together of all those who had been influential in one way or another in the grand opening of the

Lazarus Museum on the grounds of the Israel Museum. Recently a bougainvillea-covered walkway had been built to connect the two. Artifacts from the Lazarus tomb; the Gospel of John manuscript written by Lazarus, the Beloved Disciple; second-century works by Papias; and many donations from the el Said family would be housed in separate rooms of the Museum. It was too bad, thought Grace, that the Q document found at Capernaum would not be moved to Jerusalem any time soon. In any case, the ribbon-cutting ceremony would take place at the end of the following week.

The other reason for having the reunion now was that Khalil el Said was not well. His cancer was terminal and the doctors only gave him a few months to live at most. Though he still looked all right to the undiscerning eye, much of the time he had no energy due to the chemo treatments. Hannah, his daughter was looking after him, a task that was becoming a full time job.

Much had changed for all of those involved in these recent discoveries. In the interim, Grace married Manny Cohen and adopted Yelena. Art married Dr. Marissa Okur who was now expecting a child. Hannah, despite being raped by her then ex-husband, rejoiced in the birth of a son, Samuel. Grayson Johnson, for his part, was married to his archaeological work first at Caesarea Philippi and now at Caesarea Maritima, though he had mustered up enough courage to ask Sarah, owner of Solomon's Porch coffee shop, out on several dates (made possible by her divorce from Yakov). Jake Arafat was married to Melody, a Christian girl from Wilmington, North Carolina. Meanwhile, Jake, who used to play for Manny's team, Maccabi Elite, had become an NBA star. Yes, much had changed, but soon the old gang would be back together again and eager to reminisce.

Entering the biblical studies building at Hebrew University, Grace headed down the hall, her red high heels clicking on the marble floor. Today's subject was Aramaic inscriptions from the Second Temple period—Grace's strongest area of expertise. She could give this lecture in her sleep. But for some reason she was so preoccupied, she decided to take her dusty lectures notes to class.

Just as Grace entered the lecture hall, a huge explosion went off which shook the floor of the building. Grace grabbed the doorframe to keep from falling down. Plaster fell from the ceiling in the old classroom.

"Wow!" she said. "What was that?"

The twenty-five students were stunned into silence but raced to the windows. From their perch high on Mt. Scopus they looked down the

Kidron Valley and over to the Temple Mount. As their line of sight scanned the Old City they were shocked by a revelation. The golden Dome of the Rock now had a gaping hole in it! Smoke was billowing toward them.

Grace joined the students at the window and saw what they saw. No one spoke. Finally, Grace expressed what they were all thinking. "That could be the last straw, the prelude to all out war!"

Suddenly her cell phone startled everyone. Dumping her whole purse on the nearest desk, she quickly flipped open her phone and heard the one voice she most wanted to hear. "Mom! What just happened?"

CHAPTER FOUR

YULIYA'S DISCOVERY

YULIYA KARPOVA NEVER COULD choose between philosophy and art, so she simply studied both. Her first PhD came from Freiburg, Germany for her work on the philosopher Heidegger who had much to say about the Philosophy of Art. Thanks to her, many of Heidegger's works were translated into English. Her second PhD, specifically in symbolism and art, came from the University of Chicago. Combining all this with a BA and MA in religion, she was already recognized as an expert in the philosophy of art from a Christian perspective. What most intrigued her were the symbolism and aesthetic qualities of the ancient designs she found everywhere in Turkey. Her area of expertise included Greco-Roman and Byzantine art, especially the artistic patterns in the architecture, the pottery, the ceramics, and even the icons. She was now on loan from the Sorbonne as a visiting research professor in residence at the Istanbul Archaeology Museum.

Right now, she was sitting in the garden of the Museum café sipping a cup of Turkish coffee while staring at the picture she brought with her. Two uniformed men were bent over a table. They seemed to be poking at something very intently. Finally it dawned on her! Finishing her Turkish coffee, she hurried from the café and back to her small office.

Thumbing through her carefully organized, computerized picture files, a smile creased her face. She unconsciously fingered the blue and white pashmina she was wearing that morning and exclaimed to no one but herself, "They're playing a game, an ancient game! Imagine putting a picture of soldiers playing a game on a fourth century Greek urn. It's the ancient equivalent of backgammon," she exclaimed, looking at the photo she just discovered in her files, a picture Dr. Mark Fairchild, an American colleague, had sent her of a backgammon board housed in the Antalya museum in Turkey.

Just then her phone announced a text message from her very young Russian friend, Yelena Levine. "All Hades breaking loose here; somebody blew up Dome of the Rock!"

Yuliya suddenly wasn't smiling any more. Her thoughts turned from her own life in Istanbul, to her friends in Zion.

CHAPTER FIVE

TREMORS

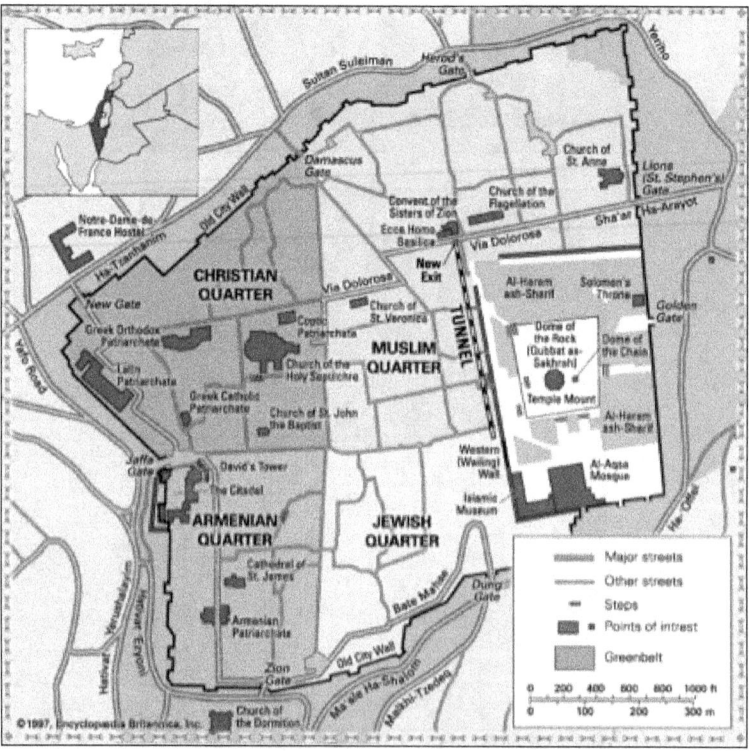

THE GROUND AND BUILDINGS shook the whole way down the Cardo, all the way to the Damascus Gate. In the antiquities shop owned by Kahlil and his daughter Hannah el Said, ancient pottery lamps fell onto the counters. Two precious lamps fell to the floor and broke. Hannah immediately locked the door and put up the closed sign. *Earthquakes bring out the looters*, she thought to herself. *Now where did I put that broom?*

"Hannah, what in the world was that?" asked a weary voice from the bedroom in the back of the shop.

"Probably nothing to worry about, Father; perhaps a little tremor. Lie back down and get some more rest. We have to take you for another chemo treatment later this morning. I've got everything under control in the shop."

Hannah thought back to all the grand plans she had to move her family to a nicer home. All that had been put on hold when Khalil was diagnosed with cancer.

There was a groan that echoed down the little hallway, followed by, "I don't see the point of any more treatments. They will not cure me, I am sure." Kahlil el Said might be an Islamic mystic but in most things he was a realist. He felt sure that he would be gathered to his ancestors before long, and he wanted to make sure that everything was in order—the will, the shop, the bank accounts—before he passed away.

"Father you never know what may help. For sure, the treatments have *not* taken away your appetite altogether."

"No, I suppose not. Speaking of which, what is for breakfast?"

Hannah smiled. If her father was still asking about food, it was a good sign. Just then another voice was heard: "Momma, Momma!" Immediately Hannah put down the dustpan with its shards of a pottery lamp, and hurried to the back of the building. Her men were hungry.

Grabbing two-year old Samuel and parking him in his high chair, Hannah poured cereal bits on the tray and Samuel immediately began stuffing them in his mouth. She filled Samuel's favorite cup with pomegranate juice and offered it to him. Two pudgy hands reached out eagerly. This would keep Samuel occupied for a bit.

Kahlil came staggering into the kitchen, yawning and wearing a robe. Hannah looked up and smiled at the scraggly beard and uncombed hair that confronted her. She told herself she needed to cherish every moment she had with her father, as it was uncertain how much longer he would be with her. Having reached his eightieth year, his hair white and his beard gray, he was quite the patriarch.

"So father, I was thinking bacon, pork sausage, and sliced ham for breakfast," said Hannah winking at Kahlil, waiting to see what sort of rise that would get out of him.

"Excellent," said Kahlil laughing. "And while we are at it, we could wash it down with some good Maccabi beer. That would make a breakfast of champions for a good Muslim like me."

"Actually father I am cooking soft scrambled eggs and warming flat bread. That should suffice until mid-day."

"But what was that noise we heard? Was it really just an earthquake tremor? It sounded more like a bomb going off."

Just then someone began pounding on the shop door. Hannah raced to see what sort of emergency could prompt such an assault. Peering by the side of the blinds, Hannah saw their old friend Omar—and Omar looked very anxious.

Hannah opened the door, and before she could say anything, Omar blurted out, "Didn't you hear the explosion? Someone blew up something on the Temple Mount—maybe even the Dome of the Rock! Smoke is rising. It must mean war will be upon us quickly."

Hannah's face went ghostly pale, and she ran to the back of the shop crying, "Father, Father, the worst thing ever has happened!"

CHAPTER SIX

THE SOCIETY OF THE MILLENNIAL DAWN AWAKES

On a normal Monday morning, the meeting of the Society of the Millennial Dawn would have been rather routine.[1] There would have been a report of whether the camera aimed at the Golden Gate, which films 24/7, had anything notable to tell the faithful. There would have been a review of regional events that might, or might not, be related to certain biblical prophecies. There would have been a treasurer's report, a statement about possible new members of the Society, and finally a Bible study led by the founder and leader of the Society, Jamison Parkes Law. Refreshments would certainly follow.

This, however, was no ordinary Monday morning. Something unexpected, even possibly cataclysmic, had happened, and the faithful were now gathered to figure out how to interpret the event in light of Scripture. Granted, there was nothing specific in the OT or NT prophecies about the Dome of the Rock blowing up, but for them hope sprung eternal that some connection could be made to the Word.

"I'm telling you there has to be some connection between this event and the prophecies about the rebuilding of the Temple," insisted Parkes Law. "After all, you can't rebuild the Temple unless that Islamic shrine is removed from the Temple Mount and the Jews reclaim their holy place."

"Granted," replied Taylor Bowles, a new member of the society who had just moved from Dallas to be in Jerusalem for the anticipated rapture of the true believers. "But, I don't see anything specific in the text about

---

1. The Society had moved their meetings from Thursday evening to Monday morning, when it dawned on them that a Society like theirs, with a name like that, needed to meet in the morning! See the first Art West adventure, *The Lazarus Effect*, ch. 9.

bombs going off, or a war on the Temple Mount leading to a Jewish take-over of that part of the city."

"Have you really not read Zechariah 9 carefully where it talks about the King coming to Zion triumphant and victorious having already cut off the chariots of the enemy and the warhorse from Jerusalem itself? This was only partially fulfilled at the first coming of Jesus, but now the part about getting rid of enemy combatants must be fulfilled before the rapture comes." There was silence in the room as the twelve members of the Society contemplated what had just been said.

"So, we need to prepare for Armageddon then?" asked Stevie Howard, the newest member of the inner circle. "I guess that means we need to send someone over to the Temple Mount to start monitoring events?"

By now Parkes Law was red-faced and frustrated by the denseness of his fellow members of the Society. "You think?" retorted Parkes Law. "We need to batten down the hatches as well. I'm sending two of you off to the grocery store. We need to stockpile supplies, lots of supplies."

"Yeah, the Mormons over at their University near the Mount of Olives are way ahead of us on that," replied Stevie and there was nodding of heads among the group. The level of excitement was ratcheting up. Could the rapture really be close at hand?

"Won't those Mormon folks be surprised when they are left behind, canned goods and all?" smirked Smith Davidson, the assistant leader of the Society. "But in the meantime, we need to prepare for the End, and supplies are the first order of business."

"But wait a minute! What about the tribulation? We need to discuss the whole pre-trib or mid-trib thing," said Taylor. "I mean, if the rapture is pre-tribulation, then what's the point in stocking up for the melee? We won't be here! But on the other hand, if it's mid-trib, then I see the point."

Trying to control his temper, Parkes Law gritted his teeth and explained, "Obviously, since we *don't know* for sure whether the Rapture is going to happen before or during the Tribulation, we need to be prepared for either eventuality. We cannot afford to be caught out if things don't develop exactly like the *Left Behind* series suggests! After all, those are fictional novels written by two people who certainly do not qualify as Bible scholars. We can't afford to make a mistake about this, which is why we are going to do some shopping—pronto!"

Two men were immediately dispatched to monitor the happenings at the Temple Mount—Stevie Howard and Graham Forbes. Two more, less excited about their assignment, were sent to the markets near the Damascus Gate. Things were about to get more interesting, especially if the prophecies began to unfold, and the one thing all the members of the Millennial Dawn Society were sure about is that the prophecies were soon going to come true, and when that began to happen, Jesus couldn't be far behind.

Later, over lunch, the chatter picked up. "I'm telling you, I don't believe the explosion at the Dome of the Rock was a mere accident. God doesn't let accidents like that just happen," insisted Taylor. Bowles was a staunch Calvinist, and he was having a heated discussion with Jamison Parkes Law about the matter.

"And yet such accidental things happen all the time all over the world. Are you telling me God planned them all?"

Bowles was silent for a moment and then said, "Perhaps it was the Devil, but God will use it for his glory. So we need to concentrate on what that purpose and aim of God is in this."

Parkes Law sighed. One of the down sides of being the head of the Millennial Dawn Society was that there were many enthusiastic members, but few understood the legal ramifications of things the way Jamison did. Zeal without knowledge worried Law; it worried him a lot. "Now that several hours have gone by, and things seem to be settling down again, I think it's safe to say this was not the trigger event when it comes to the Rapture, or else we would know about it by now."

And so went the argument, round and round and round, with no resolution. It was, to say the least, frustrating, when you had a theory in which you thought any little thing might count as verification of it, but just about nothing could falsify it in the minds of the true believers.

CHAPTER SEVEN

ABRAHAM HAS LEFT
THE BUILDING

THE MAYHEM ON THE Temple Mount was enormous after the gigantic explosion. People were running all over the large area screaming for help, and sirens were blaring as fire trucks and ambulances tried to get near the elevated site.

It is interesting where the human mind goes when fear takes over. It envisions worst-case scenarios, and replays nightmares from bad dreams. Most everyone, Jew, Christian, and Muslim, assumed that a bomb exploded. Most everyone was wondering who planted the bomb. Even the media were speculating as they raced to the scene. But in fact, it was a natural gas explosion, not a bomb.

There were bodies scattered everywhere. Many had been in the upper chamber praying at that time of morning. Many were tourists taking pictures on the Mount. There were dozens of people dead, and dozens more injured. There were Muslims, Christians, agnostics and atheists but no Jews, as Jews are not allowed on top of the Temple Mount.

The damage to the Dome of the Rock was stupefying. The rock—which was supposed to be the place where Abraham offered Isaac in sacrifice, where the Holy of Holies resided in the Herodian Temple, and where Mohammed ascended into heaven accompanied by the angel Gabriel—was badly damaged. Many of the beautiful mosaic tiles on the outside of the Dome were destroyed, and there was an enormous hole in the Dome that the King of Jordan had refurbished some years ago. In short, not even taking into account the loss of human life, this was a multi-million dollar disaster.

Since the Crusades, the Muslim community of Jerusalem had managed the Temple Mount as a Waqf—a trust fund of sorts. The Grand Mufti of Jerusalem was Muhammad Ahmad Hussein, having been appointed by The President of the Palestinian National Authority, Mahmoud Abbas. Before becoming the Grand Mufti in 2006, Hussein was the Imam at the Al-Aqsa Mosque. So far, President Abbas had been very pleased with his hard work and moderate views. The Grand Mufti had recently appointed Muktar Al-Awari to oversee the caretaking and excavations of the Temple Mount.

This morning, Muktar had been at the construction site. Workers were concerned about the condition of the natural gas pipelines. Indeed tests showed that the gas was leaking, for how long no one knew. He considered shutting down the work until assessments could be made. Muktar had just left the workers and entered the Al-Aqsa mosque to make some phone calls to the Grand Mufti about the situation. The unexpected explosion caused him to race outside and head towards the Golden Dome, or what was left of it.

One of the first persons on the scene was a Palestinian reporter named Ibrahim, the Arabic form of the name Abraham. He and his cameraman worked for a local Palestinian TV station. The Imam realized that in light of the skirmishing that was already going on between Palestinians and Israelis these days (especially after the Muslim excavations some time ago had led to the dumping of lots of interesting materials before the Jews could sift through it),[1] it was crucial for him to tell one and all, that this had been a natural disaster, not a planned attack.

Muktar found himself running and shouting to the two men. "Stop! Let me tell you what has happened!"

The pair did stop and, after establishing the Imam's identity, quickly prepared for a live interview. "Go ahead! What is happening?"

"Repairs and construction are ongoing under the Dome of the Rock. I believe our investigation will establish that a natural gas explosion occurred this morning. There is no reason to believe at this time that this is an act of terrorism. We pray that everyone will remain calm, and allow us to help the injured. Our prayers go to Allah for the families of all those who have died." Off camera, Muktar pleaded with the newsman to broadcast his message quickly. "Please, we do not need a war here in Jerusalem!"

Muktar was a devout Muslim, but he knew that if his fellow Palestinians believed the Israelis had done this, there would be war in the Middle East. The crisis needed to be defused, not least because Muktar knew that in such a war, the Israelis had an enormous military advantage. Many Palestinians would lose their lives.

Ibraham replied, "I will go immediately back to my truck, and call my Israeli counterparts and tell them at once. I understand the gravity of this situation."

But Ibrahim did not share the Imam's convictions. He longed for the day when the Palestinians would shake off the shackles of Israeli rule, and take back the land that the Israelis kept confiscating illegally and without payment. Instead of doing what he was asked, Ibrahim simply sent pictures to the Palestinian TV authorities and to Al Jazeera. In his view, things needed to get worse before they would get better.

Then Muktar interviewed as many of his workers as possible; all agreed that the explosion was a natural, not man-made, disaster. Next, he called the Grand Mufti who promised to come to the site as soon as possible. He would personally see to the arrangements for a full investigation, but would stand by the natural disaster theory for now. He also agreed to discuss the situation with President Abbas.

Muktar's next call was to someone he did not relish talking to—Prime Minister Benjamin Netanyahu. He had a direct line to his office because

---

1. This happened in 1999. The Muslims claimed there was nothing of significance in what they dumped. The Israelis cried foul.

Netanyahu was keenly interested in everything that happened in East Jerusalem, especially in the Old City. The phone rang for what seemed like forever, until finally Deborah, the secretary, put him through to the Prime Minister. A gruff voice came on the line, "Mr. Al-Awari, please tell me all you know about the explosion!"

"I am sure there was a natural gas leak under the platform of the Dome of the Rock. I have just spoken again with the workers. And we were discussing the problem just this morning and planning to shut down the work site. I do not know what set off the gas. I only wish that we had closed the site immediately. Ambulances are still arriving. I do not know the number of casualties already. Please, in the name of the God of the Bible, tell your people that while it is a great tragedy, I feel certain it is a natural disaster! Let us concentrate on the injured and not stir up more trouble!"

"Muktar, I hope you are right. We have no intel suggesting threats or even incoming missiles, nor anyone with weapons on the platform except your own guards. Personally, I worry that some rogue element of whatever faith has done this to set off Armageddon. I will certainly get on all three networks immediately, and ask for calm, and explain what you have said. Let me know how soon you can conduct a full investigation. This is one of those moments that transcends politics. A lot is at stake! I presume you have spoken to the Grand Mufti?"

"Yes, sir, and he will call President Abbas."

"Well done, Muktar. I will also call President Abbas and King Abdullah in Jordan. I must go now and plan for immediate media coverage to quell everyone's fears."

As Muktar hung up, he realized he was shaking and sweating profusely. He muttered to himself, "Hopefully, that will calm things down before the end of the day. Hopefully . . ." Meanwhile, the Al Jazeera TV van was speeding from east Jerusalem, down the Mount of Olives and towards the smoking ruins on the Temple Mount.

King Abdullah II of Jordan was furious when he first heard about the apparent incompetence that led to the explosion beneath the Dome of the Rock. He was the protector of that shrine, and he needed to make sure it was restored properly. He was drawing up a plan for its restoration with the help of the architects his father, King Hussein, had used years before to refurbish the Dome. Things were difficult in Jordan these days, especially in the squalid Palestinian refugee camps near the border of Israel. The King would have to go through various negotiations and protocols with the Israelis so his workers could come and work on the Dome. Such negotiations were never easy in this part of the world, especially when the Israeli government had the hawkish Netanyahu in control. Perhaps he would get Queen Noor to speak to President Netanyahu. As the fourth and last of King Hussein's wives, her international diplomatic abilities were well known and respected. Although busy now with the United World Colleges program, she might be persuaded to help her Jordanian people with this current problem.

CHAPTER EIGHT

PREPARE FOR LANDING,
Part I

ART, AND AN OBVIOUSLY pregnant Marissa, were over the Mediterranean coming in for a landing at Tel Aviv when the explosion happened. As a precaution, the plane was instructed to circle the new airport in Tel Aviv for thirty minutes until they received an all clear to land. The pilots had no idea what had transpired. The day was soon coming when Marissa would be too pregnant to travel, but since she realized this might be the last time to see Kahlil and Hannah and Samuel and their Israeli friends for a while, she had insisted on coming. The pregnancy had put on hold any plans she or Art might have had to work on archaeological projects in the Holy Land.

Craving chocolate, Marissa had snuck a box of chocolate-covered cherries in Art's backpack. Art was so nervous about the whole process of pregnancy that he was secretly binging on the chocolates during the flight. Art knew that his life was about to change drastically, and it would mean far less trips to the lands of the Bible for a while. In preparation for becoming a more sedentary scholar, he had firmed up his contract with Duke University Divinity School. When he and Marissa returned from their Jerusalem visit, they would be moving into a grand old home on Rosemary St. in Chapel Hill which had formerly belonged to Art's great uncle, Louis Round Wilson, for whom the old UNC library was named.

When Marissa got back from the rest room she caught Art munching away.

"Is that my box of chocolates you're pilfering?"

"Guilty as charged," replied Art with a sheepish grin. "Like a choco-late-covered cherry or two?" he asked handing over what was left in the red box. "Did I ever tell you the story of when I visited Uncle Louie after just graduating from UNC?"

Marissa simply shook her head no, as her mouth was currently stuffed.

"Well, he was about one-hundred-and-one years old at the time and nearly deaf. His two spinster daughters stood on either side of his chair, like Scylla and Charybdis, the sea monsters Odysseus had to navigate his way past, but their job was to shout into their father's ears what I said."

"Nice! Comparing your relative to sea monsters," remonstrated Marissa.

"Well, you get the picture. Anyway, I told them that my cousin Greg West had just been ordained a Methodist minister. Uncle Louie got a devil-ish grin on his face and said, 'I was once ordained a Methodist minister.'

Penelope, the elder sister, said loudly, 'Now Daddy you aren't remembering right. You were never ordained a Methodist minister!'

'Oh yes I was! I was out fishing on Jordan Lake one day with our local Methodist preacher and he reluctantly 'deigned' to give me the oars. And that was the day I was oar-dained by a Methodist minister!'

The old librarian's face broke into a big grin, spreading his wrinkles in all directions and I just died laughing. Even the two sisters couldn't stop giggling. I hope, Marissa dear, when I get to be one hundred, I still have my wits about me and his sense of humor."

Marissa smiled. "If we keep eating this much chocolate I doubt we'll have to worry about making it to one hundred."

Just then the loudspeaker crackled and the co-pilot announced, "Ladies and gentleman, we have finally been cleared for landing; please make sure your seat belts are tightly fastened and your tray tables are in the upright and locked position."

Art smiled at Marissa and whispered, "One more archaeological adventure before our family adventure."

"Finally, I get to spend some quality time in the Holy Land with you and our friends. I am so looking forward to some relaxing time in Jerusalem."

Another announcement from the flight deck set everyone on edge. "Ladies and gentleman, there has been an explosion in Jerusalem. Security will be especially tight when we land. Please be prepared for some delays."

CHAPTER NINE

PREDATORS AND PREY

THE CRIME SCENE ANALYSIS at Hezekiah's Tunnel was put on hold. Most of the local police had been pulled off the case almost immediately due to the explosion at the Dome of the Rock. The Israeli police had been unable to identify the man lying face down in the water at the end of Hezekiah's Tunnel but they had found a single shell casing from a bullet that normally would only be fired from a German luger pistol, not the weapon of choice of any of the Palestinian or Israeli criminals the Jerusalem police knew about. Because of the exotic and unusual nature of the weapon, the matter was turned over to Israeli Security, Mossad, as the assumption of the police was that this was no random killing and no ordinary crime. People did not regularly get executed in Hezekiah's Tunnel. Some sort of meeting must have been planned there under the cover of darkness. But what sort of meeting, and why this outcome? Jacob Marcus of Mossad would have to figure this out, in due course.

Malak Al-Zawari was El Tigre's half-brother.[1] Back in the days before his brother was captured and committed suicide, Malak had led a very secretive life that kept him off the police radar. While El Tigre was busy with international dealings, Malak quietly laundered the money his brother raised and made sure that it got to Hamas. El Tigre got all the glory; Malak was seldom seen. El Tigre got caught; Malak was proud of the fact that he never had—until recently.

---

1. For the story of El Tigre, see book two of the series, *Roman Numerals*.

Millions, maybe even billions of dollars, had passed through Malak's hands and no matter how hard you try to prevent it, there is always a paper trail and always a computer geek who can follow that trail. Finally, the trail led to Malak and he was arrested. For a while he thought of himself as "The Shadow" given how cleverly he snuck in an out of countries moving money quietly into Hamas coffers. However, now out of the dark and into the limelight he no longer thought it was such a great nametag. Maybe he could call himself "The King" for that was the meaning of Malak. But maybe that wouldn't go over so well with Hamas bigwigs. All this and more he pondered in his high-security jail cell.

Malak had built up a major reputation with the Muslim Brotherhood, and with even more radical groups in Egypt, including the Egyptian branch of ISIS. His ability to handle money made him a valuable asset. His recent arrest did not sit well. Money was just as valuable to them as manpower—they could always recruit more underlings who were willing to die for the cause.

Thus it was that the Israeli ambassador to Egypt had been kidnapped. Not only the Israelis but also the Egyptians were frantic to rescue Ambassador Reich and so there was considerable pressure to make a deal. The Egyptian terrorists were asking for the delivery of Malak Al-Zawari to them, safe and sound, no questions asked. While the Israelis never liked to deal with Islamic terrorists, nevertheless they figured they had better resolve this situation as quickly as humanly possible.

When the Temple Mount exploded, that was one crisis too many for the Prime Minister. Late in the afternoon, Malak was cuffed and yanked from his cell. Blinking rapidly at the blinding sun, he was escorted across the courtyard of the prison, outfitted with a black hood over his head and shoved into a Mercedes with tinted windows, destination unknown.

Hamas was an odd coalition of all sorts of Palestinians who wanted their independence, some of whom were prepared to obtain it by any means necessary. One of their more zealous undercover operatives was Abdul Abdullah, a man tall in stature but short on patience. For some years El Tigre was his mentor, but since his death, Abdul had made a name for himself. He was given to extravagant gestures and outrageous extremes—extreme violence on the one hand and extreme generosity on the other. On the dark side of things, he was a big admirer of the ruthlessness and single-mindedness of the Nazis. The German luger was his gun of choice.

It was Abdul who had shot the fleeing man in Hezekiah's Tunnel and stolen the evidence he carried, evidence that Yassir Arafat had indeed been poisoned to death, poisoned by one of his own people, poisoned by Abdul himself. This evidence could not be allowed to see the light of day, since Arafat was still widely revered by all sorts of Palestinians, both the violent and the more peace-loving. Abdul could not allow the ruination of his rising prestige in Hamas. Gaining honor and notoriety was what he lived for.

CHAPTER TEN

PERPARE FOR LANDING,
Part II

OF ALL THE STARS in the NBA, Jake "the Cat" Arafat was surely the most unassuming. Polite and helpful to a fault, no one would accuse him of being on an ego trip. Jake, apart from his obvious size, seemed like a very normal person. And now that he was married to Melody, the love of his life, he looked forward to an even mellower lifestyle focused on Melody and the possibility of family. His salary was allowing them to dream big. And his size made first-class flying a bit of a necessity! He was glad they could afford it.

Melody was quietly snuggling up to Jake as they made their way to Jerusalem. The long day and night of traveling from Charlotte to JFK to Tel Aviv was taking its toll and she felt a bit nauseous. Should she tell Jake that she had missed her period for the first time in a long time? She decided to wait awhile.

Daydreaming, she thought back to the wedding the previous fall in Wilmington. What a strange wedding it was in some respects. Jake's mother and sister, both of whom worked at a monastery in Jerusalem, flew in the week before. But there was not enough time for Melody to get to know Jake's family, not least because their English was only fair. Jake was always interpreting. This was, in part, why Melody agreed to come on this trip. She hoped to spend more time with Jake's family members, getting to know them on their home turf.

She nearly started laughing when she pictured all of Jake's Charlotte Hornets teammates sauntering timidly into the church—not one below six feet tall! Even the owner, Michael Jordan, had come. They took up about four pews in Melody's little church. It was an imposing sight!

When Melody's mother Sarah saw the RSVP from Michael Jordan, her blood pressure went up about fifty points. As a graduate of UNC-Chapel Hill and a big fan of the 1982 team that had won the national championship on a game winning shot by Jordan, then only a freshman, she could not decide whether she was more thrilled Jordan was coming, or more worried she would faint at the reception when she met him. This had produced some sleepless nights.

Melody remembered some rather terse conversations with her Mom: 1) the food (snacks versus full buffet); 2) the guest list (open door versus intimate); 3) the music (big band versus light rock). Melody, like her mother, was a micro-manager, and it was hard for her to let her Mom take charge of the planning. But in the end, all had turned out well, and the honeymoon on Baldhead Island had been terrific—quiet, peaceful, with the water still warm enough for swimming. Thank God for the Gulf Stream.

Melody did not really know what to expect of their time in Jerusalem. She knew they were going to a ceremony at the Lazarus Museum and to Jericho for a family visit but that was about it. Jake had been sketchy on the details, not least because the trip was planned just after the pro season ended in April. There was little chance of a birth in the playoffs. The Hornets were in the bottom half of the Eastern Conference, and Jake was recuperating from a torn ligament. Better to rest up for a comeback next season.

Melody and Jake had settled into life together rather easily, in spite of the fact that they came from such different backgrounds. Melody had been part of a Christian family all her life, and had embraced the faith for herself as a teen. Jake, on the other hand, had been part of Hamas, aiding and abetting terrorists and living a double life as a basketball star for Maccabi Elite, Manny Cohen's team, until the day came that his own brother Issah died because of Jake's wayward ways. Only then did Jake turn back to God, taking the Biblical name Jacob.[1]

Dozing on Jake's shoulder, Melody was startled into reality when the plane hit an air pocket and there was some dramatic shaking for a moment. Jake took her hand and smiled. "These planes can handle far worse! Shall I entertain you with scary away game flights?"

Melody laughed and said, "I'll pass the ball on that!" She began to turn her thoughts to what would transpire when they landed at the airport.

---

1. See the second Art West adventure, *Roman Numerals*.

There would be a long line through passport control, and the usual hassles getting Jake through the line for Palestinians. Then they would finally get to baggage claim. Manny Cohen had texted Jake, telling him that he would personally pick them up. They would dine the first night with the Cohens, and spend the night at their seaside place in Tel Aviv. Melody wondered where Art and Marissa would be staying, and just as she was about to ask Jake, the stewardess came on saying, "Shalom. We have begun our descent into Tel Aviv."

Almost immediately, another announcement was made from the flight deck. "Ladies and Gentleman, I've been told to inform you, and I quote, 'there has been an explosion in Jerusalem. Security will be especially tight when we land. Please be prepared for some delays. We cannot divulge any more information at this time.'"

CHAPTER ELEVEN

GRAYSON DIGS IT

THOUGH IT WAS HARD for him to believe, Dr. Grayson Johnson had now become a dig leader for the IAA at the important site of Caesarea Maritima. His days of being just a "Hippy for Jesus" student were over, and a lot of his rough edges had been smoothed over in academia. His long hair was gone, especially during dig time, and his language had evolved. He had all but given up referring to everyone as "Dude!" He had arrived and was respected for earning his doctorate under Grace Cohen and for his work at Caesarea Philippi.

Caesarea Maritima was the place where Paul had been incarcerated for two years, and had passed through the hands of two shady procurators before appealing to the Emperor and being shipped off to Rome. Grayson had helped finish the dig at Herod the Great's hippodrome by the sea, working under the leadership of Ehud Netzer from Tel Aviv University. The hippodrome had been built in 10 BC to celebrate the birth of the new city Herod had created and named for Caesar.

The dig at the hippodrome had begun in the mid-1970s, long before Grayson had ever been involved in archaeology, indeed, before he was born, but there was always more to do at a major dig. Grayson loved to imagine what the original site looked like in Paul's day, which is why he was wandering around Caesarea on a beautiful Monday morning.

Tourists were already filtering into the site. One young lady approached Grayson, who was wearing an official-looking tag, and asked for directions to Herod's Theater.

"I'll go you one better," he promised with a big smile. "I'll lead you over there. I love this place! I can tell you all about the theater. Did you know it could easily hold 3500 theater goers?"

When they arrived, she sat on one of the stone seats. "I'm not sure I would want to sit through a whole performance on these stones," she laughed.

"Apparently, one didn't have to. Scholars think that the patrons actually brought cushions. Can't blame them! By the way, my name is Grayson Johnson."

"And mine is Sarah Hopkins. I'm studying at Asbury Theological Seminary in Lexington, Kentucky. A group of us are here to start working on the site tomorrow! I came early to visit friends in Jerusalem. Our dig team is scheduled to have a tour later today, but I wanted to get a personal head start—to sort of soak in the ambiance."

"Small world! I'm in charge of your dig for the summer. And tonight I'll be meeting with your whole group! Tomorrow we'll start looking at a possible residential area behind the Theater. Rami Arav recommended ATS because they worked well before in Israel at Tel Rehov.[1] Your prof is Dr. David Hall, right?"

"It is now, but I was on that Old Testament dig also," added Sarah. "Our OT prof, Dr. Sandy Richter, also brings students to Israel as much as possible—when there's no political trouble that is. Some groups in the past have had to pick up their bags quickly and flee!"

"Let's hope life will be quieter this summer; things heated up in more ways than one last summer," said Grayson ruefully, having no idea what was now happening in Jerusalem. Brightening, he added, "Would you like to see some more of the site? Maybe the Pilate Stone?"

"Sure, this beats reading brochures and signs," she said with an even bigger smile.

---

1. Asbury students have worked at Tel Rehov in the past under the leadership of Dr. Sandra Richter.

"I wish I could show you the real thing, but the original is in the Israel Museum." When they arrived at the stone, Grayson was quick to point out the inscription in the limestone which clearly mentions Pontius Pilate, the prefect of the Roman province of Judea from AD 26 to 36.

"Don't you love it when history supports the Bible?! Everything about the inscription points to the Pilate we know from Jesus' day. He probably made his base here at Caesarea Maritima. After all, it was a military residence and headquarters at least by AD 6. "

"Did you find the stone?" asked Sarah.

"I'm not that old! It was found in 1961!" said Grayson suddenly realizing that he wasn't a graduate student anymore. He was a full-fledged PhD.

The plan was to look for some sort of residence complex, though even the radiometry studies were not clear about what was lurking beneath the sandy soil where Grayson and his team would be digging. Whatever it was, Grayson was excited because Caesarea Maritima had already contributed a great deal of information about the context of the New Testament especially various things that the Book of Acts mentions at least in passing.

Grayson was also looking forward to rendezvousing with Art and Marissa West. He had much to tell the good professor who had helped launch his career in archaeology.

CHAPTER TWELVE

DUST DEVILS

PRISONER EXCHANGES ARE ALWAYS iffy propositions, especially those done in haste. This one was done in the middle of the night, in the middle of the desert near the Israeli-Egyptian border. Neither party involved in the exchange wanted anyone seeing this event, nor any news media to report it. It was clandestine in the full sense of the term. The terrorists were all wearing black *keffiyehs* protecting their faces from the wind-blown sand whipping across the road and, more importantly, their identities. There were some nine of them, all armed to the teeth, all male, and all young.

The driver of the Mossad vehicle stopped about a hundred yards from the roadblock, the agreed upon rendezvous spot. The armored, bulletproof Mercedes with black tinted windows made it impossible to determine how many were in the vehicle. As for the wiry, bespectacled Malak, he hardly took up any space.

When Ambassador Avi Reich emerged from the back of the small black van where he had been stashed, he looked haggard, like he had not slept in a very long time indeed. The dark circles under his eyes, his unshaven face, his shirt not tucked into his trousers all bespoke a person who had been through an ordeal that totally prevented him from following any of his daily routines. Nevertheless, he was alive, and relatively intact. He would have to go through debriefing in Jerusalem, after which he would be furloughed for a while, but that was yet to come.

A burly Mossad agent emerged from the backseat of the Mercedes virtually dragging Malak, his handcuffed hands pinned behind his back. The headlights on the Mercedes lit the way to the other vehicle. It was chilly at this hour of the night in the desert, the wind was considerable and the Mossad agent had his leather jacket zipped all the way up to his neck. It concealed a Kevlar bulletproof vest. Mossad always came prepared for anything.

"Here is the package you requested," said the big Israeli man in perfect Arabic, nudging Malak along towards the rendezvous.

Walking forward with the Ambassador in front of him, a small gun in his back, Mustafa was tempted to spit in the direction of the Israeli agent, but he restrained himself. The exchange had not yet been made—time enough to vilify Israeli scum later. Mustafa did not speak Israeli Hebrew so he responded in Arabic, and without the traditional greeting. "And here is your worthless diplomat. We are certainly getting the better end of this bargain."

The Mossad agent stood motionless, not responding to the provocation just offered. Pushing Malak forward roughly, he tossed the key to the handcuffs to Mustafa saying, "You'll need this." Likewise, pushing the Ambassador forward with a shove, which caused the middle-aged man to stumble, the exchange was made with a minimum of words. Dawn was still some while away, so there was plenty of time for both parties to get away under the cover of darkness.

Helping Reich up, while never taking his eyes or his pointed gun off the terrorist, the Mossad agent gradually backed towards the Mercedes, as the wind howled and a dust devil appeared just across the road way. Noticing this, the agent quickened his pace back to the car that was still some one hundred feet away.

The terrorist was so elated to have accomplished his task that he did not notice the dust devil. Mustafa suddenly felt the surge of the wind to his left, throwing them both off balance. Mustafa lost his grip on the key and on Malak—both fell hard into the sand. Cursing his luck, he jumped to his feet and grabbed Malak by the scruff of his neck. Leaving the key behind, they both backed up toward the van.

Just then, the Mossad Mercedes did a tire screeching U-turn. All of a sudden, the trunk popped open, and a machine gun began firing at the terrorists. But the dust devil crossed the road again obscuring the marksman's line of fire. The Mercedes sped off into the night with the Ambassador. The exchange had been made, and the Israeli diplomat would have much to tell his President when he returned to *eretz Israel* several hours later.

As for Mustafa, he lay on the ground, shot twice, once in the arm, once in the leg. "They will pay for this," he murmured.

Malak, spitting out gritty sand again, hoarsely replied, "Oh yes, they will! It's time for payback for more than just this treachery. They will pay alright, pay dearly."

Two other masked faces gently helped both of them into the back of the van. It was time to get moving. Dawn was coming.

CHAPTER THIRTEEN

TROUBLE AVERTED?

AFTER THE CALLS FROM the Grand Mufti and Israeli Prime Minister Netanyahu, Palestinian President Mahmoud Abbas could not understand why neither the Palestinian network nor Al Jazeera had explained the cause of the explosion at the Dome of the Rock. What was the delay? As he looked out the window onto the streets of Ramallah in the West Bank, people were already gathering in the square—some yelling anti-Israeli slogans. He knew things could quickly spiral out of control. Better act with some dispatch, as Netanyahu was planning to do within the hour.

"It is ever thus," sighed Abbas. "We lurch from one crisis to the next, without intermission." Calling in his secretary, he asked her to summon the media at once, and to connect him with the local leaders of Hamas who lived in Ramallah. "And another cup of coffee would be nice—it's going to be a long day."

Abbas was a member of the Fatah party, the less radical of the two Palestinian Muslim political factions. Although Fatah and Hamas both wanted a Palestinian State in more than name only, they certainly disagreed on how to achieve that end. For the militant Hamas, it would mean the end of Israel; for Fatah, it could mean a two-state solution. The latter was certainly favored in reputable polls here and worldwide.

Fatah had some allies among the Palestinian Christians who were caught between a rock and a hard place, between Israelis and militant Muslims. Like the other Arabs of Bethlehem and elsewhere in the West Bank, the Christians suffered through the same blockades, the same inspections, the same rough treatment. This was one reason the population of Palestinian Christians in the Holy Land had been steadily declining. They, like President Abbas himself, were caught betwixt and between.

A decision had been made to hold the press interview on the front steps of his office building. He felt the need to get out and meet the people. Abbas, dressed in a tan suit, rubbed his graying head, and wondered just what would come next. Was there really going to be another Israeli-Palestinian war? This is what the most militant Muslims in Gaza wanted, though they had little perspective on how badly that could turn out for them, outgunned as they were by the Israelis. As Abbas liked to say, "It is not the number of men on our side over against the Israeli side, it is the number and caliber of the weapons, and on that front we have a decided disadvantage."

Thirty minutes before the press interview was due to start, representatives of Hamas arrived. Abbas briefed them as well as he could. "How do we know this is true, that it was just a gas leak?" said Mohammed, one of the Hamas leaders.

"Because the cleric in charge of the renovation work at the site had told us so. I spoke to the Grand Mufti directly. Of course, it's a preliminary judgment and a full investigation will be forthcoming, but there is no reason right now to consider this other than a natural disaster. I also spoke to Prime Minister Netanyahu who will soon make a similar announcement to all Israelis."

This answer did not sit well with Mohammed. He was miffed. "Why then did the Grand Mufti not also call us?" Of course the implication was he would not take President Abbas' word for it.

"Obviously, because he is now very busy at the Temple Mount trying to deal with death and destruction! I was the logical person to call, since I am the President of the Palestinian State! Do you want me to call your boss in Gaza, or shall I trust you to relay my message?!" growled the usually irenic Abbas, more than a little frustrated with the members of the rival party.

The Palestinian media cameras were now in place, and the Al Jazeera van from East Jerusalem had just arrived as well. His secretary handed the President yet another cup of coffee and another assistant tapped the microphone on the podium. Abbas took a long sip of the strong brew and began in Arabic. "*Salam aleichum. Allahu akbar.*"

This produced the usual enthusiastic response from the crowd. "*Aleichum salam, Allahu akbar!*"

"Today is a sad day. I have been informed by the highest authorities that it is strongly believed that there was a natural gas leak under the Dome of the Rock. This led to a major explosion. The Dome is severely damaged, as is the rock of Abraham and Mohammed, blessed be the prophet, and too many have lost their lives in the explosion. We are only now beginning to assess the damage. What we do not want at this juncture is to make this tragedy even worse by reporting rumors that somehow this was caused by the enemies of Islam. The supervisor in charge of the work at the Temple Mount has told both the Grand Mufti and the Prime Minister of Israel that they strongly believe the explosion was a natural disaster. Of course, already they are planning for a full investigation. But right now, there is absolutely no reason to believe it was other than a terrible accident. Full reports will be made available in due time. The *Palestine Chronicle* will carry a report tomorrow following interviews with the Imam and Grand Mufti.

"In the meantime, both Prime Minister Netanyahu and I are in agreement that it is important that we not make a bad situation worse. No rumor is important enough to sabotage the fragile peace we have. So, *ensh'allah* we will begin down the road to recovering from this setback beginning today. Funds will be sought to make all repairs to the Temple Mount, to aid the injured, and support the families who have lost loved ones. In the meantime I would appeal for prayers and patience. *Shokrun.* I will not be taking questions at this time."

As the President was descending from the front steps, a shot rang out suddenly, narrowly missing President Abbas, and lodging into the doorframe behind him. Many in the crowd screamed, and Abbas was quickly whisked back into the building by his security.

Standing on a nearby rooftop was a man in black, who quickly retreated across the backside of the building, dropped into the cargo bay of a pickup truck, and sped away. The sniper muttered, "The Great Appeaser has been warned. War is coming, whether he likes it or not." It was never a good thing for a President, when some of your *own* people wanted you dead.

CHAPTER FOURTEEN

DOWN BY THE SEASHORE

GRACE WAS CAREFULLY FOLLOWING the progress of flights from Tel Aviv to New York. The Arafats were due in at 9:30 but were delayed due to high airport security. The Wests were not due in until noon, having gotten a later flight out of New York. Grace picked up Yelena from her school and headed back to Tel Aviv after her class which, of course, had turned into a lively discussion on current politics. The students were too agitated to talk about anything else. The two couples would stay in the bungalow that Grace's mother used to live in, which was just down the road from the Cohen residence.

Manny finally got the call from Jake that they were ready for pickup.

"I would have been to baggage claim sooner," explained Jake, "except believe it or not, two of the passport agents wanted my autograph! Usually I get quizzed for an hour. So of course I obliged! They warned us about heightened security but it was a slam-dunk!"

"Now is when I ask you," said Manny with a grin glancing over the headrest towards Jake, "since my team is in first place, and yours continues to be nearer the bottom of the pack, are you sure you don't want to come back to the promised land and play for your old team, for a lot more money? After all, you've got a wife to think of now. Maybe this is a golden opportunity!"

"Oh no!" chimed in Melody. "Thank you for your gracious offer, but I'm a North Carolina girl who wants to stay in North Carolina, however promising the promised land may be! We are just getting settled into life in Charlotte, and we are very happy there, but thank you so much for thinking of us."

Manny laughed. "Wow—that was a quick response! Well I can see who wears the pants now in the Arafat family!"

"She may wear the pants, but I wear the basketball shorts," said Jake with a grin.

"I can see when I'm beat. You can't blame a man for trying," said Manny with a sigh. "Sit back and enjoy the short ride to your beach bungalow. You can hit the beach and then dine at our place. Grace and Yelena are really excited!"

"Oh, I *am* going to enjoy this!" said Melody, a beach girl at heart.

Finally, Grace got the go-ahead to pick up the Wests. She and Yelena went to the airport and quickly found Art and Marissa. Bundled into the car, they headed quickly to the bungalow. The conversation soon came around to the events in Jerusalem. Marissa said to Yelena, "What happened at your school when the explosion occurred?"

Yelena was quick to answer with a stream of bottled up emotions, "It was so scary! We heard the explosion from our school. Everyone thought it was a bomb going off! We were allowed to call our parents so I called Mom. You know we either drive into Jerusalem together or I take the tram. Everyone was excited. Mom had already planned to pick me up early so we could come and get you. Now what's going to happen?"

Grace replied calmly, "Remember that the news reports are saying that it was a natural disaster. I know it's scary, dear, but we have to trust that the officials are looking into everything. And let's remember those that are hurt and the families of those who lost loved ones." Yelena nodded silently.

To lighten the mood, Marissa asked, "So tell me about your school work. What subjects are you enjoying?"

"That's easy—history! Especially here in the Middle East. We were never taught that in the Ukraine. I had no idea about the long and troubled story of our past. I guess that's one reason the explosion was really scary."

"Anything else that's really gotten you excited at school?"

"I love archaeology!" replied Yelena. "We actually have a special class in that once a week—a teacher comes in from the University!"

"Wow, I wish I had those classes when I was a kid! You take after your Mom, then?"

"I guess so. She's always showing me stuff about ancient inscriptions. Someday, I hope to be a teacher too. And I have a new friend that I found on Facebook a while back—her name is Yuliya Karpova, and she is a young professor. Right now she's in Istanbul teaching art and philosophy and all kinds of things about Turkey. I want to go there!"

The conversation suddenly stopped because the SUV had pulled up in front of the bungalow. Grace explained, "I know Jake and Melody are already here. There's plenty of food in the fridge—you probably missed lunch. Let's all plan to rendezvous at the beach for a late afternoon swim. That will be followed by dinner on the patio at the main house."

"Sounds like a plan," smiled Art. They could smell the Mediterranean Sea wafting from behind the house. Gulls overhead meant the fish were plentiful.

The bungalow was absolutely charming. The outside walls were plastered white like those of the Greek isles. Shutters of bright blue striped the walls. Inside they were met with a light aqua décor splashed with daffodil yellow. The family room opened onto a huge patio overlooking the beach. Pastel curtains were blowing backward into the house from every open window. The bedrooms were pristine, each with an *en-suite* bath and king-sized bed covered with printed spreads in beach-theme patterns.

Art and Marissa quickly discovered that Jake and Melody were out exploring the neighborhood and shoreline. For now, Art and Marissa unpacked, raided the fridge, and sat on the deck. "Ah, there's nothing like a beach to soothe the soul," sighed Art.

"Ah, there's nothing like a bathroom to relieve a pregnant woman," said Marissa as she got up yet again. "I'll be glad when this pregnancy thing is over."

"But you look so beautiful, like you're blooming," replied Art as she crossed the patio.

"And you're a bloomin' idiot to admire a fat lady like me," said Marissa in jest.

Meanwhile, Jake and Melody had discovered that great beaches are the same everywhere—soft sand, lapping waves, blue sky. "Oh, I'm ready to stay here for a while," said Melody.

"Just not permanently," quipped Jake with a smile. "You made that clear."

"I hope I wasn't too forward with that remark, but after you told me how aggressive Manny could be in pursuing something he wanted, I figured I'd better stop that plane before it took off."

"Stop it you did, and that's fine. Honestly, I don't want to come back here long term. I never did. Too many bad memories. Let's head back—I'm hoping Art and Marissa have made it to the bungalow. I'm guessing they're relaxing on the patio. Shall we join them?" And indeed they were on the patio—and everyone was abuzz with news about the flight, the events in Jerusalem and old friends. With icy drinks in hand, the foursome looked out over the Mediterranean.

"You know, we should get in touch with Grayson. I would like to see what he's up to down the coast at Caesarea Maritima. I hear the hippodrome is amazing."

"Is that where the hippos used to race?" asked Jake with a wink.

"*Hippos* is the Greek word for horse, silly," said Art. "But it does make for an interesting mental image—hippos trundling around the track!"

Marissa jumped in. "Rather like pregnant ladies waddling around the track!"

About this time the Cohen clan showed up. "It must be tough to live right here on the beach," said Art. "Maybe I could open a Bible school here. We would specialize in recreational theology and beach ministry."

"You wish. Instead we are going to live in Chapel Hill, nowhere near enough to the coast, sighed Marissa."

Jake, Manny, and Art set up the beach chairs on the sand. Balancing a tray of lemonade like a veteran, Grace navigated her way around various sunbathers, and deposited the tray safely on the little table next to the chairs. "Drinks all around," she announced with a flourish.

Just then a little trolley bell rang. A brown-haired girl was peddling ice cream. "We'll have seven," called out Manny confidently, opening up his wallet.

"What do you have for us?" asked Melody when the girl arrived with her cart.

"The best! Magnum ice cream! There's Classic vanilla, double chocolate, mint, white chocolate, almond, espresso, and fistik, otherwise known as pistachio. I've got bars and cones. In short, something for everyone!"

"Make mine the double chocolate," said Melody enthusiastically.

"Fistik for me please," smiled Art. For the next ten minutes, conversation ceased. All anyone could hear was slurping and crunching. The gulls were hoping for leftovers, but they were disappointed. The sand was so hot that everyone had to wear flip-flops except when they dared to make a run for the ocean.

"Race you to the water, Jake!" challenged Art.

"Not without me!" hollered Melody.

"My racing days are over," laughed Marissa.

"I was so hoping you would say that," Grace replied. "I'm more than happy to sit here and enjoy the scenery and catch up with you."

Manny was so deeply engrossed in his sports section of the local paper that he was caught totally off guard when Yelena grabbed the paper, tossed it to Grace, and scampered to the water. Manny was soon in hot pursuit! And so the afternoon quickly slipped away, the couples staying on the beach until it was time for dinner.

CHAPTER FIFTEEN

LIFE AND DEATH DECISIONS

YET ANOTHER TRIP TO the chemotherapist had resulted in Kahlil being utterly exhausted, and not his usual cheerful self. Indeed, he had become quite grouchy, even at points surly. Cancer is a horrible thing, like a kind of evil animal that lurks in deep crevices waiting to attack. In this case the deep crevices were in the pancreas, and one cannot survive without a healthy pancreas. The chemotherapist told Hannah yet again that the prognosis was not good. All the chemo could accomplish was holding the inevitable at bay and making Kahlil generally miserable. She asked to have a private talk with Dr. Ebenezer Schwartz.

"What do you suggest?" Hannah asked tentatively.

"I suggest we stop this process here and now, but it is entirely up to you and your father."

"He's sick and tired of being sick and tired, and he attributes a fair bit of that to the treatments."

"And he would be right about that," the chemotherapist said. The man sitting before Hannah was over seventy years of age, tan, wrinkled and with hair that looked like the standard pictures of Einstein. He had seen a lot of patients in his forty years of doctoring. Rather than letting technicians do this part of the job, Ebenezer Schwartz had insisted that as an oncologist he should be the one doling out the cell-killing chemicals. This was in many ways remarkable, not least because it was out of the ordinary, but especially because Ebenezer's parents had both died from chemical injections at Buchenwald. Through a clerical error, Ebenezer, having been confused with another child, had not been killed, and finally had been rescued in the last days of the Third Reich. He was nearly four at the time when the liberators showed up in 1945. Ebenezer knew all about death. And he knew when it was time to give up the fight against the inevitable.

"So you are saying, I should let him go. I should leave him alone but keep him comfortable until the end with pain killers?"

"Exactly! Let him enjoy his favorite foods, his family, his friends, and let him say goodbye to everyone over a period of time."

"Are you a religious man, Dr. Schwartz?"

"If you mean do I believe in God, I think I do. I pray from time to time. Listen, Kahlil has lived a wonderfully full and interesting life. And he has enjoyed it all, still talks endlessly about your mother, Sheena, about you and little Samuel and about your work in antiquities. He would be the envy of many people, when you compare lives. Isn't it better now to enjoy what you have left, rather than regret what you will not have in the future?"

Hannah began to cry. "I suppose so, but it's so hard to let him go. Just facing the reality of it has been hard enough."

Hannah felt the doctor's hand patting her shoulder as she bent over in grief. "What you must do now is seize the moment. By tomorrow he will begin to feel better again, at least a little. Feed him anything he wants, and tell him the good news, no more sickening treatments. I know you and your father are religious people, so by all means pray. Perhaps God will give you both more time. Perhaps not. Who can say? But whatever you do, be careful not to let yourself withdraw from him before he dies. He needs you right to the end. It's not about you. You will have plenty of time to deal with 'you' and 'your grief' later. For now, it's all about him, making him happy and comfortable. Apparently, you are very good at that. So, just keep going."

Wiping away the last tears and blowing her nose, Hannah stood up and extended her hand to thank Dr. Schwartz. "You have given me the right advice I think, and I intend to follow it. Thank you for all you have done." The doctor nodded, and let her out the door into the lobby where Kahlil sat waiting.

"Well?" said Kahlil.

"Well, we are going home, and you do not have to have any more of those sickening treatments."

"Hooray!" shouted Kahlil. "I was hoping you would say that. They probably didn't do an old man like me much good anyway. Let's go over to our favorite coffee shop, Solomon's Porch, and enjoy ourselves on the way home."

"Are you sure you are up for that?"

"Are you sure you still like Sarah's coffee?"

"Alright, then it's settled—the coffee shop and then home." Hannah sighed a big sigh as she glanced sideways at her father walking slowly towards their car in the hospital parking lot, and then resolved within herself, "Stay in the moment and enjoy the days we have."

CHAPTER SIXTEEN

DIGGING BY THE SEASHORE

By kind permission of Ferrell Jenkins

CAESAREA MARITIMA WAS PROVING to be a gold mine of archaeological treasure. The site was so well funded and protected that new finds should keep pouring in. Being such a huge seaside site, the supervisor of the dig always said, "There's more history under the water than above it."

For someone like Grayson, quotes like that were music to his ears. He figured this was his chance to find something significant, not that his work at Caesarea Philippi hadn't been productive. To the contrary, it had been, but now he was truly in charge of digging a particular area, with his Asbury students' help.

On this morning, Grayson was taking a walk up the beach by the Roman aqueduct, waiting for his students to arrive at 7 a.m. He had them working early, until the heat of the day really got beastly after lunch. Even in May, digging and hauling was exhausting for anyone, however fit they might be.

In his head, Grayson vividly pictured how Herod's harbor must have looked when it was completed. "Spectacular!" he thought.

Just then he heard the van pull up to the parking lot, with six Asbury Seminary students, including Sarah Hopkins whom he had met yesterday. They were dressed right—lightweight, light-colored cotton attire, good sneakers and socks, and the essential hat. Gloves are optional. Each carried a refillable water bottle. Their leader, Dr. David Hall, had prepped them well before coming. Each was expected to keep a journal if they wanted academic credit for their work. Each had read background material on the site and planned to study further if they wanted to pass the exit test! All had greatly enjoyed the tour of the whole of Caesarea Maritima yesterday. And each had listened intently last night at the hostel as Grayson gave them a pep talk about their upcoming summer work. However, they were all basically new to archaeology, and each site is different in its approach.

David Hall, spoke first. "We are ready to get our hands dirty! Point us in the right direction!"

"Welcome to the dig site! First, I will show you the piece of real estate we'll be dealing with! It's not a beauty spot, but I hope it's a productive spot." Leading them to a sandy patch behind the theater, he pointed and said, "Behold our little piece of dirt!"

"This is it?" said Sarah. "I'm glad you didn't show me this yesterday, or I probably would have gone home!"

"You should be glad this is all there is. The site has been generally surveyed for size, so we have a map, using GPS of course. It's pretty flat, so height isn't an issue. It will take weeks to dig even this small plot down to the first century layers—our real goal. To accomplish this, our tools have arrived for the day."

Everyone surveyed the equipment as Grayson methodically gave a brief explanation of each: mattocks and shovels, wheel barrels, hand brooms and dustpans; soil corers, buckets, screens, plastic bags and waterproof nametags; tape measures, stakes, line levels and plumb bobs; 4" trowels, paint brushes, screens and small took kits with toothbrushes, dental picks, etc. "And let's not forget the cameras," smiled Grayson.

"And knee pads!" exclaimed Sarah to everyone's amusement.

"Yes, there's a stack over by the Porta Potty. Feel free to use either!" laughed Grayson and everyone groaned. "So, are you ready to work?" Nods all around. "Great, but we are going to pray first!"

Grayson knelt down on the ground and said, "Dearest Jesus, we are your people. And we are prepared to work hard. We know that history matters to you and to our faith, and we would ask for your guidance as we dig and sift and sort and wash and collect and label and do all the things that archaeologists do. We do this to your glory and for the learning and benefit of all people. In your sure name, we all pray, Amen!"

A chorus of "Amens" followed. Grayson looked up to find his troop kneeling in prayer with him. "It's good to have a godly bunch. It really is. Sarah was right about the kneepads. This job brings you to your knees repeatedly. And now it's time for our radiometry survey."

"Cool," said Anna Underwood, as she handed Grayson the viewing device that was stored in the back of the van. "I saw them use that thing on one of the History Channel specials. It can actually see underground!"

"Mostly it just shows us shapes of things, and sometimes it's just rocks," explained Grayson. The radiometry survey took a good hour, with one student taking measurements, another recording, another photographing, another staking spots, and others installing fencing.

"I am happy to tell you, there is indeed something under the surface other than dirt and rocks," announced Grayson. "There is some sort of man-made structure, who knows how old. But man-made it is. There is also a wall. So, we will begin over in the northwest corner where we got the clearest results. No more than a couple of feet down, it would appear."

For the next three hours digging was done with vigor. Anna hit something with her hand trowel. "Got something boss!" she hollered. Grayson knelt down and dug away around the spot. What surfaced was a rusty Maccabi beer can. "I give you the beer that fired the Maccabean revolt, Maccabi beer!" said Grayson in mock triumph.

"Please don't tell President Tennent the first thing I dug up in the Holy Land was a beer can! It's against the seminary ethos statement," said Anna with a grin.

"No worries," said Grayson. "This goes in the recycling bag over there. Maybe next we will find a vintage Coke can. You can tell him about that!" And so the first day of surveying, marking and digging came to an end with no exciting discoveries at all, but everyone's appetite was whetted for more, hopefully much more.

CHAPTER SEVENTEEN

TRACKING A NEW TIGER

MALAK WAS HAVING A bit of trouble adjusting to his sudden change of venue. He was used to being on his own—coming and going as he pleased—unfettered by family, friends and associates. The only interruption had been his recent unpleasant stay in the Israeli prison. But even there he had kept to himself—except for the one day he got jumped by a bunch of thugs. That episode was best forgotten as far as he was concerned. As of yesterday he was now bedded down in Gaza—which some consider the biggest jail in the world, keeping thousands of Palestinians behind its walls. This would also curtail his freedom of movement. He watched as Hamas soldiers came and went from the safe house owned by Ibrahim.

While radical Hamas supporters had rescued him, they had their own agenda and were hoping to get him to help them once again move money. In particular, they wanted him to help Abdul Abdullah, El Tigre's former underling, now a leader in his own right. But Malak was not a man who could be co-opted easily. He was used to being his own boss. He had begun to call the members of his half-brother's extended network but discovered that most of them had moved on to other things, even to loyalty to Abdul, knowing El Tigre was dead and buried. He was old news to them, and that actually infuriated Malak. He thought his half-brother's memory should be held in higher esteem.

On top of that, he was having difficulty figuring out where he would make his home base. He could not return to Bethlehem or East Jerusalem, so where exactly should he set up his base of operations in Palestine? And how would he pick up where he left off? Many of his contacts would be quite shy given Malak's new prison record.

Hamas wanted him to get the money train flowing again in their direction so they could buy more grenades, more guns, more bullets, more rockets, etc. While Malak agreed because this was making him rich, he was also thinking of revenge, especially against folks like Jake Arafat and company who were responsible for his half-brother's death.

His initial thoughts were along the lines of a Big Bang. In jail he had read about the Lazarus Museum in the local papers which he devoured whenever possible. All the characters involved in El Tigre's downfall were involved. All of them would be attending the Lazarus Museum festivities. Hamas and bombs go hand-in-hand. So why not send a suicide bomber to blow up the museum right when the celebration was in full swing? He imagined the bodies of his family's enemies. Or maybe he should go for a larger target—the Knesset perhaps. He imagined the bodies of Israeli politicians, the ones who ultimately sent him to jail. Or maybe . . .

Malak was not a religious man; he didn't care much for Hamas any more than he did for the Israelis. He was a businessman and war was good for business. He began to think big.

The locator was beeping. A little red flash kept pulsing on the screen that Joshua Lentz was watching, while eating his doughnut and slurping his coffee. Yelling to his partner, Daniel Goran, in the next cubicle Lentz said, "Well, it appears Malak is in Gaza City. At least that's what the tracker is showing. He will never know that we know where he is at all times! The surgery was so successful he might never figure things out."

Goran stood up and glanced around the wall of the cubicle with a grin on his face. "I never got the full story after my vacation; explain it to me," he urged.

"Love to! So this Malak guy, the brother of the famous El Tigre, finally gets caught. And he gets roughed up in prison which required some minor surgery and some stitches to his head and so forth. Obviously he's anesthetized—out cold. Mossad decides to have the doc insert a tracking chip beneath the skin on the back of his head—deep enough so that nobody notices. It's new tech stuff, but apparently a success! The guy never noticed. The transmitting chip should do its work for years. Hopefully the chip leads us to all sorts of thugs in the terrorist underworld. This monitor was set up while you were gone."

"That's cool," said Goran. "So how does the tracking actually work?"

"Come have a look at the screen. It's a basic radar grid, but when our man begins to move, say in a car, this road map pops up and shows us where."

"I'm betting the Geneva Convention hasn't weighed in on this yet," said Goran.

"It's still experimental, and the US doesn't use it—or at least they don't claim to!" laughed Lentz. "It's supposed to be an info storage unit, or a way to track children. Anyway, the ethics are above my pay grade."

The two men smiled at each other, confident that they had the situation under control. All of a sudden the red light stopped beeping on the monitor.

"What just happened?" cried Goran. "The screen just went blank!"

Lentz shook his head nervously. "Not sure. No way he yanked it out of there!"

"Maybe the system crashed. Let's face it, technology is great—except when it isn't," moaned Goran.

Abdul Abdullah himself stretched out his arms to embrace the half-brother of his old friend El Tigre! "Welcome to our enclave. I hope you are being treated well here. I'm confident we can work together again. Maybe you have good ideas? Ah, but for now I have brought you this new black beret. Notice the workmanship. Many of us wear them proudly. You will fit right in. We need you!"

By now Malak's ego was already swelling. Maybe he should take more credit for all that he did in the old days with El Tigre. Maybe his half-brother's former allies were working with Abdul for a good reason. He admired the hat with care and then put it on his head with a flourish. The Hamas leader was beaming.

"You do remind me of El Tigre himself," he cried. "I shall call you that—with your permission, of course!"

The new and improved El Tigre beamed back. A "mutual admiration society" had suddenly sprung up. It was settled. Not The Shadow, not The King, but El Tigre himself was back in business.

The new El Tigre puffed out his chest and said, "You have done well in Hamas I understand. Thank you for this beret."

"Wonderful! I think we can do business together to our mutual satisfaction. You can stay with my friend Ibrahim for as long as you want. Anything you need, you let me know!" promised Abdul.

CHAPTER EIGHTEEN

A TOAST TO LIFE

It was sunny and warm on Ben Yehuda Street and the sidewalks were packed with shoppers, tourists, police, kids, vendors, street artists—a little bit of everything. Putting a bit of a damper on the scene was the disconcerting presence of teenage soldiers trolling the street. Solomon's Porch was doing a brisk business at this hour and when Sarah saw Kahlil and Hannah squeeze their way into the front door, she immediately whisked them upstairs to a private room where she served special guests. Kahlil could not be expected to stand in a long line waiting for his favorite white chocolate mocha.

"Here we go friends. Sit right down, and I will join you in a bit. What are you having to drink?" asked Sarah, pushing her bangs off her forehead which glistened with beads of sweat.

"You know me Sarah, a tall white chocolate mocha with whipped cream," said Kahlil softly with a weak smile.

"I want a double espresso, please!" said Hannah.

"I'll be right back with the drinks. Then we can chat."

Khalil leaned his head against the wall and closed his eyes. "I'm beyond tired, but I am sure the mocha will perk me up."

Hannah looked with concern at her father, and wondered how much longer this could go on. The upstairs window of the coffee shop was open letting in the rather warm breeze and the sounds of the day. She could hear Vivaldi being played by a violin duo on the sidewalk below competing with a police siren in the distance. Sarah appeared after a while with a tray of three drinks and a smile.

"Did you think I would never come back? Honestly we are slammed downstairs, and my barista is about to pull her hair out." Sitting down with a big sigh, Sarah said, "How is little Samuel?"

Hannah brightened up at the mention of her son and said, "The little prophet is nearly two and the terrible twos have started early. So we are constantly toddler proofing an antiquities shop, which is next to impossible." Hannah put her hand gently on the arm of Khalil to wake him. "Father, your mocha is calling you."

A grin spread across the old face, and he said before he opened his eyes, "And what, pray tell, is that drink saying—'Come ye who thirst?'" Khalil opened his eyes, and there before him was a steaming red mug of white chocolate mocha with whipped cream on top. A bit greedily, he began taking large sips.

Sarah was grateful he still had his appetite—at least for some things. "So what have you been doing lately?"

"You don't really want to know Sarah."

Khalil roused himself and said, "It's alright, we don't need to beat around the bush. I was having chemotherapy, and praise be the One, it was my last session, ever!"

"Good! *L'Chayim*," she toasted raising her cup of macchiato on high.

"Indeed! To life! A good gift from Allah," said Khalil now beaming.

Hannah could hardly bear this conversation. Tears welled up in her eyes, and she barely whispered as she raised her cup with the others. The conversation turned to questions about other events. Do you really believe the bombing was just an accident? Do you think there's a cover up? Do you think they'll be more bombings? Are you going to the Lazarus Museum opening? Have you heard that Art and Marissa are in town? Do you know if Melody and Jake made it also? Do you think they'll be able to visit Jake's family? The list was endless but not all the questions got answered.

The coffee was good, the company was better, but the time came to get Khalil home and relieve the babysitter. "Come on Father, it's time to move on. Sarah needs to get back to work." They stood up and gave each other hugs, and as Hannah and Khalil walked out on the street, Khalil said quietly, "This is a day Allah has made for us. We should rejoice in it and be glad, even when we are sad."

CHAPTER NINETEEN

NEWLY RED LOBSTERS

"I could get used to this," said Jake, snuggling in with Melody.

"Ouch!" cried Melody, "That sunscreen didn't really do the job." Swinging her legs out of bed she tiptoed across the stone floor to the mirror. What she saw was a pretty but sunburned lady. "I was afraid of that," moaned Melody. "Just look at me! I look like a lobster."

"So long as you don't get your claws into me, we could take a shower," joked Jake.

"No, you go first. You like the water too hot, and that will not work with this sunburn I've got. I'll follow you," said Melody.

Across the hall, the Wests were waking as well, and discovering the same dilemma. Despite the use of sunblock, there was still sunburn. Art especially looked pink. Turning on his side, he said quietly to Marissa, "I guess today we have to be more careful about the sun."

"I guess today we stay out of the sun, period! What's on our agenda?"

Art scratched his head. "I think Grace means to take us up to Caesarea Maritima and see what Grayson Johnson is up to. But that's later this morning, not now. You can bring an umbrella or hide in the inevitable tent."

Meanwhile, just down the street in an upstairs room, Yelena and Grace were enjoying pomegranate juice while reading on a soft yellow couch that faced the bay window overlooking the sea. Yelena was engrossed in P. D. James' *Original Sin*, while Grace was scanning the *Jerusalem Post*.

"Says here, the Imam Muktar Al-Awari has now said repeatedly in public this explosion was caused by a gas leak, and that's all. He was there, after all, and none of the workers are saying otherwise either! The government and even the Palestinians are agreeing. That in itself is remarkable! Glad to know Armageddon isn't right around the corner. Maybe that will amount to a little rain on the Hamas parade. They are always spoiling for another fight."

"Mother, I don't really understand that. I mean, Hamas has to know they are outgunned ten to one. Messing with the Israeli military is like messing with a huge hornet's nest. Do they really have such self-destructive tendencies? What's up with that?"

"Unfortunately, there is a long history of violence between Palestinians and Jews and both sides are to blame. And every time the Israeli government gives permission for another Jewish settlement to be built on what is, or at least was, Palestinian land, it's like taking a match and throwing it into a petrol can. Let me recommend a book for you to read when you finish that one. It's called *The Lemon Tree* and it tells the story of a Palestinian family who lost their home that was later occupied by Jews who discovered the history and tried for a little understanding and reconciliation. It will show you some of the dynamics of all this mess. And frankly, Yelena, this ongoing struggle has me worried about your future in this land. What will things be like in ten more years? In my more worried moments I've actually thought about moving to the US."

Yelena's eyes got big and she put her coffee cup down, "Really, Mom?"

"Yes really! Would you like that?"

"Maybe I would, though I've no experience of America of course. I've been texting with my friend Yuliya and she is loving Istanbul. Maybe somewhere exotic like Istanbul would be a good place for me. Yuliya says that there's a large Jewish community in Izmir. That's right down the coast from Istanbul."

"I was thinking more along the lines of Massachusetts, specifically Boston. There's lots of nice Jewish communities there too! But we can talk more about this later. Here come our breakfast guests. Wow, what lobster pot did you folks crawl out of?"

"Don't remind me," moaned Melody. "Everything hurts."

Grace stood up and said, "Not to worry. I prescribe Ahava cream for the lot of you and no beach this morning! Let's go into the breakfast nook where Yelena has everything nicely laid out for us this morning. And then we are off to Caesarea by the Sea! And yes, I have some parasols perfect for a dig site."

"Where's Manny?" asked Art.

"He went off to the office an hour ago. Seems that there are some trade rumors out there he needs to track down."

Jake added, "But they don't involve me!"

"Not yet anyway," winked Grace. "But you never know!"

Jake just groaned and sat down, and after Art had said the blessing, they all dove into a breakfast of bagels, cream cheese, lox and scrambled eggs—but no bacon.

"One thing for sure," said Art between bites, "Lying on the beach certainly gives you an appetite. Are the morning papers available?"

"Oh yes, I've scanned all the important stuff, so I can report on yesterday's explosion." Everyone went quiet as Grace filled them in.

CHAPTER TWENTY

MEETINGS IN HIGH PLACES

WHEN PRESIDENT ABBAS DISCOVERED who had been swapped for Ambassador Reich, he arranged for a meeting. He was interested in meeting El Tigre's half-brother who, apparently, had a real knack for amassing and moving money.

The new and improved El Tigre came sauntering into President Abbas' office as if he owned the place. Flush from his newfound friends and fame, he flopped down in a chair across from the President, took off his new beret and nonchalantly began to light up a cigarette. The President was not pleased.

"Excuse me, but there's no smoking in this building and especially not in *my* office. I have allergies if you don't mind! You do remind me of your arrogant half-brother. I hear they're even calling you the new El Tigre. Be careful! Unless you want to end up in a Palestinian jail after suffering in an Israeli cell, you better lay low!"

Malak realized he had probably overstepped his bounds and began to revert back to his old self, the serious banker, the shadowy figure. "We are surely on the same side in this war against the Israelis and their friends, even if officially you cannot acknowledge that. But I understand. You must be the public face of the Palestinians. Every state has and needs its secret operatives, so why not let us work together?"

President Abbas was twirling a pen in his hand as he tried to figure out this split personality. "I hope Abdullah knows what he's doing. Your talents as, shall we say, a banker, have been invaluable in the past. The real El Tigre became a liability, however. I hope you plan to be the former, despite your new nickname!"

"Yes, Mr. President. I plan to resume my career as a banker. But I will not tolerate those who defame my half-brother. They should pay for what they did!"

The President said in more menacing tone, "If you want to help the Palestinians, then I suggest you forget about personal revenge! If you come up with any plans, any plans at all, you *will* work carefully with the Hamas leaders. Go rogue and we'll bury you ourselves!" Just then, the phone rang. It was Abdul Abdullah.

Neither Lentz nor Goran could figure it out. The chip was only working intermittently which had these two Mossad officers very worried. Thus far they had not told their superiors about the glitch for fear it would make them look incompetent. They realized they had better figure this out before long or there would be hell to pay. Mossad had gone to a lot of trouble to get Malak wired up. In fact, had they not done so, they would not have released him. Thus far they were sure that Malak was still in Gaza City.

All of a sudden the locator beeped again—the coordinates pointed to the West Bank, specifically to Ramallah. Finally they narrowed their search to none other than the office building of President Abbas himself!

"The Gaza border isn't as tight as we thought. This could be big," understated Lentz. "I think it's time to notify our boss." Now they had something to show for all the money paid to keep Malak on their radar.

The Prime Minister left his residence, Beit Aghion, early Thursday morning. The daily commute to his office reminded him that the plan for combining the residence and office, a la Washington's White House, had been abandoned for budget reasons. But he didn't mind the commute; it provided quiet time.

His office was a beehive of activity as usual. At his huge desk he perused papers and fielded phone calls. He had just finished some calls about the Syrian situation when the knock came on the door. An aide announced that Ambassador Avi Reich, newly rescued from Hamas, had arrived.

The Ambassador to Egypt looked like a changed man when he walked through the door. He was neat, shaven, moussed, and dressed in his usual red tie and black pinstriped shirt. Netanyahu strode over and shook Avi's hand with a strong grip.

"So glad you are home safe! How was your debriefing with Mossad?"

"I honestly didn't have as much to tell them as I would have liked, but that's the way these things go, unfortunately. They keep you blindfolded in a dark space and even when they take off the blindfold, you have no idea where you are, and you are so disoriented that it's difficult to figure out which end is up. Then there comes the verbal and physical abuse as well, which doesn't help," said the Ambassador ruefully.

"I am truly sorry about all that. How exactly did they capture you in the first place?' Netanyahu had already read the reports, but he wanted to hear it first-hand.

"It was strange. I was scheduled to be at the opening of the new Egyptology Museum in Cairo, but then I got a call to come home immediately, that my wife had taken ill. I rushed out of the embassy and jumped into my car and headed home. When I got there all the lights were out, and I should have realized something was amiss, but my wife has been ill off and on for the last year or so, so I am afraid my anxiety was such that I wasn't paying as close attention as I should have. Before I even got up to the door, there was a black bag over my head and handcuffs on my wrists. I was thrown into a car and driven off at high speed, destination unknown. That is really all I can tell you. Oddly, the voices in the car were not just Egyptian Arabic; I distinctly heard a Syrian dialect as well."

Netanyahu leaned back in his comfortable lounge chair, and rubbed his chin. "Now that piece of information could be most significant. Strange things are going on in Syria, as you know, and among the many splinter groups are some fundamentalist Muslim rebels. I wonder if this means that the Muslim Brotherhood in Egypt has an alliance with them?"

"Your guess is as good as mine. I'm relying on Mossad to ferret out the facts. And I understand they are keeping a close watch on Malak Al-Zawari. I'm told he's the half-brother of the notorious El Tigre. Is that right?"

"You are quite right. Yes, we are keeping him under surveillance. Meanwhile, you and your wife are going off on holiday I gather, and the Vice Ambassador will remain at his post in Cairo while you are gone."

"Correct. We are going to southwestern Cyprus, the birthplace of Aphrodite, for some R&R," said Avi with a wink. "I fancy myself a bit of an archaeologist. The Hellenistic and Roman periods are well represented at

Paphos. I'm looking forward to studying their beautiful mosaics," smiled Avi, imagining the upcoming trip.

"A silver lining to your ordeal then," laughed Netanyahu. "I doubt you would be heading there if it wasn't for the kidnapping!"

The phone began ringing and the Prime Minister stood up. The interview was over. Ambassador Reich was ushered from the office as Netanyahu grabbed the phone.

CHAPTER TWENTY-ONE

ANTIQUES AND OLD FRIENDS

HANNAH WAS SORTING THROUGH old cups and pots earlier deposited on a top shelf in the antiquities shop. Khalil was out drinking tea with Omar, his longtime friend who also owned a shop in the Arab *souk* (market) that sprawls across the Christian and Moslem Quarters of Old Jerusalem. Today the locals were scurrying through the alleys and the tourists were slowly winding through the Via Dolorosa many on their way to the Church of the Holy Sepulchre. Serious shoppers were genuinely looking for archaic and artistic treasures amidst all too many junk shops.

Photo by Elaine Sears-Dennehy

Omar sold fruit of every kind imaginable, and today he was peeling an orange to share with Kahlil.

"Here, you need the vitamins. Take this orange," urged Omar.

"You are right," said Kahlil. "And praise be to Allah I still have my appetite. I love the fruit you have in your stall. Are Haifa oranges your favorites?"

"Actually, I like bananas the best, but it's all good, and all good for you. Changing the subject, what do you make of what happened at the Dome of the Rock? Things seem pretty quiet now, and King Abdullah said he would help us all rebuild, but what a disaster! Let's hope nothing like that ever happens again!"

While these two were enjoying each other's company, through the Damascus Gate came Art, Marissa, Melody and finally Jake, towering over everyone. Jake had not been back to Jerusalem since he left for America. He was taking it all in and explaining things to Melody who had never been to Jerusalem. He enjoyed being the tour guide.

"Melody, we're walking on the old Roman street, the Cardo. It goes straight on to the Wailing Wall, the very center of the old city. We'll be going into the covered market, the souk, pretty soon. Later we can go into the Christian Quarter and see the Church of the Holy Sepulchre before we end up at the Wailing Wall."

"Will we be able to go up on top of the Temple Mount?"

"I'm afraid not. Everything is closed for repairs up there. Let's just hope things stay quiet for a while."

Art and Marissa were slowly leading the way, winding through familiar areas so they would end up at the Antiquities Shop precisely when they promised to be there. Kahlil had arrived back just in time and was sitting on a low stool in front of the shop. Art arrived first and broke into a big smile, but with a tear in his eye. He realized this would likely be one of the last times he saw his old friend and his mind flashed back to many shared adventures.

"*Salam aleichum!*" said Art in a loud voice as he approached Kahlil who struggled to stand up and give Art a hug. He looked so gaunt, so pale, but he was still tall and there was still that warm smile.

"My dear friend, marriage appears to be agreeing with you! You look a little sunburned but otherwise well."

"We are well, and here is Marissa and Jake and Melody."

"So you are the famous antiquities dealer," said Marissa. "I'm guessing I could spend hours in your shop."

"If I get any older, Hannah will set me on a shelf as an antique for sale!" said Khalil with a big laugh. My friend, Omar, gave me a plate of oranges for you all. Let's go in and find Hannah. I know she has put them on the table with the rest of the food. Ah, what a cook she is!"

Hannah had fixed some tea and baked treats for their guests. Little Samuel was peeking out at all the grownups from behind Hannah's skirt. Art bent down, put out his arms and the boy let himself be swept up.

"Want milk," said the tot quite seriously. Hannah provided a cup of milk which disappeared quickly. The empty cup was offered to Art. "All gone," sighed Samuel.

"So this is what a young prophet looks like! Maybe we can have one of our own."

"Or prophetess," countered Marissa. "Miriam, Deborah, and Huldah come to mind. How about those as potential names for a little girl?"

The friends all settled down to an enjoyable lengthy visit, after which the plan was to do some sight-seeing and shopping in the Old City. Art was especially determined to remember this day. It was more than hard to say goodbye to old friends. It was heartbreaking, but death calls on everyone in due course.

CHAPTER TWENTY-TWO

THE JERICHO MEETING

EL TIGRE WAS INSUFFERABLY pleased with himself. He had found the perfect hideaway on the backside of Jericho, and the authorities never bothered anyone on this little side street near the Hebron Glass Shop.

On this morning El Tigre had a meeting with a Jew, a Jew who hated Muslims, a Jew who had access to the Temple Mount—just the kind of Jew El Tigre was looking for. Menachem had no problems meeting with a man who promised to help him fulfill his dream of removing Muslim occupation from the Temple Mount. They would meet in a public venue, a well-known tourist restaurant across from the ancient site of Jericho. Thanks to Dame Kathleen Kenyon who led the excavation of Jericho in the 1950s, the city is recognized as the oldest continuously occupied settlement in history. El Tigre II felt that he too was destined to influence history. What better place than Jericho to make those plans?

Menachem Sharansky, though Orthodox, believed himself to be a brave radical. He was just the sort of zealot El Tigre found most useful, whether Jew or Palestinian. The clock in the town square struck twelve. El Tigre took off his beret and waved at the young man. Settling down in a chair opposite El Tigre, Menachem furtively looked from side to side, and then began to speak quietly, pulling at his beard.

"So, do I understand you to say you can give me the materials I need?"

"Yes, indeed. What I have in mind is the use of C4 explosives which will stick to any surface. You can embed a transmitter in it, and detonate from up to five hundred yards away. But how you will gain access?"

"That part is easier than you think. I am on the IAA archaeology team that is allowed to work under the Temple Mount. I have dreamed for years how I would blow up the Mount. I know every nook and cranny and just where to place the C4. More importantly, I have been able to make a copy of the key to the main site. We must do this in the middle of the night."

"Aren't you afraid of doing damage to the Western Wall?" asked El Tigre.

"No, I'm not. The explosion will be entirely upward in direction. Some of the platform on which the Al-Aqsa Mosque stands will fall in, but both it and the Dome of the Rock are more than far enough away from the Wall to leave it intact."

El Tigre smiled and said, "So let's talk details." Over cups of coffee, the two planned a disaster, down to the precise date and time, and the amount of C4 explosives to be delivered to Menachem at his home in Jerusalem.

"Why are you doing this?" asked Menachem. "And how will I get in touch with you?"

"My name and my reasons are of no concern to you!" said Malak a bit menacingly.

Menachem decided to bravely push the issue. "But I can't work with someone who doesn't believe as I do! We must end Muslim tyranny! We must have our Holy of Holies back! We must build a new temple!"

"Calm yourself, my friend, before you draw attention to our plans," warned El Tigre. "Of course, of course, I believe as you do! Yes, of course, we must return the Temple Mount to the true Jews." El Tigre was impressed with his own theatrics.

Then suddenly he jumped up and grinned at Menachem. "Don't you love it when a plan comes together? It must be the will of God. I am sure of it!" Vigorously, he shook hands with Menachem who at this point was feeling a bit leery of the schizophrenic man. But he so much wanted to accomplish his great goal, that he convinced himself that this man was his benefactor, the man that would make his dreams come true.

Across the square, Mamonides, a man who definitely *looked* like a tourist, had been taking many pictures of the pair. He also photographed Malak talking on his disposable cell phone for nearly thirty minutes. He also followed the ex-con as he hurried out of town, turned up toward St. George's Monastery, sat in his car for three hours, and seemingly followed a young couple all the way back to Tel Aviv. He also got great photos of the couple, a tall Palestinian, and a pretty young woman who was definitely *not* Palestinian. Then he followed his assigned prey back to his room in Jericho. Since the tracking device wasn't proving to be reliable at times, Mamonides decided that he would personally fill in as many gaps as possible!

A fly was buzzing around the office where Lentz and Goran worked in Jerusalem. It was generally annoying everyone, rather like the pictures sent by their Jericho agent, Mamonides. Who in the world was that man talking to Malak in Jericho? What were they talking about? Goran was the only one who thought he looked somewhat familiar, but he couldn't place him. Mossad ran the picture through the criminal database with no hit. Without a name, they were dead in the water.

Goran knew it was going to drive him crazy until he figured out where he had seen him before. Meanwhile, he would keep searching databases. Malak was cooling his heels in Jericho, and Mamonides was tracking him still. Something just didn't seem right. Despite the lack of Orthodox dress, they were sure that the bearded mystery man was just that, an Orthodox Jew with his side locks tucked up under a cap. Why would Malak, a man important enough to Hamas to be swapped for an Ambassador, be talking to an Orthodox Jew? "Oil and water," thought Lentz.

"Got a hit on the couple! And you won't believe this!" cried Goran. "Lentz ran over to Goran's computer. There on the screen was a press photo of none other than Jake Arafat and his new bride, Melody.

"Why in the world is Malak interested in Jake Arafat? I remember him when he was a basketball player! Get El Tigre's file. Find out everything you can!"

Menachem had driven home from his meeting with Malak / El Tigre on an adrenaline high. He lived on the west side of Jerusalem in an apartment complex with his young wife and son, Aaron. On the surface of things, he was a very normal orthodox Jew who attended synagogue weekly. His wife, Rachel, kept a kosher home.

His day job was working for the IAA under the Temple Mount, a job he enjoyed immensely. Menachem's uncle and aunt had been killed by a rocket from Gaza a long time ago. All he ever told his wife was that they had died tragically when he was a boy. But Menachem remembered every detail. He had been with them when the rocket hit the house, and he alone lived to tell the tale. Uncle Daniel and Aunt Sarah had been looking after the young Menachem while his parents went on their one week summer holiday abroad. It was their seventh wedding anniversary present to each other. They had gone to visit Austria. It was the first time they had ever left Menachem with anyone for any length of time, and needless to say the experience turned out to be truly traumatic for the boy. Only a lot of prayer and counseling and love had brought him out of his shell-shocked condition full of anger and bewilderment about what had happened to Daniel and Sarah. Menachem had solemnly promised himself that the day would come when he would have an opportunity to avenge the death of his loved ones. That day was about to dawn, and he was excited.

Of course, he couldn't tell anyone about it—not a single soul. The nameless man had simply told him to expect the C4 by special courier on Monday. Menachem would have no more contact with the man who was supplying him with explosives. Upfront he asked El Tigre for safe passage out of Israel, money to set up a new life elsewhere for his family, plus an anonymous gift to his synagogue. Of course these perks came with a caveat. Menachem's wish list would never be fulfilled if he in any way implicated the wiry man with glasses. Menachem was truly on his own.

CHAPTER TWENTY-THREE

THE SANDS OF TIME

THE ADRENALIN WAS PUMPING. Unexpectedly, on day four of the dig, the lip of a vessel had been found and, hopefully, the rest of the vessel was still submerged in the soil. The work now required the most delicate of operations possible, using only toothbrushes and spoons.

The pot was some four feet down from the surface of the dig, lying on its side. Slowly, very slowly, the vessel, seemingly on a shelf of sorts, began to emerge. Ashley was busy taking dozens of photographs as the work progressed. David Hall was down on hands and knees slowly digging around the perimeter of the jar. It was soon apparent that the upper side of the jar was actually cracked through and some loose shards could be lifted up like puzzle pieces. Anna carefully recorded each piece and placed them into a box. Now they could see inside the pot that seemed to be filled with light-colored sand. Slowly, David began to remove the sand from inside the pot as well.

Looking at the shards, Grayson decided, "This vessel is not that old by biblical standards, by which I mean it's much later than first century. It looks like it might have originally been used for water or wine or the like. Hopefully we can remove the whole vessel by lunchtime."

Grayson himself took a turn removing the sand from inside the jar while David brushed the dirt from around the outside. As they continued, Grayson uncovered the top of what looked like a scroll. "Look here," he announced excitedly. "There's something inside! It looks like someone left us a message!" As the sand gradually was moved from around the scroll, Grayson could tell that there would come a moment of truth where he would need a little help.

"Jeremy, put on gloves and hop down here beside me. I'm going to ask you to lift the scroll out. Then we can remove the whole jar and take everything back to headquarters. Anna, please have some boxes ready!"

Jeremy's hand was shaking from nervous energy and then came the moment when Grayson said, "Now, but ever so gently!" Jeremy carefully removed not one but two scrolls and laid them in a box. Soon after, they were able to lift the rest of the vessel from the dirt.

"We are going to take our prizes directly to headquarters!" exclaimed Grayson. They all headed for the van and soon were huddled around a table staring at the scrolls. Grayson began to unroll one scroll and soon clear lettering came into view—lettering he recognized. The first line of text caused him to gasp!

"I believe we have at least a copy of a manuscript written by Eusebius of Caesarea!

"It will take some time to put a date on this, but the vessel itself suggests that it's very old indeed! Eusebius was born around 260 and died around 340. He was the Bishop of Caesarea for a while and a very prolific writer! If this really is one of his manuscripts we may have found where he lived or worked, although it could just be a copy that happened to find its way here to Caesarea Maritima. I promise not to jump to conclusions!"

"But let's face it," laughed Sarah. "We're all starting to imagine ourselves as famous archaeologists! What if we really did find his house and some early scrolls? Wouldn't that be a real find? The stuff of history books?"

"For real!" laughed Grayson. "And I promise you'll all be named if we go to press with this! But let's not get ahead of ourselves. In fact, let's just step back right now and have lunch!"

"And over lunch, I'm going to quiz you on the life of Eusebius!" threatened Dr. Hall. After a collective groan from the students, he amended, "How about I use this as a teachable moment, and just go over the basics."

"You're on," said Grayson. And as they munched on lunch, David reminded them that Eusebius is now called the Father of Church History.

"Eusebius was a native of Caesarea and spent most of his life in the Holy Land. In about AD 314 he became Bishop of Caesarea Maritima. Eleven years later he went to Nicaea in Turkey where Emperor Constantine convened a church council. That should certainly sound familiar!"

"Absolutely!" piped in Jeremy. "The Nicene Creed came out of that conference."

"Ah, ten points to Jeremy! Eusebius was a scholarly exegete of biblical texts, a defender of the faith and a good pastor from all reports. He was also good with languages. Grayson, of all his works, what would you hope to find?"

"Well, there are two front runners here. He wrote two treatises, one called *Demonstrations of the Gospel* and another called *On the Discrepancies between the Gospels.* The fragments we currently have were not found here, and are from a much later period. Who knows, these could be earlier copies or even originals! But that's still in the daydreaming stage.

"You have to remember that when Eusebius lived here it was a pagan city, with a large population—maybe up to one hundred thousand. So he had his hands full defending the Gospel. Remember, before Constantine really became Emperor, Christianity was still considered a *superstitio,* a dangerous and in some cases even illegal eastern religion. Emperors Decius and Diocletian persecuted Christians, and Eusebius says that he recalled seeing Diocletian pass through Caesarea with his army. This happened about AD 296. In other words, the environment was hostile or at least volatile, and people like Eusebius had to be defenders of the faith. But to truly understand Eusebius you need to back up and deal with his famous predecessor in Caesarea—Origen.

"Origen, who died just before Eusebius was born, was educated in Alexandria, one of the great centers of learning in the whole ancient world. Origen became one of the most famous and even controversial scholars in church history. He started a school here, where he trained Pamphilius, who in turn trained Eusebius. It was Origen who was largely responsible for the collection of various manuscript copies of the books we now call the New Testament. It was Origen who began a list of approved apostolic writings. I'm sure Eusebius's later list was largely based on the earlier work of Origen.[1]

"And where did all these books come from? Origen was a traveler and in his travels he found out which apostolic books were accepted in the various churches in the Mediterranean world. Origen built up a library and Pamphilius continued the work of collecting. So Eusebius had access to all of this. Over time, despite persecutions, a great Christian school was established in Caesarea, and just maybe we will have the privilege of excavating it. But for today, class is over. Take the rest of the day off! I've got some people to contact if we are ever going to figure out exactly what we have found."

Ashley suddenly said, "Wait until the folks back at Asbury hear about this!"

Grayson cautioned, "Sorry folks. For now, mum's the word. Do I have your word on that?"

Everyone agreed and then there was general silence among the students who were in awe of what they had just heard. Imagine digging up documents important to the study of early Christianity! They all wished it were so.

---

1. Cf. Eusebius's *Hist. Eccles.* 3.25 and 6.25.

CHAPTER TWENTY-FOUR

HEART TO HEART

WARM BREEZES WERE BLOWING off the Mediterranean late Friday afternoon. Yelena had decided on a quick dip in the water, but within thirty minutes Grace spotted her scurrying back to the house. Grace was puzzled.

"Honey, why are you back so soon—sharks in the water?"

"No Mom, nudists on the beach! I told those girls off. They were just showing off. They flipped me the finger and told me to get lost! I complained to the lifeguard, and he just laughed at me. So, I'm back—not wet and not happy!"

"Trust me, your father will have a word with the city government and the police department! But, meanwhile, I would like to have a word with you!"

"About what?" asked Yelena cautiously.

"About us moving to America. Say, the East Coast. Say, near a beach—and I guarantee it won't be a nudist beach!"

"But I was just starting to enjoy school in Jerusalem. The beach isn't my highest priority you know!" said Yelena with some exasperation.

"And you think there aren't good schools in America?" countered Grace.

"Of course there are, but it was enough of a trauma to move here, if you know what I mean, and now you want me to go continent hopping."

"I've also done my share of that. I'm sure you haven't forgotten I lived in the Boston area for some time," reminded Grace as she pointed to a painting of the Cape Cod seashore that hung in the living room.

"Nope—haven't forgotten. I'm wearing your Red Sox cap if you haven't noticed," said Yelena laughing as she pointed to her own head.

"Getting back to priorities, here's the deal. You know and I know that this place is a tinderbox that could explode at any time. I truly sense that things are going to get worse, not better, because we have ideological militants involved on both the Israeli and Palestinian sides. There are too many zealots and too many hot heads not directly involved with either government who are prepared to take matters into their own hands. No amount of security can make us all safe here in Israel where Palestinians and Jews live on top of each other. That's just a fact. So, I think we ought to consider moving."

"Is that your way of saying you've already made a decision," challenged Yelena.

"Actually, no! We've talked but we haven't come to an absolute agreement about where, when and how to move. And that's partly because we want to include you into the discussions at this point. It's only fair. Your father has a lot to consider—like his company and his basketball team. Of course he realizes that the team is mainly a hobby—but one that is near and dear to him. It would not be easy to walk away. As to the company, he could actually run it from the States and expand his base, which would be a good thing. In fact, there are many opportunities in the States for a man of his technical talents."

"And what about your talents," said Yelena pointedly. "Your work is all tied up here with Hebrew University and the IAA. You're needed here! Your students would miss you!"

"That's very sweet, honey. But I've learned no one is irreplaceable. And I like to think that a woman of my talents, as you say, can also find a niche anywhere!" smiled Grace. "However, jobs are not my priority at the moment—safety is!"

"Is anywhere safe?" asked Yelena in a very serious voice. "I mean America is a dangerous place as well, isn't it? I've watched American television—it seems to be a 'shoot first, ask questions later' mentality. The crime rate is really high—admit it!"

"Television is a far cry from reality. You should study the actual statistics on gun ownership and crime rate. Yes, Americans can own guns legally, but mainly it's criminals with illegal guns that cause the problem—and primarily in the big cities. It's complicated. The type of violence I'm talking about isn't due to crime or random shootings. I'm talking about race and religion—larger issues that are more and more becoming the root of violence. The problems are very different here with Palestinian and Israeli governments showing no signs of finding a peaceful resolution. There will be more trouble," she explained solemnly.

"Wow, I didn't realize you were so freaked out about all this. Are you sure it isn't just the blast on the Temple Mount that's got you so jumpy?"

"Honestly, no, but I see why you would think that. Your father and I see a bigger picture—and we don't like what we see. Again, we want to keep you in the loop but know that ultimately, we must decide what's best for our family."

"You're right—this is big. My brain's tired! I'm going swimming in the pool in the backyard. Would it be okay if I talk about this with Yuliya. She went to school in the States. And she always says I should consider all my options."

Grace smiled. "I need to meet this Yuliya someday. For now, I'll race you to the pool!"

CHAPTER TWENTY-FIVE

THE LAZARUS MUSEUM

WORKERS WERE BUSY POLISHING glass, labeling displays, checking guest lists, and testing security at the Lazarus Museum. Art and Marissa were enjoying free access and a leisurely walk through before opening day.

The main room housed the ossuaries of Mary, Martha, and Lazarus. Also displayed was the stone encrypted with the words "Twice dead under Pilate; twice reborn in Jesus, in sure hope of resurrection." In his mind, Art reminisced about nearly losing both his life and the stone. The opening day would also feature the Aramaic Gospel of John. Scholars, including Art and Marissa and Grace, all believed that the Beloved Disciple, aka Lazarus, provided the source material for this Gospel.[1]

Another longer room now housed a whole series of Egyptian artifacts that Khalil and Hannah El Said had donated. There were alabaster bowls, lapis lazuli perfume bottles, a Pharaoh's necklace, a replica of a funerary barge, cartouches with hieroglyphics and much more.[2] Glass cases lined the walls and for now a comfortable row of low benches filled the center of the room. They would be replaced with buffet tables for the reception.

1. See the first Art West adventure, *The Lazarus Effect.*

2. Museum pieces shown are displayed in the Metropolitan Museum of Art, New York, New York.

"You have to hand it to the Israelis," said Marissa. "They certainly know how to build a state of the art, climate-controlled museum. I only wish we had some museums like this in Turkey. Maybe the new building at Aphrodisias rivals this."

Art sat down on the long padded bench in the middle of the room and just said a prayer of thanks while Marissa wandered around examining the showcases. He knew this room would be a crowning achievement for the el Saids and their life work in antiquities. Art reckoned there was over a million dollars' worth of precious items from Egypt alone.

"Marissa, do you think perhaps we could persuade Israel Stein, the curator, to name this hall after the el Saids? Do you think there would be time enough to get a plaque made before the opening?"

Marissa smiled, "I saw him working away at his desk when we came in. You wandered off, but I stopped in to let him know we were here. I doubt it would be a problem, but let's go find him."

Israel Stein was the perfect man to be a curator of a museum. He spent his young adult years working with people like Kathleen Kenyon who died in 1978 and Yigael Yadin who died in 1984. In his last years as an archaeologist he mentored Lee Levine, now a professor at Hebrew University with Grace. Now in his seventies, he was often called upon to speak to groups about the prizes and perils of archaeology—his stories were full of anecdotes and revelations. Being curator here was better than retirement. He had an excellent working relationship with both Art West and the IAA, and was well respected by everyone, including President Netanyahu, who was planning to attend the gala ceremony.

As Art and Marissa came into Israel's office, Art smiled wryly at the fact that Israel's desk was absolutely covered with paperwork and the like. Hardly looking up from the letter he was now signing, he said, "How do you think things are shaping up?"

"Excellent, just terrific, but I have a small request."

Israel laughed and said, "Art I didn't know you were capable of small requests."

"Listen to this one and you decide. Do you think we could dedicate the long hall to the El Saids? After all, the majority of the artifacts were donated by them, especially the Egyptian collection."

"I'm sure we could, but I'm guessing you want more," mused Israel putting down his pen finally.

"Right you are! I was thinking of a plaque—for opening night!" suggested Art.

"Is that all? If you draw up a rough draft of what you want on the plaque, I certainly know of a small company that could make that happen in a short time. My friend Amos Sukenik, the owner, once made an entire archway sign for a museum in less than twenty-four hours. This should be easy for him," promised Israel.

"See, that wasn't so hard," laughed Marissa. "I think we are ready for the big night. We'll just add the unveiling to the list. Of course, we better triple check that Kahlil and Hannah will be there."

The three friends continued to talk for about another thirty minutes and then agreed to visit Kosher Pizza on the edge of the Jewish quarter.

CHAPTER TWENTY-SIX

EXCITEMENT AT THE MONASTERY

WITHOUT QUESTION, ST. GEORGE'S Monastery in the Wadi Qelt is one of the more breath-taking structures in the Holy Land. Hanging on a cliff, in a deep rift valley near Jericho, the compound gives new meaning to monastic isolation. If one can't be contemplative here, one should abandon all hope. The winding, deep valley parallels the route of the old Roman road to Jericho and certainly brings to life the story of the Good Samaritan in Luke.

Fortunately, the buildings were renovated at the end of the nineteenth century through the efforts of a Greek Orthodox monk named Kalinikos, but it was John of Thebes in the late fifth century AD who began construction here. He was apparently seeking the place where, according to one tradition, Elijah had been fed by ravens and restored in the desert. Needless to say, the monastery has a colorful past.

The monastery had granted asylum to Jake's family to escape the death threats of El Tigre and his gang of thugs.[1] Jake's mother, Ruth, and sister-in-law, Rachel, along with her two children, Tamar and Amin, now lived here. The children, however, were now safe at a nearby boarding school although they frequently were taken across the footbridge to be with their mother and grandmother.

Since the two of them had come to the monastery, they had lived out of the public eye, and while not quite cloistered they had lived a very orderly, ordinary, quiet life. After the horrible turmoil of the death of Issah, Jake's brother, St. George's Monastery seemed like Eden for the family.

On this early Friday morning everyone, including the monks, knew something special was happening. Jake and his new bride were coming for a visit.

"Cooking yesterday for Jake and Melody was a lot more fun than messing with this pile of laundry!" exclaimed Ruth as they labored away after breakfast.

"We don't get to use the kitchen very often. The cook is very possessive of his pots and pans," laughed Rachel.

"The bread and baklava are done with extra set aside for the monks. I know one in particular that has a real sweet tooth! Jake's favorites are waiting in the kitchen to surprise him!" smiled Ruth.

"I'm so glad we went to the wedding! Imagine Jake being rich enough to send us an escort! It sure was nice to have someone steer us through airports and security. He was such a nice young man! And so patient with the children despite being so intimidating! Tamar and Amin, little imp that he is, certainly behaved well. Jake and Melody will have interesting children. Imagine, my two will actually have cousins one day, God willing."

"All in good time," mused Ruth. "For now we need to make a big dent in this mound of laundry—all these bed sheets and pillowcases! It's like the monks have been saving them up all month and only today gave them to us."

"Don't worry. We'll have the washing, drying, and folding done by ten. Then we can finish up in the kitchen. The trip to the market yesterday morning was refreshing—at least once in a while we can go to the real world," laughed Rachel.

Ruth countered, "This laundry and this monastery seem pretty real to me thanks be to God." She was happy with her life apart from "normal life"

---

1. A tale told in the second Art West adventure, *Roman Numerals.*

and had no interest in going back. But she longed for a day when it was safe for Rachel and the children to have a more "normal life."

Jake was clearly excited. Melody could tell because his left leg was jiggling while he was driving. She was taking mental notes of the whole journey. The roads from Tel Aviv to Jerusalem were no problem. From there they took the Dead Sea Highway (Road 1). Fortunately, St. George's is located in the Israeli controlled part of the West Bank. It was a peaceful trip uninterrupted by checkpoints. Turning left off the main highway, they continued the short drive alongside the Wadi Qelt up to the entrance where they parked and then walked about fifteen minutes on foot. They decided not to ride the donkeys that are provided by some of the locals.

"What a place to live," said Melody. "I really don't understand this withdrawing from the world. Christianity is supposed to be a missionary religion. You can't convert people if you withdraw from the world and hide out in the desert."

Jake smiled and said, "That's not quite the idea. The idea is that the church needs some people to dedicate their life to prayer. You call them prayer warriors. So monastics go to a place where they can pray without any distractions or interruptions, a place like this. Think of the monastery as being a power station for the church. It takes lots of different kinds of Christians and ministries to make a whole church, and this is but one part."

"I never thought about the church that way, but it makes sense of the metaphor of the Body of Christ. Different body parts have different functions," she mused.

"Exactly," replied Jake. "And here we are. I promised Mom I would get here by lunchtime.

Standing on the stairs just above them was Ruth. Jake leapt up the stairs two at a time and bear-hugged his mother. "I have been so looking forward to this day." Melody was right behind him, and Ruth made a point of going over and giving Melody a welcoming hug and a little Middle Eastern kiss on both cheeks.

"Welcome to our home. It is indeed a holy place, and it is an honor to live here. Our quarters are down this slope a bit, in a separate building, so we don't bother the monks."

"How many residents are there?" asked Melody.

"Only twenty-three, and most are elderly," said Ruth. "You won't find them hanging out in some of the cliff prayer areas as in years gone by. The monks have a hard time recruiting new members. Indeed, there's a shortage of priests as well in Palestine."

At this point they reached the little house where Rachel and Ruth lived, and Rachel, who had been finishing up the lunch preparations, came out and gave both Jake and Melody a hug. "Welcome. We are so glad you are here. We have a feast waiting in the kitchen!"

"And then we'll give you a tour to remember!" promised Rachel. "The Chapels are beautiful and contain relics of orthodox saints."

The "holy corpse" of Father John the Romanian (1913–60) preserved in the Chapel of St. George's Monastery and canonized by the Romanian Orthodox Church in 1992.

CHAPTER TWENTY-SEVEN

C4 AND THE CIA

IF YOU NEED AN effective explosive, then use C4. The advantages of C4 are that it can easily be molded into any desired shape while remaining very stable and insensitive to most physical shocks. For example, C4 cannot be detonated by a gunshot or by dropping it onto a hard surface or by stomping on it. It does not explode when set on fire or exposed to microwave radiation. Detonation can only be initiated by a combination of extreme heat and a shockwave, such as when a detonator inserted into it is fired. It can be detonated from a distance by radio signal if it is connected to a radio transmitter or a clock with a set alarm time.

El Tigre was convinced that he knew all there was to know about explosives. He knew the best ones for any and all occasions. He knew the dealers in the Middle East. He had brokered many deals with them in his role as "banker" to Hamas. He knew that no one was going to detect C4 in a backpack, unlike say a hand grenade or a gun. He knew all about C4—but he had never *used* C4.

When the package of C4 arrived at Menachem's doorstep by special courier early Monday morning, he immediately snuck it into the basement. Inside the package he found a detailed explanation of how to use the C4 and live to tell the tale. There was only one chance to do the job right, no trial runs, and if it failed, then it failed. There would be no second attempt.

One of the difficulties Menachem was going to grapple with was how to calculate where he was under the Temple Mount, since cell phones and GPS devices did not work that deep underground. So today Menachem planned to start pacing off distances, discreetly, when others were working out of sight. He was confident that he would be able to cram several blocks of C4 into the crevices in the roof at the right two places, then leave, then detonate the charges, and then walk through the Jewish quarter and out Jaffa Gate. It was a bold plan, but it certainly could work. In his mind, he imagined the Temple Mount cleared, the Muslims gone, and a new Jewish Temple gleaming white in the sunshine.

Menachem quietly put the package into his safe. He began to chant, "We want Messiah, we want Messiah now" in Hebrew. He had no doubt that war would come, that the Israelis would win, and that the Temple Mount would be reclaimed. And he, Menachem, would set those events in motion.

"Menachem, what are you doing down in that dirty old basement," said his wife Rachel. "You need to get ready for work!"

"Yes, my love. I am on my way."

Neither Lentz nor Goran had made any progress figuring out the identity of the Jewish man who met with Malak Al-Zawari. El Tigre for his part was content to simply stay in Jericho, and seemed to be up to nothing special. Indeed, Mossad's sources learned that Malak had signed up for a glass-blowing class at the local Hebron glass factory! What in the world was that all about? Could he really be easing into retirement in Jericho? Surely not, but try as they might, neither agent could remember if and where they had seen that Jewish man before.

When Mossad needed a fresh view, they frequently called their go-to guy in the American embassy in Tel Aviv, Bob Cunningham. Bob had been in the CIA since the early Reagan years and was finishing his last assignment in Israel before retirement. He was a font of information and had no problem working with Mossad.

He was sitting at his desk munching on a doughnut and downing coffee when his phone rang.

"Cunningham!" he confirmed in a booming voice.

"Bob, Lentz here! Need a favor. I'm sending you a photo of a guy we need to track down, a Jewish guy here in Israel. He had a meeting with Malak Al-Zawari today."

"That guy you swapped for the Ambassador? Yeah, I know about him. I have a contact who says he's calling himself the new El Tigre. Guy must have delusions of grandeur!"

"Really! We didn't know that. Makes sense though, given he's the real El Tigre's half-brother. We've got an electronic tracker on him, but it's giving us grief—sometimes it works and sometimes it doesn't!"

"Ain't technology grand?" sighed Cunningham. "Yeah, I've got the picture already. Your terrorists really wanted that Malak guy? He's just a low-life businessman on our radar but I guess he must have brought in the big bucks for Hamas. Anyway, let me look at the picture and I'll get back to you soon if I can find anything on him. So you don't think he has a criminal record?"

"Not guilty on any counts yet," said Lentz laughing. "But anyone meeting with Malak looks guilty of something. I just don't know what!"

"Well that helps, just a little. There are only about a million suspicious Jewish males with a beard in Israel. No insult intended," said Bob knowing that Lentz was very proud of his beard.

Lentz just started laughing. "Shoot Bob, you should be able to figure out this one before you even get to your second doughnut and coffee."

"I love a challenge! Later gator," he replied and the phone went dead.

"Later gator?" said Lentz shaking his head. "I'll have to work on that one." Bob was full of weird Southern colloquialisms that kept Lentz puzzled.

Goran just shrugged his shoulders. "Now we have the CIA's best blood hound on the trail. Hopefully, he will come up with something soon, real soon. It makes me nervous that Malak is calling himself El Tigre. I wouldn't want Malak to pick up where El Tigre left off! And if I'm not mistaken there's a lot of other people hurt by El Tigre in the past that wouldn't want him back either!"

Reaching over to his in box, Lentz pulled out the El Tigre file. "It just arrived this morning. Let's spend lunch poring over it. And remember, we requested the file to find a connection between Jake Arafat and Malak. So let's start on page one!"

While Lentz read bits and pieces, Goran began to map out the connections between all the players on a large erasable board. Pieces were fitting together.

"The bottom line—Jake Arafat is in danger," said Lentz solemnly.

CHAPTER TWENTY-EIGHT

LIFE AND BEYOND

HE DEBATED AND DEBATED with himself whether to tell Hannah or not. He was coughing up blood. He was tired of the whole thing. Enough doctors, enough pills, enough injections—enough. He and Hannah had quietly made arrangements with the local funeral director just outside Damascus Gate near the bus station. Khalil was ready to go, and he was tired, oh so tired.

Hannah had seen her father gradually losing his appetite. This time it had not come back after the treatment. This time he began eating less and less. Hannah had given up knowing how to pray—for God to take him quickly, for a miraculous healing, for a few more quality days? What she did know is that she wanted to attend the Lazarus Museum gala with her father. Art had called to make sure they were going to be there; in fact, he seemed rather insistent which was odd. But he certainly made her feel as if he really wanted them both to come and, after all, many of the artifacts on display had come from their own collections. She had carefully catalogued each one that had been sent to the Museum.

"Father, it's time for breakfast," said Hannah, knocking on the bathroom door. "Are you alright?"

"Fine," said a tired voice. "Be there in a moment." Khalil was having a hard time moving about quickly this morning. Whenever he looked down he felt light-headed. Samuel was standing outside the door, waiting to take his grandfather by the hand and lead him to breakfast. Hannah raced back into the kitchen to rescue Khalil's favorite cheese omelet.

Breakfast was a quiet affair, and Hannah was encouraged a tiny bit because her father had tried to eat all she gave him, putting a good face on things, and at the end of the meal he said, "Hannah that was wonderful. I have a poem to read to you and Samuel, if you can give me a moment." He pulled out his favorite book by Kahlil Gibran, *The Prophet,* and read the following:

> Then Almitra spoke, saying, "We would ask now of Death."
>
> And he said: "You would know the secret of death.
>
> But how shall you find it unless you seek it in the heart of life?
>
> The owl whose night-bound eyes are blind unto the day cannot unveil the mystery of flight.
>
> If you would indeed behold the spirit of death, open your heart wide unto the body of life.
>
> For life and death are one, even as the river and the sea are one.
>
> In the depth of your hopes and desires lies your silent knowledge of the beyond;
>
> And like seeds dreaming beneath the snow your heart dreams of spring.
>
> Trust the dreams, for in them is hidden the gate to eternity.
>
> Your fear of death is but the trembling of the shepherd when he stands before the king whose hand is to be laid upon him in honor.
>
> Is the sheared not joyful beneath his trembling, that he shall wear the mark of the king?
>
> Yet is he not more mindful of his trembling?
>
> For what is it to die but to stand naked in the wind and to melt into the sun?
>
> And what is it to cease breathing, but to free the breath from its restless tides, that it may rise and expand and seek God unencumbered?
>
> Only when you drink from the river of silence shall you indeed sing.
>
> And when you have reached the mountaintop, then you shall begin to climb.
>
> And when the earth shall claim your limbs, then shall you truly dance."

Hannah was crying by the end of this recitation, and Samuel slipped his hand into his mother's. "Father, I do not want you to die. I want you to stay with us forever, but I know it cannot be. I know you are trying to prepare me in your gentle way."

"Daughter, think of it this way. Would you not want me to draw closer to Allah in my old age?"

"Well of course, but . . ."

"The only way I can get closer to my Maker is by meeting Allah in person. And I believe I will go into the presence of everlasting joy and peace and love. I know you would want that for me, now and forever. And besides, it will not be forever. You remember what the great prophet Jesus said to the bandit on the cross, 'Today you will be with me in Paradise.' Someday you, and even Samuel will go into the presence of the Everlasting One, blessed be his name. So, you will only be without me for a short time, when you look at it from Allah's viewpoint. I have entrusted you both to Allah, who will take care of you. Do not worry. Do not be afraid. Life is good to the very last drop. So, please let us enjoy the rest of this time we have together. And soon we will go see the Lazarus Museum. It will be a blessing to see our treasures become everyone's treasures."

CHAPTER TWENTY-NINE

UNDER THE TEMPLE MOUNT

FOR THE PAST ONE hundred and fifty years, both the Israelis and the Arabs have carried out excavations and restorations under the Temple Mount. This has resulted in extensive controversy and criticism. For example, in 1996, the Waqf trust began construction in the area known as Solomon's Stables, widely believed to have been built by King Herod himself at the south end of the Temple Mount. The vaulted arches are distinctive. The excavated area was opened up as a Muslim prayer room, the Marwani Musalla, large enough to house seven thousand worshippers! This repurposing of the sacred site did not sit well with the Israelis.

No matter which group excavates under the Mount, the opposing side always protests. Some of the arguments reach international tribunes. The IAA especially complained about the use of bulldozers along the Southern Wall in 1997. The excavations apparently led to a bulge in the Southern Wall that necessitated repairs. The large white patch in the wall is considered unsightly to say the least.

In 2005, the Israeli authorities inaugurated the Temple Mount Sifting Project dedicated to analyzing the three hundred truckloads of soil removed by the Muslims from the Temple Mount and dumped in the Kidron Valley. The Sifting Project recovered some remarkable artifacts: 1) a coin minted by the Zealots during the revolt, c. AD 67, with the Hebrew inscription, "For the Freedom of Zion"; 2) a cornice stone from Herod's Temple; 3) a first temple period bulla or seal from one of the priestly families, c. 1000 to 586 BC; and 4) a Babylonian arrowhead, no doubt used during Nebuchadnezzar's siege on Jerusalem, c. 587 BC. That names but a few.

Menachem, of course, supported all IAA incursions under the Temple Mount and railed against all excavations carried out by the Waqf. He also knew that the true Temple could never be built until the Muslim structures on top of the Temple platform were destroyed. Of course, Menachem had imagined blowing up the Mount for years. He had often thought about the best way to destroy the Mosque and the Dome of the Rock that, for him, defiled the original location of the Jewish Temple. Now, however, his dreams would become reality. Now he was armed and dangerous. He was familiar with all the nooks and crannies in the underground labyrinth. He knew the best places to cram the C4, and he wasted no time doing it.

Menachem did not expect to hear from the mystery man again. He asked for safe passage out of Israel if necessary; money to get re-established until it was safe to return; and a large but anonymous donation to his synagogue. El Tigre laughed and promised, "Sure! Whatever you want!" If politics can create strange bedfellows, this is all the more the case when dealing with religious terrorism in the Holy Land.

CHAPTER THIRTY

THE MISSING MAN

MARK FAIRCHILD WAS BEGINNING to worry. He had not heard from his buddy Sean Singletary in a good while. And this was not like him. They had been friends for decades and they talked or emailed regularly. What was especially worrying to Mark was that he had looked at Sean's video file of someone putting something in a cup of Turkish coffee that was drunk by the then President of the Palestinian territory, Yassir Arafat. At the very end of the video was an uber-quick shot of the mystery man, a swarthy figure with a big moustache. Though clearly Palestinian and not Jewish, he was otherwise unrecognizable to Mark.

Where was Sean, and why had he sent him this particular video? After all, Arafat had been dead since November 2004. Why was this surfacing now? Mark decided to turn over the video to the authorities, but which one—Palestinian, Israeli or both? For sure, it made no sense to turn it over to the Turkish authorities in Izmir where he was currently residing as a guest of Levent Oral, the owner of Tutku Tours. While he was mulling this over, Levent, who was sitting in the same room with Mark, received a phone call from Yuliya Karpova.

Mark didn't want to intrude, but he could overhear that the conversation was about some of Yuliya's discoveries about ancient games and patterns on vases. But then Levent said. "Mark is right here. Would you like to speak to him?"

Mark readily took the phone. He and Yuliya had exchanged photos and information on archaeological sites in Turkey for some time. Levent employed both Mark and Yuliya to lead tours especially to the early Christian sites in Turkey. Having highly knowledgeable experts on trips was a hallmark of Levent's booming tourist business both in Turkey and in the Holy Land.

"Mark, I have a concern. I was talking with Yelena recently and she told me about a man found in Hezekiah's tunnel who was shot. The newspaper description of the man matched that of our friend Sean Singletary, but the Israelis authorities, namely Mossad, haven't yet released any information. Apparently, there's a pretty intense investigation going on. Have you heard from Sean?"

"No, I haven't, and I was getting worried. He sent me an odd video clip on a flash drive, a clip involving Yassir Arafat. Wasn't there some talk about Arafat dying under suspicious circumstances?"

"Absolutely, but that was about ten years ago."

"And that's why I'm wondering why this video surfaced now. And I'm hoping that the dead man is not our friend Sean!"

"Contact the Israeli police. I'm sure someone there will listen if you say you have information on the dead man in Hezekiah's Tunnel."

"I'll do that right away. But I have a sick feeling that Sean is no longer with us."

"And you may have a key piece of evidence to find his killer if that's the case!"

"Let's change the subject," said Mark wearily. "I suppose life is settling down in Jerusalem after the explosion on the Temple Mount proved to be caused by a gas leak."

"I suppose. Yelena hinted that her mother is especially upset and might want to move away. I said they were more than welcome to come here to Istanbul! But I think a lot of people are very shook up. And the Prime Minister has been trying to get expatriates to return to Israel. This explosion won't help his cause even if it was an accident," said Yuliya.

Mark agreed and went one step further. "In some ways that makes the matter worse, especially if the government insists that returning Jews build homes on what was supposed to be Palestinian land. It seems like a volatile situation. I think I'll put it higher on my prayer list."

"Me too. For now, *Slava bogu* [God be praised]".

CHAPTER THIRTY-ONE

BOMB ON BOARD

NEWLY MARRIED COUPLES HAVE a remarkable propensity for tunnel vision. They often seem to be oblivious to most anything going on around them because they are so absorbed in each other. Last Friday, Jake never noticed that they had been followed from their first visit to St. George's Monastery back to Tel Aviv by a man in a beret. Abdul's many scouts had reported that Jake Arafat was back in Israel and one of his men had not only followed them to the monastery but had quickly called El Tigre to let him know. From his meeting with Menachem in Jericho Friday morning it was a short hop over to St. George's and a pleasant Friday afternoon was spent waiting for the pair to return from their visit inside. He wanted to see the Arafats for himself. It wasn't hard to follow the pair back to Tel Aviv.

On this Tuesday morning, Abdul's scout, Mohammad, notified El Tigre that Jake and Melody were on the move. He reported that they once again headed to Jerusalem, out the Jericho Road, and down the lane toward St. George's Monastery. The couple left their car by the side in the parking lot, hopped on a pair of donkeys, and disappeared into the monastery grounds. This was the second trip in five days, and El Tigre was beginning to guess that Jake's family was staying at the Monastery—possibly since his brother's death. Regardless, El Tigre drove to the Monastery and easily found the car. Few tourists were about that day and Mossad had decided not to waste manpower trailing him. They would rely on the tracking device for the time being.

Jake and Melody came out of the monastery just after lunch. Melody joked that things were going "relatively" well after this second visit.

"Okay! I get it," laughed Jake. "But seriously I'm glad you feel that way, Melody. I was hoping to visit as often as possible while we are in Israel." As they walked back down the path to the car, Jake added, "I sure do like this car that Manny gave us for the day. She's a beauty!" And he clicked the door opener on his keyless fob.

Instantly, there was an enormous explosion, lifting the front end of the car off the ground. Shattered glass and metal fragments sprayed in all directions. The blast knocked both Jake and Melody to the ground, and Jake covered Melody as shards came raining down here and there after the explosion. Monks on the grounds heard the explosion; Ruth and Rachel raced down the path. No one noticed that at the very end of the access road a Mazda headed off rapidly, so focused were they on the now burning car.

"Are you alright!" cried Rachel arriving first on the scene.

"I think so, but Melody is shaking all over," cried Jake as he hugged his wife.

"But you're bleeding!" exclaimed Melody. Jake then noticed glass embedded in the back of his hand. Rachel pulled it out, and Ruth wrapped a clean handkerchief around Jake's hand.

Rachel, with phone in hand, said, "Obviously we need to call the authorities in Jericho and get a fire truck out here pretty quickly!"

Jake opened his own phone. "I'm calling Art!" Soon the police arrived and whisked the pair off to Jericho's police station.

Art relayed what he had just heard on the phone to Manny who went immediately into action, sending a car service to rescue Jake and Melody. Of course, still shaken, they told the authorities they had no idea at all who would do such a thing, but somewhere in the back of his mind, Jake wondered if his past might be catching up with him. The Palestinian police told them that the report would be sent on to Mossad. Paperwork was finished and by late afternoon the chauffeur had deposited the young couple safely back at the Cohen compound.

Needless to say, the evening was spent with the three couples all trying to make sense of what happened. They tossed around a number of scenarios. Random bombings of this sort weren't that rare anymore—maybe Jake and Melody were not specifically targeted. Grace worried that Manny was the real target given that the car belonged to him. Everyone wondered how anyone would even know that Jake and Melody were at the monastery. Art reminded everyone that El Tigre was dead. He doubted that Jake was important enough to be on the Hamas radar anymore. Besides, if they wanted him dead, they would have done more than blow up a car. But Jake wasn't convinced and neither was Manny who assigned a bodyguard to the couple.

Malak was furious with himself. "You don't deserve the title El Tigre! I am not my brother—I'm just an accountant! What an idiot I am! I had them both—they should be dead! Where did I go wrong?" All the way back to Jericho he loudly berated himself for the botched job. Somehow the detonator had been set off too soon—a mere ten more seconds and both of his prey would have been dead. When he calmed down he realized that the so-called botched bombing might work in his favor. "After all," he mused, "Two deaths would send Mossad into a frenzy and my trail isn't that hard to follow. Maybe the scare alone will send Arafat packing. Any more blood, and I might not be a free man much longer!" He smiled and turned his thoughts to bigger matters.

Menachem was arguing with his wife. She was angry that he was going out again at night instead of helping his son with his homework.

"Look, I told you! I've got to finish up something at work, and I can only do it after hours. I will be back later tonight. No problem."

"No problem for you maybe! Promise me you'll be in no later than eleven."

"I promise," said Menachem trying to placate his wife and kiss his child.

"Good. Now give me a kiss too and I'll let you go."

The sun was setting quickly. With his keen knowledge of the site, he easily slipped into the dark passageways under the Temple Mount. It would take him the rest of the evening to carefully set more of the C4 packs and detonators. Everything had to be carefully concealed. If he was satisfied that everything was in place tonight, then tomorrow would be a day to remember. He prayed to the God of Abraham to bless his work. He prayed that the God of Abraham would rain fire upon the Muslim heathens just as he had rained fire on the prophets of Baal and Asherah on Mount Carmel (1 Kings 18). And he prayed that the God of Abraham would be restored to His rightful place in a new Temple, the Third Temple, on the Temple Mount. Then he went home to his wife and children as he promised.

CHAPTER THIRTY-TWO

SCROLLS AND SKELETONS

GRAYSON JOHNSON WAS LEAVING the digging to his students for the moment. Right now he was back at IAA headquarters still housed in the Rockefeller Museum. He was looking forward to the "new digs" as he liked to joke. Yes, the National Campus for the Archaeology of Israel sounded like a good plan and he hoped to get in on the ground floor. He would also have ready access to the Israel Museum. He sighed and returned to the scrolls.

The IAA's well-trained staff had set up a clean room and all the proper tools to unroll and analyze the scrolls. He was poring over the Greek manuscripts still convinced that he was looking at the earliest complete copies of two Eusebius manuscripts: *Demonstrations of the Gospel* and *On the Discrepancies between the Gospels*.

Two things fascinated him about the *Demonstration of the Gospel*: 1) Eusebius was concerned to show how Christ fulfilled even obscure Scriptures, and 2) he was equally concerned to find rich symbolism in the Gospel accounts. The latter was not surprising since Eusebius was influenced by the Alexandrian approach to interpreting the Bible which was often highly symbolic and allegorical. Grayson found a passage entitled, "Christ walking on the Sea of Galilee" and began reading:

> These words also can only apply to our Lord and Savior, as the Creator of the Universe, God's Word. For He is the only One ever said to have walked on the sea, which He did when Incarnate, having taken the body and form of man, when He constrained his disciples to get into a ship, and to go before him unto the other side, while he sent the multitudes away. And when he had sent the multitudes away, he went up into a mountain apart to pray. And when the evening was come and the disciples saw him walking on the sea they were troubled, saying, It is a spirit; and they cried out in fear. But immediately he spoke to them saying, "Be of good cheer: It is I; be not afraid."
>
> Now it would not appear to agree with orthodox theology to understand the oracle—what propriety is there in talking of the God of the Universe walking on the sea? How could He be thought to walk on the sea? Who includes all things, and fills heaven and earth, and says, "The heaven is my throne and the earth my footstool?" And "I fill heaven and earth, says the Lord?" But our Lord and Savior "emptied himself and took the form of a slave, and being found in fashion as a man," offering a proof to His disciples of His Divine Power which eluded the multitude, is described as having walked on the waves of the sea, and to have rebuked the storm and the winds, when they who saw Him were astonished and said, "What sort of man is this, that even the winds and the sea obey him?" And this was a symbol of something greater, that other spiritual sea, in which a dragon is said to have been made to be mocked by the angels of God, on which also our Lord and Savior walked and is said to have crushed the head of the dragon (447) therein and of the other subject dragons, according to the words, "You have bruised the heads of the dragons in the water, and you have bruised the heads of the dragon": clearly of another spiritual sea of which He says again in the Psalms, "I went into . . . .

~ ~ ~

"Have you gone to the spring of the sea, and have you walked in the steps of the depth? The gates of death did they open to thee in you, and did the gate-keepers of Hades fear when they saw you?"[1]

Thus when He walked on the sea in our human life, and rebuked the winds and the waves, He performed a natural symbolism of something unspeakable.

Grayson then turned to a lengthy explanation attempting to harmonize the genealogies of the Lukan and Matthean birth narratives. He could see immediately that Eusebius is clearly aware of the difficulties, and tries to find a reasonable explanation for the differences in the two accounts. Eusebius once said that every "believer" had personal views about the differences but, more importantly, it wasn't a bone of contention that kept believers apart or cast doubts on the historicity of the birth narratives. "Today's liberal theologians ought to read Eusebius," laughed Grayson.

Suddenly, his phone rang. An excited David Hall cried, "Please get over here quickly. We found bones—maybe human bones. And don't worry, we won't disturb anything!"

"Wow! I wish I could, but I'm here at the IAA and there's no way I can leave Jerusalem right now, especially with the Museum opening this evening. I'll see if I can find someone to come out with me tomorrow morning—someone who knows more about 'dem dry bones'! In the meantime your team should knock off early. I think the beach is calling you on this really hot day!"

"Well, it will be hard to steer their excitement away from this trench, but I will promise them an afternoon of beach and Magnum bars!"

Grayson whipped out his cellphone and dialed Ada Yardeni who was overseeing several dig projects this summer including Grayson's.

"Shalom Ada, this is Grayson. Have you got a minute? As you know I've been working on the dig out at Caesarea Maritima. Last Friday we found two scrolls connected with Eusebius. I've got them set up here at IAA. And just now I got a call from my team claiming they have found some bones at the site!"

Ada replied, "Your timing is great! I just got back from Caesarea Philippi up north. So now I have time to help you and your team. You can't be too careful about those Orthodox rabbis. They will be upset if someone

---

1. This is my modification of the out-of-print Ferrar translation of Book 9, Chapter 12 of the *Demonstration of the Gospel.*

has been messing with Jewish bones that should be left interred as they are. I'll call the team now and get them out there tomorrow morning."

"Excellent, we will all meet you there. This will be a real teachable moment for the Asbury students. Meanwhile, they get a beach day! And I presume you are going to the gala at the Lazarus Museum tonight?"

"The IAA staff has been invited—don't know how many are going, but I certainly will be. The Prime Minister should make his grand entrance around seven o'clock. Regardless, I will see you tomorrow!"

After hanging up, Grayson muttered to himself, "My one suit is pressed. But I guess I'd better get a haircut this afternoon. Time to put away the scrolls and get ready for a party!"

CHAPTER THIRTY-THREE

A NIGHT TO REMEMBER

By six o'clock Hannah had managed to get Khalil properly dressed in his new robe. He looked the part of an Arab sheik. Despite his gaunt looks, he was in high spirits and could hardly wait to see his friends and the exhibit. Hannah was dressed modestly in a long black dress plus a beautiful print head scarf (*hijab*). Her friend Sarah from the coffee shop had arrived an hour earlier to do the baby-sitting.

"Thank you so much, Sarah! This will be our version of Night at the Museum!"

"No problem, girlfriend. Samuel and I are going to read some books and then he is straight off to bed. In fact I already saw the first harbinger of sleep—a big yawn. Take your time! I'll enjoy the evening with your little prophet!"

Art was not the fretting kind, but he was really worried about the car bombing—were Jake and Melody really the targets? He wondered if it was a preview of bad things to come. But he kept his thoughts to himself as he, Marissa, Manny, Grace, Yelena, Jake, and Melody rode quietly in the large limousine hired to take them all to Jerusalem. Art knew security would be tight, not least because President Netanyahu was putting in a brief, ribbon-cutting appearance. He took hold of Marissa's hand and squeezed tightly. He was worried, uncharacteristically worried.

Grayson was now dressed in style, in his freshly-cleaned Jeep, driving to Jerusalem and listening to a Christian rock CD by Skillet. He was excited about spending time with friends and seeing the finishing touches on the new wing at the Lazarus Museum. Tapping his fingers on the steering column, his mind turned to his excavation. He needed to call Simon Kalman, his journalist contact, and start offering press releases about the dig. Maybe this would generate more revenue from the IAA. Art and Marissa's visit last week would be good for PR also. And that reminded him that he should update everyone on the recent findings—skeletons and scrolls.

Simon Kalman stood outside the front entrance waiting for the doors to open. A red carpet had been rolled out the front door and down the front steps. Inside the lights were already blazing. Dr. Israel Stein, the curator, dressed in a black tuxedo, came down to greet Simon. He was so glad that both the *Jerusalem Post* and *Ha'Aretz* were covering this gala event to the max. The valets were also standing by. Guests would be arriving by 6:30 p.m.

Art, Marissa, Grace, Manny, Yelena, Melody, and Jake all emerged from the limo to a round of camera flashes. Grace wore her latest Italian outfit, a floor length silver gown with her trademark red heels. Yelena was wearing her first-ever gown in Russian red. Melody, still not used to spending money, thriftily borrowed one of her bridesmaids gowns in a truly southern peach shade. Marissa's electric blue gown was specially made for her very pregnant body by a Russian seamstress back in Charlotte. Manny had arranged tuxedos for all the men in the group.

Within minutes, Grayson drove up in his Jeep and Art gave him a hefty slap on the back. "So very glad you could make it. What's happening with your dig? When we stopped by the first time, you were just getting started." There followed an animated five-minute conversation about skeletons and scrolls until Marissa interrupted with, "Boys, no more shop talk; we need to go inside!"

At that very moment, Khalil and Hannah arrived by taxi. When Art turned to greet his old friend his heart stopped. He looked so pale, and was using a cane to get up the steps. Coming down to help him, Art said, "I know this is costing you, but I am so very, very glad you are here old friend."

Khalil tried to smile through the pain. "I would not have missed it for the world."

As the old friends were gathering in the gleaming lobby, sirens could be heard nearby, presaging the coming of the Prime Minister and his entourage to the opening ceremony. Israel looked fairly calm but underneath he was sweating.

As the motorcade pulled up at seven o'clock, security emerged and cordoned off the semi-circular driveway. The door of the stretch limousine opened, and Benjamin Netanyahu emerged with his wife Sara who looked elegant in dark sky blue and white, the colors of the Israeli flag.

Grace remembered when Sara finished her master's degree at Hebrew University in 1996. Ever since, she had followed her career as an educational psychologist.

A red ribbon now separated the lobby from the new museum rooms. Dr. Stein stepped forward, called everyone to attention and announced: "It gives me great pleasure to welcome you all to this special unveiling of the new wing of the Lazarus Museum. We want to give you plenty of time to enjoy the many exhibits, but first we have two ceremonial tasks. To begin, I would like to ask Professor Art West and Professor Grace Levine to come forward.

Israel quickly turned the microphone over to Art who began by saying, "This is the surprise portion of the evening, and I want to ask Khalil el Said and his daughter Hannah el Said to come forward."

When they arrived, looking somewhat confused, Grace continued. "Khalil and Hannah, I know you are not expecting this, but we all owe you both an enormous debt for your contributions to our museum. You have been examples of how to work in the antiquities trade with fairness and integrity. On this night we have chosen to honor you by naming the new wing of the Lazarus Museum the el Said Hall." And at that moment, Art pulled the cord to reveal a gleaming name plaque. The applause was loud and long because many had known the el Saids for many years. The Israelis in the room had nothing but praise for these Palestinians.

The el Saids stood speechless, Kahlil leaning on his cane and looking up at the plaque. For Kahlil especially, this was the crowning achievement of a life's work. Hannah urged him to say a word. Moving slowly to the microphone, Khalil spoke softly but clearly, standing as tall as he could. "Hannah and I say thank you. We have tried to live in such a way that Allah would be honored and our fellow human beings would be edified by what they learn through studying our antiquities. From the bottom of my heart we thank you all, and especially Dr. Arthur West and Dr. Grace Levine, our friends and partners in many archaeological adventures. May you all be blessed here in this place." Once again there was a large round of applause.

At this juncture Israel came back quickly to the microphone and said, "And now our Prime Minister will cut the ribbon."

He strode to the microphone confidently and said, "Shalom!" and the audience all instinctively responded in kind. "The advancement of learning about our past has accelerated in the last four or five decades in *eretz Israel* because of the tireless efforts of faithful archaeologists like many of those here. Tonight, I would especially single out Dr. Arthur West and Dr. Grace Levine, who along with Dr. Sammy Cohen from the IAA were responsible for finding and displaying many of the archaeological treasures in this museum. This is where they belong and so we are dedicated to the eradication of antiquities thefts and forgery in this land. And we are indebted to the el Said family who again show us how the antiquities trade can be our ally in preserving our history. This museum shows what is possible when there is honesty and integrity in archaeological work and trade in the Holy Land. It is right that we are here tonight to celebrate the opening of this new wing of the Lazarus Museum."

Israel handed the Prime Minister a gigantic pair of scissors, and as cameras flashed, he quickly cut the ribbon and said, "I pronounce The el Said Hall now open!" The press, continuing to take pictures, followed the President into the new wing. As soon as the formalities were over Bibi Netanyahu, as he is called by his friends, quickly found Manny and the two instantly turned their thoughts to sports until the Prime Minister was reminded that he had to leave. Grace had a short chat with Sara about her work in education before Sara was whisked away.

Meanwhile, Khalil said to Art, "Did you ever think when we were dealing with the theft of the Lazarus stone years ago, that this Museum would contain so many new and marvelous artifacts?"

Art, munching on kosher hors d'oeuvres, responded, "No, especially when we had authorities questioning me, and then there was that nightmare of a trial. I never expected to be praised by the Prime Minister, never mind have a museum like this connected to all of us. Not in a million years!"

Yelena was, as usual, tagging along after her hero, Grayson, who was happy to tell tales about the exhibits. Grace caught up with Hannah, Marissa, Jake and Melody. She began to explain each ancient object and answer any and all questions. As the sun was going down, things could not be going any better.

While viewing the ossuaries of Mary, Martha, and Lazarus, Grace raised her wine glass for a toast but just then an enormous explosion was heard. The sound shook the very foundations of the building and rattled the windows. Not fifteen seconds later, there was another blast, and another one, and another one. The lights flickered; people crouched; all chatter stopped. And just when it seemed to be over, there was one more blast.

Israel Stein said in a loud voice. "Please, everyone, stay calm and stay inside the museum!" With a nod to Manny and Art, the three ran out the front door. But they saw nothing. Running back inside, they bounded up the stairs to the roof. And what they saw was horrific. Smoke rose from the Temple Mount. Even in the darkening sky they could see that the al-Aqsa mosque had sunk right into the ground, with only the top of its dome visible at all, and as for the Dome of the Rock, it was no more. Just then Simon Kalman arrived on the rooftop. The reporter took one look at the horizon and began calling his sources in the police department to find out what happened. The only thing they could confirm—it had been a surprise attack.

Israel, Art, and Manny went back into the museum only to find cell phones ringing and a clamor of voices. Israel grabbed the microphone and appealed for calm and quiet. He then addressed the gathering. "I am sorry to tell you that a terrible catastrophe has happened in Jerusalem tonight. Much of the Temple Mount seems to be on fire. From what we could tell from the rooftop, the Dome of the Rock is no more, and the al-Aqsa Mosque may have collapsed also. I think it would be best if you slowly and calmly leave the building and make your way to your homes. With great regret we will end our evening immediately."

The shock of the situation was so great that people moved in slow motion. Khalil sat with his head in his hands weeping and saying, "This cannot be happening. Not after all the work we have done to make peace!" Art had his arms around Khalil, but he was shaking violently.

Hannah frantically called Sarah and was relieved to discover that she and baby Samuel were fine. The building shook, some artifacts were broken, but overall the damage to their shop and home was minimal. Hannah promised to be home as soon as possible. Art arranged for the limo driver to take them home first.

"Father," said Hannah in tears. "We must go now and just pray, pray again for the peace of Jerusalem."

"There is no peace for Jerusalem," said Khalil. "This probably means war. But who would attack the Temple Mount? Who?"

"Who indeed?" whispered Grace and Art almost in unison. "Who indeed?"

CHAPTER THIRTY-FOUR

MENACHEM'S MISTAKES

As a child, Menachem Sharansky loved to blow things up—at least in his active imagination. He built forts—and leveled them. He built model cars—and demolished them. He set up cans and "shot" them up with his cap pistol. Of course, his furtive activities were kept well out of sight of his deeply conservative Orthodox parents. To them, their middle child was a bookworm, a quiet, wimpy child who studied Torah and later archaeology behind thick glasses.

As he was huffing and puffing up the stairs into the Jewish quarter he realized his child-like fantasies had come true—the C4 had indeed done its job on the Temple Mount. The explosion, fire, and smoke triggered a flashback to when he was crawling out of the rubble of the house of his aunt and uncle. He felt some measure of payback had been doled out for their violent deaths. He remembered all the days in elementary school when kids had teased him for being weak and mousy. Today, finally, he felt strong and heroic.

Today he made a difference for his people. For years, he had prayed vigorously for Messiah to come, but his rabbi had taught him that until the Temple could be rebuilt on Zion that was not likely to happen. What Menachem had failed to think about was what would happen if war broke out and Israel did not take control of the Temple Mount. Or what would happen if peace broke out and Israel decided to work with Palestine!

For Menachem everything had gone perfectly this evening, and now he needed to go home and return to being the person he always was—a good husband and family man. He was pleased; he believed he had made no mistakes. But he was wrong. He had made several.

His first mistake was in trusting El Tigre. He also made the mistake of leaving his backpack under the Temple Mount. Now it was under a pile of rubble. And he failed to read the memo about the new security cameras very recently installed. Finally, he failed to check the duty roster. There were bodies on the Temple Mount, all victims of the blast. But it was the first mistake that produced immediate consequences.

El Tigre realized from the beginning that not everything was likely to go according to plan. After all, he had already flubbed up yesterday. Blowing up a car, without Jake and Melody actually in it, was not the plan! His second plan, to blow up the Lazarus Museum was scrapped; the security was more than he bargained on. Plans for attacking the Knesset were also scrapped. He was trying to accomplish too much too soon. He was working without the support of Abdullah and Hamas, and he was warned by President Abbas not to do anything stupid! So he had settled on the Temple Mount. This wouldn't wipe out his intended targets, but the greater ramifications would deeply affect all of his enemies.

It was an enormous risk to trust such a mission to someone like Menachem. Yet, that was the only kind of Israeli who would be bold enough to do something like that, and it had to be an Israeli, because El Tigre was going to make sure this man got caught. He was going to make sure it was clear to the whole world that a Jew blew up the Temple Mount. He made some phone calls.

"Mossad Headquarters. Who's calling?" said Sharon, who was on call at the desk at the Mossad office in Jerusalem. "You wish to report what? I'll put you right through to an agent!"

While munching on Cheetos, Daniel Goran grabbed the ringing phone. The voice on the other end wildly related an amazing tale!

Goran put his hand over the phone and said to his partner, Josh Lentz, "I've got some nut job on the phone who claims some guy named Menachem Sharansky bombed the Temple Mount!"

"Yeah, well don't laugh, because apparently it's true! I just got the first report. There's been a huge explosion at the Mount! Take down the info while I start the tracer. Keep him talking!"

But when Daniel went back to his phone, the caller had hung up before the trace could be completed. Menachem Sharansky—why did that name ring a bell? Suddenly Goran began scrambling through papers on his desk. A photo popped up. He grabbed it along with a today's memo from Bob Cunningham, his CIA contact.

"Look at this," Daniel yelled to his partner. "Here's that photo of the Jewish guy with El Tigre. Bob Cunningham said it was Menachem Sharansky!"

CHAPTER THIRTY-FIVE

HIGH LEVEL TALKS

MUCH AS HE DID not like the man, Benjamin Netanyahu did realize that President Abbas was the lesser of several evils compared to some people involved in Hamas. The minute he heard about the explosions at the Temple Mount he called Abbas from his limo which was still driving away from the event at the Lazarus Museum.

The President was very cool when the Prime Minister called. "I presume you are calling about the horrendous events now happening on the Temple Mount! You better have a very plausible explanation. Choose your words carefully. And remember, there will be repercussions, no matter what you say."

"I am going to say this just once! The State of Israel, the government I represent, had absolutely no official role whatever in the bombing tonight at the Temple Mount. And it has to be a bombing; there's no way we are having gas explosions this time! I am only beginning to get the reports of the damage. And we will find out who is responsible!"

"And I will tell you just once! The State of Palestine, the official government I represent, did *not* plan or carry out this attack! We, of course, have no reason to do such a thing! I have already been in touch with the Hamas leaders in Gaza. Both Acting President Duwaik and Prime Minister Haniveh categorically deny that their members officially planned or participated in any plot against the Temple Mount. But I will investigate every faction of the Palestinian movement, no matter how radical. Right now I believe it was orchestrated by a rogue third party."

"For now, we have a truce. But Mossad will track down any and every lead, I can assure you," said the Prime Minister firmly.

"Agreed," said a grim Abbas, gripping the phone tightly.

As Netanyahu's limo sped toward his office, he said, "Living in Israel is like living on top of an active volcano! And it just erupted!"

News travels fast, and bad news travels faster. London is two or, at some seasons of the year, three hours behind Jerusalem. When Number 10 Downing Street got the news that explosions had demolished the Temple Mount, Prime Minister Cameron called the President of the United States and then his own counterpart in Jerusalem. It took some time for the connection to be made, because the phone lines into Netanyahu's office were humming with incoming and outgoing calls.

"Good evening Benjamin," said the Prime Minister of England.

"No sir, I am afraid not. It's been a very bad evening indeed, and we are trying to prevent it from getting worse. The Palestinians are already rallying outside Damascus Gate."

"Not good. I just wanted you to know that if you need anything, don't hesitate to call on us. We have troops on Cyprus, as you know. I spoke with President Obama as well. He reminded me they have troops in Adana, Turkey."

"Yes, I appreciate all the support, but this appears to be the work of a third party. So far, no one has taken responsibility, and the Palestinians, including Hamas, have denied all responsibility. Convincing the Arabs that we Israelis had no official role in this disaster will be paramount. It has to be a rogue faction! Mossad already has a lead but it will take time to track down any suspects. Right now President Abbas and I are working towards the same end—avert war and find the perpetrators! Justice will be swift! Whoever has done this is going to pay, and pay dearly. The damage to the holy place is irreparable! If someone thought we the people of Israel would now regain ownership of the Mount, they are sadly mistaken."

The English Prime Minister was glad to hear that a hawk like Netanyahu was not going to dole out instant reprisals before he discovered who the guilty parties were. "Thank you. I hope I can quote you on that. Both President Obama and I will be going live soon to talk to our people. We are monitoring the situation and if MI5 finds out anything useful, I will personally call you with the data."

"Thank you. I must leave. I have incoming calls from Jordan and Egypt!"

CHAPTER THIRTY-SIX

THE FALLOUT

THE LIMOUSINE BROUGHT MANNY, Grace, Yelena, Art, Marissa, Jake, and Melody home in silence. Each was deeply pondering the meaning of tonight's events for the people of Israel and Palestine, for their close friends, and for their own families.

Once inside the compound, Manny and Grace comforted a now crying Yelena who finally went to bed. Manny and Grace sat in the family room, sipping a glass of port just to calm their nerves.

"Manny, this is precisely the sort of thing I've feared for some time. What kind of safe haven or home or future can we provide for Yelena if WWIII is coming to a theater near us? I am tired of it, almighty tired of all the hostilities and the danger and the explosions." Grace began to cry.

Manny was quiet, which was quite characteristic of the tall, dark, business-like Manny. He thought maybe Grace would blow off more steam and he gave her plenty of time to do just that. But it didn't happen. She sounded uncharacteristically defeated.

"Call it prophetic or call it pathetic, I've already had a talk with Yelena about moving to the States even before this latest disaster. I think it's time we faced reality. Things are never going to be entirely stable here. Never! Not ever! Did I mention never! You have a global business. You could run it from the States just as well as you could run it from here. And we would be safer; Yelena would be safer. Picture our daughter graduating with honors from Harvard. It could be good! We are all in good health with few family ties. A move like this is manageable at our age and time of life. And I could always get some kind of lecturing post. I would not be idle!" she added, beginning to rally to her old feisty self.

Manny realized he would have to think seriously about this. He loved his work and his team, the Maccabi Elite. He was on the cusp of winning another championship, hoisting another trophy. But at the same time, he knew in his heart Yelena's future must come first.

A still stunned Art and Marissa, and a very silent Melody and Jake sat quietly listening to the local TV reports back at the Cohen's beach house. Jake thought that no matter what, his mother and sister were safe in the monastery complex. He really wasn't worried about that. But in light of the car bomb, he figured he and Melody had better get out of the country sooner rather than later. This prompted a thought and Jake was the first to break the intense concentration on the news.

"Do you think Manny would put us on his private jet and get us out of the country quickly?" asked Jake to no one in particular.

"I will certainly ask him," said Art pensively. "I have a feeling that the airport will be under close scrutiny, however. Even a private jet leaving could draw suspicion."

"That might be a bit paranoid. But after yesterday's car bombing, getting out quickly might be the way to go. Art, you and I could go to Istanbul for a while. Maybe Manny's pilot could drop us off there," said Marissa with an attempt at a little humor.

Melody surprised everyone, "Let's wait and see what the next few days bring. I feel safe here in Tel Aviv near Grace and Manny. At the very least we do need to see Jake's family once again. Manny already arranged for a body guard." Jake was impressed with this new and strong side of Melody. He still had a lot to learn about his bride.

"Each day's trouble is enough for itself," said Art.

"Amen to that," said Marissa.

Young Muslim Palestinians were gathering outside the Damascus Gate. Each one brought dry wood. Their plan was to start a literal fire to light a figurative fire under the Muslim community. They were already "sure" of what had happened. How was this any different from the Israelis taking their land and then putting up walls to protect new Jewish settlements? This was just one more land grab, only this time they had messed with a holy site. And Muslims around the world would be incensed. Something had to be done. At present twenty young Palestinians were chanting, "*Allah akbar* ("God is Great")!"

Hannah and her father were safely delivered by the limo company back to the Damascus Gate. The evening had been filled first with joy and then enormous sadness. Emotionally, it was just too much to take; Hannah was afraid. Holding on tightly to her father, she guided him along past the chanting crowd and through the gate. The sheer volume of people coming in and out of Damascus Gate made things difficult, very difficult. She kept encouraging her father, "We are almost home; we are almost home. Keep going; keep going." Finally, when she turned the key in the lock, there was Sarah to help her get her father into his easy chair.

Khalil sank deeply into his chair, murmuring to himself, "I am going home, finally going home. I am going home."

"You are home father. We made it." But Khalil was already fast asleep in his chair, breathing very deeply. The evening had taken its toll.

"Is Samuel still asleep?"

Sarah smiled and said, "He's a little angel. He slept through the explosions somehow, but I can tell you everything rattled big time and I was surprised only one of the glass cases broke. The whole floor shook at the second blast and I've been watching the news hoping for some little ray of hope that the madness would soon stop."

"Sarah, I don't think it's safe for you to go out from here tonight. Let me lock up and you can sleep in my father's bed. He will sleep very well in his recliner. We will deal with things in the morning."

Sarah sighed and said, "You're probably right. Both the Israelis and the Palestinians have been on the TV calling for calm, and apparently the Israelis are going to enforce a curfew for the rest of the night. Good luck with that. Without the co-operation of the Palestinian authorities in east Jerusalem it won't work. It will lead to violence."

It had indeed been a night to remember or, as Hannah realized, a nightmare she would never forget the rest of her life.

FIELD TRIP

As HE WAS DRIVING back to Caesarea Maritima, Grayson was in something of a fog. His instinctive reaction had been to pray for Jerusalem and for both the Israelis and Palestinians, but then human nature set in and he began to worry about his job. If there was war then probably archaeological work would be halted for the time being by the IAA. Grayson would have to help the Asbury students get out of the country. But where in the world would *he* go? Israel was now his home. He had not been back to the United States in several years, and had no gainful employment there if he went. These were the things he contemplated as he rode down out of the Judean hills along the main highway to Tel Aviv and then up to Caesarea Maritima.

The Thursday morning papers carried one lead story—the disaster on the Temple Mount. In the *Jerusalem Post*, the museum opening was pushed to the next to the last page with one picture of the Prime Minister cutting the ribbon. *Ha'aretz* decided to delay coverage of the museum gala until the weekend edition.

Around 7:30 the group gathered at Grace's house for breakfast. The news broadcasts were surprising—other than a few bonfires, the night had been much calmer than expected.

Art said, "I'm not sure why things are so quiet. No shots have been fired—no missiles have been sent off. Is everyone just in shock? Both governments have denied any participation. No one has claimed responsibility. This is indeed strange."

"I just hope it's not the calm before another storm—like Carolina thunderstorms—just when you think they're over, another one thunders in," said Melody.

Then Art suddenly remembered that he had talked to Grayson last night about visiting Caesarea. "Grayson was telling me about scrolls and skeletons, that is, before Marissa ended the shop talk!" said Art with a kidding smile aimed at his wife. "I'll give him a call but last night he was hoping we could come to the site this morning. What do you all think?"

Marissa added, "I think that would be a great way to get our minds off our problems! Let's do it!" Suddenly, everyone perked up!

At about nine o'clock, Art and Marissa, Jake and Melody, and Grace and Yelena piled into the Cohen van. At Manny's insistence, the bodyguard followed in a second car. Despite this, in many ways, being outside Jerusalem proper, all seemed normal. They tried to imagine life in the Jerusalem today—schools closed; businesses shut; people hiding behind closed doors. As they drove to Caesarea, a caravan of jeeps and tanks were seen heading toward Jerusalem. Art said a silent prayer that the guns would remain silent.

It was a hot sunny morning as usual, but everyone was wearing what any smart archaeologist would wear—khakis and light-colored t-shirts, bandanas, large sunglasses and brimmed hats! Melody had come prepared with a big bottle of sunblock. When they arrived at the dig sight, they were met not only by Grayson but also by Ada Yardeni and her "bones team" from the IAA. Absent for now, the Asbury team was meeting to discuss their immediate future—stay and work or get out of Israel ASAP.

The bones team seemed particularly on edge and the group stood well back while they did their work in the bone-filled trench. They were particularly interested in a ring encircling the index finger of the skeleton.[1]

---

1. This silver, third century ring was found at the Vinovia (aka Binchester) Roman Fort archaeological site outside of Bishop Auckland in County Durham, England. It has an inset with an intaglio, a carving into the flat surface, showing two fish suspended from an anchor.

Once they were sure that the symbols were Christian, they were ready to sign off on this being an early Christian, not Jewish, set of bones. Dr. Yardeni consulted with Grayson. Both felt that the skeleton was of no concern to the "guardians of the tombs" as the IAA called the Orthodox who protected graveyards. Yardeni and her team beat a fast retreat back to Jerusalem, leaving within minutes of signing the necessary forms so that Grayson could continue the dig.

"Grayson, now that the archaeological police have headed back to Jerusalem, how about we remove the ring from the gravesite and have a closer look?" said Art as they all peered into the trench.

"I thought you'd never ask. I was just holding my breath and waiting for them to confiscate it, but even Ada seemed distracted obviously by what's happening in Jerusalem. She shrugged and said it could stay with the bones." With his little whisk brush, Grayson dusted off the bony hand and ever so gently slid the ring off the index finger of the right hand of the skeleton. Back in the tent, Yelena was asked to draw the symbol that they could see on the ring—an anchor with two fish dangling. There could be little doubt this was a Christian ring, but whose?

Marissa said, "I've seen similar rings in Turkey. It's certainly not a signet ring to be used for wax seals. It's clearly an interesting mix-match of Christian symbols."

"I agree," said Grace, admiring the drawing that Yelena was diligently creating. Yelena suddenly looked up and said, "How come the bones aren't in a bone box? I thought everyone was buried in ossuaries."

"Good question, Yelena!" said an impressed Grayson. "The use of ossuaries ended after the Second Temple period with the destruction of Jerusalem around AD 70, though it probably continued into the second century. But I think our skeleton is later than that."

"I remember a lot of bone boxes were found recently; that's why I thought about it," explained Yelena.

"She's right. Eleven boxes were retrieved by the police just recently. One of these days I want to go over to IAA and have a look at them," said Grace realizing how time flies.

"Okay, so you found just a skeleton with a ring. Anything else," asked Yelena who, at her age, was hard to impress.

Grinning, Grayson fetched a metal cylinder and slid out photocopies of the two scrolls. Unrolling the first one he turned to Grace and said, "What do you think?"

"Not my period, and not my language, but clearly early Greek."

Grayson agreed. "In fact, it's a very early copy of Eusebius' *Demonstrations of the Gospel*, including chapters missing in the forms of that document that still exist today." He then showed his friends the translation he had been working on."

"So," said Art, "You reckon you've found the Father of Church history?!"

"I sure hope so," beamed Grayson. "We need more dough for this dig!"

"Who's the Father of Church History?" asked Yelena.

Grayson responded. "His name was Eusebius! He lived from about 260 to 340. Actually he was Roman but he lived right here in Caesarea and became a bishop around 314. And he was a scholar who wrote books on the Gospels as well as church history. One of his books was called *Ecclesiastical History*."

"So you really think those bones belong to Eusebius? How cool is that! I have got to tell Yuliya all about this! Wow! That means he's been dead for—let me think—1674 years!"

CROSSING OVER JORDAN

It had been a short night, much too short, but when the sun came up Sarah figured it was time to get up and get out quickly. The noise from nearby Damascus Gate had finally subsided about four in the morning when the young men had gone home, having finally run out of energy. Not wanting to disturb the others, Sarah wrote a little note and left it on the kitchen table. Khalil was lying back in his recliner and did not stir as she tiptoed past. As quietly as possible she turned the latch on the front door of the shop, being careful not to hit the bells that hung in the front door, and slipped out into the still streets. The coast was relatively clear and the light was beginning to stream in from the east.

Hannah awoke an hour later to the cries of a wet and hungry Samuel. This she attended to as quietly as possible in the kitchen in the back of the shop, trying not to bother her father. When finally she set Samuel down in his playpen where he was soon preoccupied with his toys, she went into the shop, into the little alcove where Khalil was sleeping. She gently went over and kissed her father on the forehead and whispered, "Time for breakfast."

But Khalil did not respond. She gave him a gentle shake—no response. She laid her head on his chest—no sound. She put her finger on his carotid—no pulse. She stepped back, cocked her head, and realized he had died peacefully sometime in the night. Hannah sat down on the floor next to her father, and just held his hand for a while. It was cold, very cold. She wept, but remembered to thank God for his life and love and so many good times. What was it he had said the previous night before drifting off? "I'm going home. I'm finally going home." And it was true. He had crossed over Jordan into a heavenly promised land.

There is a silence when death is present in the room, a deathly silence one could call it, and it causes all those around to step quietly, speak softly and act reverently. In Hannah's case this was a natural response. But how would Samuel respond?

Hannah looked again at her father's face and saw only peace. She was so relieved, because he had been so upset last night over the lack of peace in the supposed Holy Land. Hannah believed that her father was experiencing true peace now. Though Sunni and Shi'a Muslims have their differences, most Muslims believe that the good deeds one does in life will allow one to enter Paradise on the Last Day or Judgment Day. Hannah believed her father would lie peacefully in his grave and eventually enter Paradise because of his good deeds.

Since no one had been with Khalil when he died, she now recited the *shahada*—"There is no God but Allah and Muhammad is his messenger." Then she said aloud, "Verily we belong to Allah, and truly to Him shall we return. Please forgive any sins of my father." Finally, she fetched a clean cotton sheet and covered his body.

Hannah had many emotions at the moment, and one of them was relief. Her father no longer suffered. She was prepared for this; the problem was, Samuel was not. She decided it was important for him to go and give his grandfather a goodbye hug and kiss before he was taken away by Ibrahim, the funeral director.

Hannah lifted Samuel out of the playpen and headed back but not before grabbing her camera from the desk. Gently explaining to him that his grandfather had been "gathered to his ancestors and was going to be with Allah in paradise" she sat him down gradually into Khalil's lap after removed the cloth from his face. Samuel stared intently at his grandfather. Then he reached forward and pressed his cheek to his grandfather's cheek with both little arms around his neck. Hannah took a picture that she and Samuel would cherish the rest of their lives.

Khalil was a mystic poet, an antiquities expert, an honest merchant, a loving spouse, father and grandfather, a friend to many, a philanthropist in his later years, and most of all a compassionate man who loved Christians, Jews, and Muslims alike. His guiding stars had been prophets—Abraham, Jesus, and Mohammad. Art would have said, "He had fought the good fight, run the race, and now he had finished the course, and was inheriting his reward." She reached for the phone to call Art West.

CHAPTER THIRTY-NINE

DESECRATION

WHEN MUKTAR AL-AWARI REACHED the Western Wall, the military far outnumbered the praying Jews. He slipped into the now demolished area, waving his security badge at one guard after another. Muktar had spent the last thirty years of his life working in and around the Temple Mount, supervising what went on in both the Dome of the Rock and the al-Aqsa Mosque. He was, as the old Ottomans would have said, the Mufti in charge.

Even though he had seen pictures taken early this morning from an Israeli news helicopter, he still could not take in that those enormous structures on the Temple Mount were largely destroyed. When he reached the Dome of the Rock, he saw yellow caution tape extending in all directions. He saw beautiful blue mosaic tiles lying in pieces as if someone had maliciously strewn them to the wind. The Dome itself was gone. And on the famous rock itself there was nothing but wreckage that would take weeks, maybe months, to clean up and sort.

As for the mosque, he could just barely see the top of its dome poking out above ground level. Its superstructure had been destroyed, but somehow the dome had simply fallen on top of the rubble when the foundation collapsed. There might be something salvageable there, but at this point Muktar was not hopeful.

Muktar was neither a violent man nor a vengeful man. He was a deeply spiritual man but he could not remember a time he had been this angry. Whoever did this should pay dearly—with his life! Hundreds of years of history had been destroyed in a single night. He had been reflecting on how easy it was to destroy a thing of beauty. He remembered reading a poem by a mystic writer about this very subject. It was called "China Doll".

The china doll perched, perilous, upon the fireplace ledge

Her beauty unquestionable, but pale and with an edge
Her outlook seemed serene, surveying her domain
As if there were no challenges, no antagonists remained.

Shining bright in morning light, no equals met her gaze
She glimpsed an unimpeded path to always brighter days.
Yet watching dark and dangerous, a creature lurked below
Silently he stalked her, ignoring her obvious No.

The leap on high took seconds,
The fall was just as quick.
The china doll came crashing down
The dust rose up quite thick.

The labor of the artist destroyed forever more
A thousand tiny pieces lay scattered on the floor.

DESECRATION

The cat, with devilish grin, now surveyed *his* domain
Seeing the havoc wreaked, and counting it as gain.

Beauty, like art, is fragile
And easily undone
Molded in a multitude of minutes
Destroyed in less than one.

Muktar memorized this poem when he was young because he found it so striking, and so true. Great art, architecture, and human beauty are fragile, easily destroyed. He remembered the outcry when someone deliberately tried to deface the Pieta, the image of Mary and Jesus in the Vatican. The only word that seemed appropriate was desecration.

In his hearts of hearts, he was not sure he or anyone would be up to the task of rebuilding the Temple Mount and the holy sites. He was, quite simply, heart-broken. He found he had little energy, little enthusiasm for anything right now. In the distance he heard the Muslim call to prayer. Muktar summoned his last bit of strength, sank to his knees at the edge of the rubble, and emitted a loud, long, low scream to Allah.

CHAPTER FORTY

IN MEMORY

WHEN ART TURNED OFF his cell phone and turned back to Marissa, she could tell something was profoundly wrong. "He's gone," he said.

"Who's gone, Art?" asked Marissa, but deep down she knew.

"One of my best friends in the whole world—Khalil el Said has been 'gathered to his ancestors' and the funeral will be tomorrow morning near the Golden Gate, just outside the walls of the old city."

Grace came over and gave Art a hug. "We knew this was coming didn't we? We had so many wonderful adventures together!" Grace began to cry. "I'm so glad he got to be at the museum last night for the dedication! I think it meant a lot to both of them. He seemed totally surprised!"

"But I noticed how often he withdrew from the crowd. Being Sufi at least in heart, he went often to his mystical place to cope with his physical problem."

"What's a Sufi?" asked Yelena.

Grace replied, "Sufis believe in a deeply spiritual, often mystical, form of Islam. They are not political and certainly no threat to anyone—unlike the radical ISIS Muslims. All Muslims believe that they are on the right path to knowing God and they all hope to be with God in Paradise after death. But Sufis believe you can draw close to God in this life. To travel this path they usually study with a teacher. I have never met his teacher. Maybe he will be at the funeral."

"Didn't Mr. el Said donate a lot of artifacts to the Museum? He must have had a lot of money! How come he lived in the back of the shop?" she asked thinking about how different her life was at the Cohen compound.

"Sufis strive to live a simple life that is not filled with material possessions. We could all learn a lot from that. Although he wasn't an ascetic, he certainly did not believe in living high. He gave much of his money to charity," said her mother.

"We can attest to that," added Marissa. "Khalil generously supported Art's archaeology work to say nothing of the gifts to the Museum."

"I remember him trying to explain Sufism to me one day. Sufis believe they are seeking the perfect form of worship as revealed by Gabriel to Muhammad. 'Worship and serve Allah as you are seeing Him and while you see Him not yet truly He sees you.' Khalil quoted that to me several times," explained Art.

"Something we could all strive for—Jews, Christians, and Muslims," said Grayson. "When you know all the details about the funeral, let me know and I'll be there. I got a text message a few minutes ago. Right now, the dig has been suspended. Apparently, the Asbury students will be returning to the States as soon as possible."

The friends parted after a few more minutes and Grace drove everyone but Grayson back to her house for a late lunch. Grace first brought out cold drinks for everyone—a choice of lemonade or champagne. "To Khalil," said Grace, raising her glass of bubbly.

"To Khalil," they all said as one.

"Grace if you don't mind, I'd like to say a little thanksgiving prayer right now."

"Of course," said Grace, and she bowed her head with the others.

"Lord, Khalil has been a true friend of us all for so many years and we will miss him sorely. But we would be amiss if we did not thank you profusely for his life and all the ways he enriched all of ours. He was definitely one of a kind, someone very special, a gentle and gracious and compassionate person. Please give Hannah strength and wisdom to make the right decisions going forward. Help us to maintain a memory of all that Khalil meant to us, and cherish that memory in our hearts. Finally, we ask that the funeral tomorrow will not be interrupted by trouble of any kind, despite all the chaos in Jerusalem just now. Let Khalil be laid to rest, and rest in peace."

And everyone said, "Amen."

CHAPTER FORTY-ONE

POLICE WORK

AT MOSSAD HEADQUARTERS, JOSHUA Lentz and Daniel Goran were looking at the photo of El Tigre and Menachem Sharansky, the latter having been identified by their CIA contact, Bob Cunningham. Goran was still trying to remember where he had seen that face before. Now they were dealing with the anonymous phone call that claimed Sharansky had something to do with last night's bombing at the Temple Mount.

"How much do you wanna bet those two are both involved?" pondered Lentz.

Just then Goran's eyes opened wide and he waved his hand wildly at his partner. "That's where I've seen that guy in the picture, working at the Temple Mount digs! I saw him when I was on the Mount after the gas explosion!"

Lentz got excited. "I'm going to call Joe Epstein. He heads up the IAA security at the underground operations on the Mount." Soon he made contact.

"Joe, it's Lentz at Mossad. How are you managing at the Temple Mount?"

"It's bad, really bad. We've lost some good people. And the destruction is beyond belief," said Joe very somberly.

"Do you have a Menachem Sharansky on your team at the Mount?"

"I do indeed! And I think his brother died in the explosion! But I don't have all the details yet. I haven't seen Menachem for a few days. He's on holiday I think. The odd thing is, he didn't turn in his keys before he left. He's usually very reliable."

"What else do you know about the guy? Did he seem okay to you?"

"He's a quiet guy. Kinda' mousy. I will say, he's a Zionist. I've been with him at lunch when he's been in heated discussions over the future of Israel and the rebuilding of the Temple. I know he has a wife and kid and seemed like a quiet family man most of the time."

"Last I heard about one-third of our people believe in rebuilding the Temple. The Golden Dome sitting on top of the Temple Mount is a reminder to all Jews that Torah cannot be fully practiced or fulfilled until we have a Third Temple. So I have to be careful about jumping to conclusions. Being a Third Temple advocate, which I am, doesn't make me a terrorist, which I'm not. I'll get back to you, Joe." Lentz hung up.

"Yeah, I'm all for the Third Temple myself," added Goran. "I'm more worried about the fact that Sharansky was hanging out with El Tigre—a chance meeting in a café? I doubt it!"

"Let's contact our agent in Jericho and locate El Tigre. The beeper indicates he's in the area still but I'd rather have a visual," said Lentz.

Next, calling their boss, Lentz said, "Remember that picture I told you about—the one with El Tigre having coffee with a Jewish man? He's been identified as Menachem Sharansky who works under the Temple Mount for the IAA. He had keys and access and my contact, Joe Epstein, says he's not been at work for several days. Also, Joe thinks he's a more radical Zionist. In short, we may have a lead on the bombing. I've got an address for this guy."

"Then head out there and find out what you can. Take a team and bring him in! And I'll send another team to bring in that Malak guy for questioning—does he really think he's the new El Tigre? He's dangerous if he really thinks so. But before you go, turn on the news—the joint Israeli/Palestinian leaders are on the air."

In an unprecedented gesture, both Israeli Prime Minister Netanyahu and Palestinian President Abbas were on camera. Netanyahu was speaking.

"Both President Abbas and myself assure you that neither government was responsible for last night's horrendous attack on the Temple Mount. And both of us vow that if any Jews or Palestinians are involved, we will track down each and every one. I deeply apologize for the desecration of the Muslim holy site. I further pledge that the Israeli State will contribute to the fund for the repairs."

The two Mossad agents listened carefully to the speeches and then left to investigate their target, Menachem Sharansky.

Though there had been several mass rallies by some radical Palestinians, in a development no one predicted, the appeals for calm by Presidents

Abbas and Prime Minister Netanyahu seemed to have had an effect. People were scared enough to believe the reports that this was done by some outside agency with no connections to either the government of Israel or Palestine, in part because both governments repeatedly denied such a connection and promised to help each other recover. Deep down the people wanted peace, not war.

It was a nice afternoon, a normal afternoon, when a knock came on the Sharansky front door in New Jerusalem. When Mrs. Sharansky opened the door, there stood a sea of policemen in full gear.

"I am Detective Lentz. Are you Mrs. Sharansky?" After she nodded, he continued, "Is your husband, Menachem Sharansky, at home?"

"Wait here, I will fetch him," promised Mrs. Sharansky. Rachel ran to the back garden where her husband was playing with his five-year-old son, Aaron.

"Is there some reason why policemen should be at our front door asking for you?"

Menachem looked up and smiled, "Well maybe something to do with my work at the Temple Mount perhaps? The IAA knows I'm on holiday, but I suppose they are interviewing everyone connected to the Temple Mount after last night's bombing," he said without batting an eyelash.

"What are you not telling me?" replied a panicked Rachel. "Where were you last night?"

Menachem slid past his wife and jauntily walked toward the door looking every bit the self-assured young Israeli. But Menachem was not expecting armed guards surrounding his front door. His smile disappeared instantly. Lentz took the lead.

"Mr. Sharansky. You work at the Temple Mount, do you not? We have reason to believe you are also involved with this man," barked Lentz as he showed him the picture of Menachem with El Tigre in the Jericho café. Menachem swallowed hard when he saw the picture. "Mr. Sharansky, we are taking you in for further questioning. But I'm going to let you say goodbye to your wife."

Menachem found his tearful wife sitting in the kitchen, holding a cup of tea in her shaking hands. He sat down and looked her in the face. "Don't cry honey; I will be alright. No one will blame you. What I did, I did for the good of our cause."

"Your cause, not our cause! Your first responsibility is to your wife and child, not some crazy idea about rebuilding the Temple! I knew you were involved somehow!"

He was silent and then said, "I have to go with these men." As she stood up, she dropped the teacup which shattered on the stone floor. He put his arms around her and kissed her on the cheek. "Don't worry, you'll see me again."

She looked down at the floor and said, "I don't think so, but I still love you." He went to the backyard and called Aaron. Aaron came running and leapt into his father's arms. "I love you Aaron," Menachem whispered in his son's ear. "Someday you will understand and be proud of me." He grabbed his Torah and black hat and headed out the front door in the custody of the policemen.

Rachel walked to the front door and watched them go. Deep in her heart she knew it would be the last time they would ever be a family. Deep in her heart, she knew what he had done, and there would be no forgiveness. Then came the final blow. Menachem's mother called in tears wailing that Jacob, her older son, a security guard at the Mount, was found dead in the rubble.

Back at headquarters, Menachem was placed in an interrogation room and allowed to sit and stew for an hour while Lentz and Goran watched from behind the two-way mirror. Menachem sat quietly praying the whole time. Finally, Goran entered, played the "good cop" and offered him a cup of coffee with a warm smile. When his guard was down, Lentz stormed in and threw pictures of the Temple Mount destruction on the table.

"Okay, Sharansky. Let's look at a little security footage and tell me if you recognize anyone!" The footage ran, and sure enough there was a man running like crazy from the left end of the Wailing Wall area heading across the square towards the steps leading up to the Jewish quarter. Then the huge explosion knocked out the camera and the footage stopped cold. Menachem was silent.

"I repeat," said Lentz. "Do you recognize yourself in that camera shot?"

Menachem's brain was running a mile a minute. If he co-operated he might be seen as a hero by many Jews. He truly believed that what he did was a good and honorable act for an Orthodox Jew of his persuasion. But for now, he remained silent.

CHAPTER FORTY-TWO

FUNERAL FOR A FRIEND

THE GOLDEN GATE LIES on the eastern slope of the Temple Mount overlooking the Kidron Valley and the Mount of Olives beyond that. This oldest of all the gates to the old city, seven of which are still open, was the only one not rebuilt by Suleiman the Magnificent in AD 1539–42 when new walls were erected to fortify the city. In AD 810, twelve centuries ago, the Arabs walled up the Golden Gate. Some of the stones surrounding the gate date to the sixth century BC, the time of Nehemiah.

The Golden Gate is actually two gates representing repentance and mercy. Traditionally, judgments were rendered at the gates of the city, especially the Golden Gate. For Jews, Messiah will come eventually, and he will arrive at the Golden Gate. For Christians, the Golden Gate is the site of Palm Sunday and the future site of Jesus' second coming at the end times. For Muslims, Allah's final judgment will occur here also. To be buried near the Golden Gate means you are the first to be raised and greet Messiah/Jesus/Allah, according to your faith.

In the Muslim tradition, a person must be buried as soon as possible—autopsy, embalming and cremation are not allowed. Sharia (Islamic religious law) requires ritual bathing and shrouding of the body in simple cloth followed by prayer before burial. Khalil had been granted the honor of being buried near the Golden Gate with the old Muslim saints.

According to Muslim tradition, the corpse must be thoroughly washed, usually three times but always an odd number, according to the local Palestinian traditions. In Khalil's case, it happened within hours of when the funeral arrangers came and collected his body from the antiquities shop. Normally the washers would be male members of the same family, but since Khalil had no male relatives, the funeral director himself had performed the service for free, as a gift to the family. Once bathed, Khalil's body was wrapped in three sheets of plain, cotton cloth. Some perfume was added to retard odor. All was now ready for Friday's funeral.

The first stop was the mosque where Khalil had worshipped. *Salat al-Janazah* (funeral prayers) was performed by the Imam and other members of the Muslim community in the courtyard—always facing Mecca. Art knew enough Arabic to realize that this was the prayer for the forgiveness of the sins of the deceased.

From the mosque, the body was transported to the cemetery outside the Golden Gate. Fortunately, in Khalil's worshipping community, women were allowed at the graveside. A host of other people, especially their neighboring shopkeepers, had walked down from the old city and arrived just as Hannah and Samuel alighted from the limousine. The Muslim cleric was waiting at the burial site. The wind was blowing rather stiffly down the valley. Everyone, including the cleric, was dressed in black. Looking up Art saw at least fifty people lining the wall above the gravesite, looking down from above, like saints in heaven waiting for Khalil.

Once everyone was in place, all the Muslims began saying more prayers in Arabic, including Jake. Art recognized the fourfold repetitions of "God is great" (*Allah Akbar*), but also noticed there was no bowing and no prostrating during this prayer. Normally Muslims get on their knees and bow their heads to the ground in the direction of Mecca when they pray. Everyone maintained a high level of decorum; wailing is not a Muslim tradition. It is a solemn ritual.

The burial itself happened quite quickly. The grave was aligned per-pendicular to the direction of Mecca so that Khalil's body would be facing the holy city. Khalil's old friend Omar performed the ritual of burial. He jumped down into the grave; accepted the body as it was handed down; and gently laid the body on its right side facing Mecca. He then placed a fist-sized clump of packed soil under the head, chin, and right shoulder. Finally Omar said, "In the name of Allah we bury Khalil el Said according to the ways of the prophet of Allah."

In the Muslim tradition, the grave marker is plain and small, no more than twelve inches high. A few flowers can be placed on the grave, but elaborate wreathes are discouraged. For her father, Hannah had requested his favorite purple and white pansies.

At this point the cleric and Hannah herself poured three fistfuls of dirt into the grave and then recited the traditional prayer, "From Allah we have come, and to Allah we return." The prayer for the forgiveness of sins of the deceased was then repeated, followed by some more prayers.

Then the gravediggers came and covered the body completely. Sod and flowers were placed over the topsoil. Hannah handed Omar a copy of Gibran's *The Prophet*. He began reading the passage:

> Then Almitra spoke, saying, "We would ask now of Death."
>
> And he said: "You would know the secret of death.
>
> But how shall you find it unless you seek it in the heart of life?

Omar had a deep, resonating speaking voice reminiscent of Khalil's and everyone was enthralled with the reading of Gibran's famous poem (see Chapter 28, "Life and Beyond").

Mourning can last up to forty days, but the first three days are set aside for the family to receive guests. Everyone went back to the el Said shop where many of the local shopkeepers had already brought food for all the mourners. For three days, Hannah and Samuel would be looked after in very special ways.

CHAPTER FORTY-THREE

TIGER ON THE LOOSE

LENTZ AND GORAN WERE given full reign by their superiors to interrogate Menachem and continue the investigation. Friday morning they sat opposite Menachem in a drab room with bars on the windows and doors. Goran began by showing Menachem a picture of his dead brother, Jacob. Menachem was stunned and began to cry uncontrollably. The two agents actually felt sorry for him—but just for a moment.

Next they showed him the picture taken in Jericho of him having breakfast with El Tigre. Menachem obviously recognized the man, but it was also obvious that Menachem had no idea who he really was. Lentz finally told Menachem that his lunch mate was Malak Al-Zawari, alias El Tigre. "I just had lunch with him. He is a fellow zealot, or so he implied!"

"Never trust Hamas," said Lentz.

"I didn't know he was Hamas. If he's Muslim, why would he want to destroy the Temple Mount," asked Menachem with great anxiety.

"Ah, that's what we want to know also. Why indeed? We know he has close contacts with Abdul Abdullah, a bigwig in Gaza. We plan to ask him the same question!"

At that point, it was obvious that they had to find El Tigre—quickly! So far, surveillance on El Tigre had not led to any recent Hamas contacts. They knew he had been in Gaza, presumably with Abdul Abdullah, immediately after his release from Egypt. But Abdullah was an unlikely suspect in the bombing. They also knew he had met with President Abbas, although Mossad was certainly not planning to implicate the President in the recent bombing! Surprisingly, El Tigre seemed to be operating alone.

The beeper had been useless of late, and Maimonides had not seen El Tigre since Wednesday morning. So no one knew El Tigre's whereabouts.

The team sent to find him on Thursday returned empty handed. Mossad was beginning to get nervous.

To be on the safe side, Malak did not return to his apartment Wednesday night. Making very sure he wasn't followed, he had checked into a small hotel outside of Jericho. War, not peace, was his goal. He craved a real war between Palestinians and Israelis. He couldn't believe the commitment of Netanyahu to help with the rebuilding of the Temple Mount. El Tigre also realized that the police had probably caught up with that naïve Zionistic zealot, Menachem, already. His anonymous phone call to Mossad would nearly ensure that outcome.

He had no reason to believe that he would be implicated. But Menachem might break and tell them about the mystery man who supplied him with the C4. Even an artist's sketch could bring the police down upon him.

For now, he was laying low on the outskirts of Jericho listening intently to the news releases. He waited hoping that the authorities would tell everyone that an orthodox Jew blew up the Temple Mount. He waited in the hopes of war. Unlike Menachem, he didn't really care who won. War was good for business. His enemies would suffer in multiple ways. That would have to suffice in terms of revenge for his brother's death.

By Thursday night it was clear that the two governments were more interested in peace than war. That made El Tigre very nervous indeed. He decided to execute his escape plan—cross over into Jordan. His lock box contained all the paperwork, some legal, some forged, to allow him to travel freely through the Middle East. The question was, should he risk crossing the Allenby Bridge? Would the authorities be on the lookout for him? He decided to risk it.

El Tigre shaved his head, donned a new suit, changed his license plates, and headed toward the Allenby Bridge with a passport and license reading Kamal Gibran. "El Tigre is dead," he mused. "Long live El Tigre!"

Multiple bank accounts assured his financial survival. Contacts in Jordan assured a safe house when he arrived. Bribery at the border was also a possibility. Thinking about security cameras, he said to himself, "Remember to keep your head down!" Early Friday morning, Malak Al-Zawari crossed the Allenby Bridge and drove into the countryside of Jordan.

While munching on pistachios, Lentz saw the ping again, east but off the grid. And that surely must mean El Tigre was in Jordan, the only country he could quickly get into from Jericho.

At that moment, Goran came into the office. "Remember I promised to review the real El Tigre's file? Apparently, Jake Arafat had a lot to do with his arrest. There's our link to the bombing at the monastery. Now we have two reasons to bring him in."

"Easier said than done," moaned Lentz. "We've lost him. Maimonides can't find him and, well, look at the screen. He's off the grid."

"Looks like Jordan to me," said Goran. "And that means a call to the GID! I'll clear it with the boss."

As soon as he got the go-ahead, Lentz called the headquarters of the Jordanian equivalent to Mossad—the GID or General Intelligence Directorate. Fortunately, they were considered an elite group, one of the best in the Arab world when it came to international security. MI5, the CIA, and Mossad all listened when GID spoke! Western countries were especially cautious when dealing with Jordan, one of their few allies in the Middle East. Jordan plays a central role in maintaining stability. True, the GID was still a little upset over the 1997 attempt by Mossad to assassinate a Hamas leader, Khaled Mashaal, in Amman, the capital of Jordan. Best to work with the GID on this case, especially since the suspect was definitely involved in the bombing on the Temple Mount! Soon, Lentz was put through to General Hasam.

"Sir, this is Agent Joshua Lentz. Mossad needs your help. We believe that a major criminal, probably responsible for masterminding the attack on the Muslim buildings on the Temple Mount, is now in Jordan. His real name is Malak Al-Zawari. He is the half-brother of the infamous El Tigre who died some years ago. But Malak has been referring to himself as El Tigre. My partner is faxing you the whole file right now. I have to confess we've lost him. He seems to have crossed the Jordan at Jericho, probably using the Allenby Bridge. We can check security cameras, but I wouldn't put it past him to go through with a fake passport, fake license, a disguise—you know the tricks. Technically, we have a homing device on him, or actually *in* him, but it hasn't been reliable. We're sending you all the details. He was last seen Wednesday morning. We know he made contact before the bombing with Menachem Sharansky who is now in custody."

General Hasam listened carefully, taking notes. "We have most of the details from the police. And we were waiting to hear about Al-Zawari. If we find him, I'll notify the head of the police and Mossad myself. There's going to be some legal tangles in terms of who will prosecute."

"That's above my pay grade," granted Lentz. "Happy hunting."

"Trust me, King Abdullah would like nothing better than to be able to say his people arrested the man who blew up his Golden Dome."

CHAPTER FORTY-FOUR

THE BUSINESS OF BASKETBALL

THE CAR EXPLOSION, THE destruction of the Temple Mount, and the death of Khalil el Said remained very much in the mind of Melody Arafat. Though she tried to stay calm, even strong, she really wanted to go home—to her home. The Holy Land, however, was Jake's home, his family's home, and he did not seem to have any thoughts about leaving early. The initial plan had been to stay for three weeks for family visiting and sightseeing. But she was feeling very uneasy and very queasy of late.

But today, Saturday, Jake was going with Manny to the Maccabi Elite arena to rev up the team that had a real chance to win the championship this year. Tomorrow, they would head north with Art and Marissa to tour the Galilee. Grace personally assured her that life in the Galilee would be greener and more peaceful than in Judea.

Manny, being the early riser, was sitting in the breakfast nook on the patio devouring bagels, lox, cream cheese and the *Jerusalem Post*. Jake loped into the breakfast room and quickly noted that the maid had set out a breakfast bar for everyone: scrambled eggs, kosher sausage, bagels, cereal and fruit. Jake decided he would have all of it.

"So the Cat's awake? grinned Manny.

"Barely. Maybe after some good coffee."

"When we go to Menora Arena, I want you in on this conference call to Kevin Love so you can answer any questions he might have about playing here. I've decided he's the player who will put us over the top, and he's available too! Will you do that for me?"

"Happy to do so. I like Kevin. He's a terrific player and this would be a good rehab stint if the Minnesota Timberwolves allow it."

"I've already cleared that hurdle. I'll be paying a pretty sum for this 'rent a player' deal. He will play maybe thirty games, and that's if we get to the championship. But today we have to convince him to come. So that's the big item on this morning's agenda. So here's a copy of information on Kevin—history, stats, the usual. Read up—quickly. And by the way, the others can catch up later. Grace will bring them down to the complex."

"Right," said Jake. "Eat quick; study quick. Got it!"

At exactly 7:45, Manny's Porsche was revved up and ready to drive to the office. Jake hopped into the passenger seat wearing his Hornets uniform and hat. He looked every inch the tall NBA basketball star that he was.

With a zip in his step, and rubbing his hands together, Manny sat down in his swivel chair, pointed to a similar one for Jake, cued his legal aide Sam (short for Samson) Adelman to crank up the conference screen on the wall and said, "I just love making deals!"

"So long as they're legal," added Sam nodding wisely.

Suddenly, there on the screen was the bearded power forward sitting on an enormous plush sofa looking relaxed and confident.

"Jake, you're on first," said Manny.

"So Kevin, you're up late? How's things in Minnesota?"

"I'll let you in on a little secret. I'm about to be traded to the Cleveland Cavaliers!"

"That is news, especially since you set an NBA record to become the first player to record 2,000 points, 900 rebounds, and 100 three-pointers in a single season!"

"You know your stats," said Kevin grinning.

"I did my homework, man! And I'd like to follow in your footsteps some day!" said Jake with a side wink to Manny. "Meanwhile, we've both had rehab troubles. My rehab finishing date is still too far away for me to be useful to the Maccabi Elite team, but for you the timing is good I hope."

"Yes it is! So tell me about Maccabi Elite. Is this like playing in the Instructional League or the D League here?"

"Not at all. It would be like playing for Barcelona. The European style of play is more physical, less fouls called."

"Good. That suits my bump and grind inside game."

"Exactly! I'm the shooting guard; I stay away from the big bruisers. You should feel right at home on this court."

"But what about the political situation? Is it even safe for me to come to Israel at this point? I read the newspapers this morning, and things look pretty grim."

"You will not be playing in Jerusalem. Tel Aviv is a big city, relatively quiet, right on the Mediterranean. That's where we are staying. Apparently, neither the Jewish nor Palestinian governments had anything to do with the bombing of the Temple Mount. People are too scared of war. Contrary to expectations, this bombing seems to have set them on the road to peace, not war! But it will be awhile before the tourists return—all the traffic is headed out of Israel right now. The Old City is crawling with military—and rightly so."

Kevin took this all in and said, after a pause, "So let me talk to Mr. Cohen."

Manny then appeared on the screen and said, "Nice to meet you Kevin. All my scouts and my friend Jake tell me only great things about your work ethic and skills. So what will it take for me to entice you to play about thirty games for Maccabi Elite?"

"Well, if you were to break down my current contract, per game, counting all the seasons involved in the contract, I reckon I make about fifteen thousand dollars a game."

"That's a nice chunk of change for a per diem. So here's my offer. I will give you ten thousand dollars a game for the remaining regular season; twenty thousand a game for the playoffs if we make the championship series; a twenty-thousand-dollar bonus if we win the championship with your help; and another forty thousand dollars if you're named MVP!"

Kevin scratched his beard and said, "My girlfriend is not going to be pleased, but I see it as a once in a lifetime trip. So when do you want me there?"

"Yesterday, of course! Seriously, next week I'll send my jet to the Minneapolis airport. Sam, my legal assistant, will have you sign the contract on board. He'll be in touch with all the details."

"And Melody and I will be in Tel Aviv to meet you. You made a good decision, Kevin."

After ending the call, Manny was pleased. "I like the boldness of this plan. I can see the sports page headlines: 'All You Need is Love!'"

"I'll bet he's never heard that one before," said Jake a bit sarcastically. "Let's get down to the court. The boys are already working out and I'm raring to go!"

Jake loved the world of basketball. Watching a wheeler-dealer like Manny at work was an education in itself. Someday, thought Jake, I would like to be a businessman. He was sure Manny would help. Jake made a mental note to tell Melody that Manny was confident enough things were cooling down that he was sending his plane to Minneapolis to pick up none other than Kevin Love for the basketball team. Obviously, thought Jake, that should put her mind at ease.

CHAPTER FORTY-FIVE

GRAYSON'S GRAVE DECISION

ON THIS SUNNY SATURDAY, Grayson was also out and about. He decided to go to Bethlehem to learn more about another famous Church Father—Jerome (AD 347-420)—who was born shortly after Eusebius died. He wondered how much Eusebius had influenced the life and work of Jerome.

All of the major Church Fathers—Origen, Pamphilius, Eusebius, and Jerome—seemed to have a lot in common. They wanted to study the earliest possible New Testament texts. They wanted to harmonize all of the accounts or at least to find a way to reconcile problem passages. They all had a knack for allegorizing the Old Testament texts, assigning symbolic meanings to literal events. They all seemed to be very suspicious of anyone who engaged in eschatological predictions—foretelling the biblical future. They shied away from charismatic types like Papias.

Jerome was not from the east. He was educated in Rome in rhetoric and philosophy, and only came to the Holy Land later in life. One of the things that had struck Grayson about Jerome was how he would often meditate on the Christian dead. He would visit the ancient sepulchers in Rome, and often came away repenting of the sins of his youth as a student in Rome. The following quote was one of Grayson's favorites when it came to Jerome. It seemed like a script from a Hollywood horror movie.

> Often I would find myself entering those crypts, deep dug in the earth, with their walls on either side lined with the bodies of the dead, where everything was so dark that almost it seemed as though the Psalmist's words were fulfilled, "Let them go down quick into Hell." Here and there the light, not entering in through windows, but filtering down from above through shafts, relieved

the horror of the darkness. But again, as soon as you found your-self cautiously moving forward, the black night closed around and there came to my mind the line of Virgil, *"Horror ubique animos, simul ipsa silentia terrent* [the horrors and the silences terrified their souls]."[1]

When he got to Bethlehem, Grayson did not follow the long line of tourists into the Church of the Nativity. Instead he made a beeline for the newer Catholic Church of St. Catherine next door. Passing the statue of St. Jerome, Grayson went in the back door of the Cathedral. Grayson then

1. Jerome, *Commentarius in Ezzechielem*, c. 40, v. 5 and *Patrologia Latina* 25, 373.

carefully descended down the narrow steps into the crypt area beneath the church. Altars, niches and lit candles filled the area. Here he planned to meet with Father Abbas, the Franciscan cleric now in charge of St. Catherine's.

While waiting for his friend Father Abbas, Grayson picked up a brochure and began reading more about the life of Jerome. Most importantly for Bethlehem it seems Jerome arrived around AD 388 and spent his life living as a hermit until his death in 420. In his underground cave, Jerome spent thirty years translating the Scriptures from Hebrew and Greek into Latin—the so-called Latin Vulgate—the first official version of the Bible not in the original languages. During those years he was assisted by two noble Roman women, Paula and her daughter Eustochium.

Although he was originally buried in Bethlehem, legend says his bones were moved to Santa Maria Maggiore in Rome. Strangely, his head is said to be in the Italian town of Nepi, although another tradition claims it is in El Escorial, an historic residence of the King of Spain north of Madrid!

"My goodness," mused Grayson. "It seems as if poor Jerome has lost his head! No wonder the most famous painting of him has him staring at skull on his desk!"

As much as anything, this trip was a spiritual pilgrimage for Grayson. He was doing a little soul searching after the death of Khalil and the disasters in Jerusalem. His heart was heavy, and he had become rather convinced that he was not going to see a great deal of his friend Art any more.

And he had heard rumors that Grace wanted to move to the States as well. His mentors were leaving, and one of his friends had died.

Father Abbas entered the crypt. A big smile spread across the cleric's face when he saw Grayson.

"What brings you to Bethlehem? It can't be the Roman census, as was the case with the Holy Family."

Grayson laughed, "Good one, Father, but I have a grave matter to discuss with you—literally, a grave matter. It is possible that at my dig in Caesarea Maritima we have found the skeleton of St. Eusebius."

"That would be quite the find, my son, especially since tradition has it that Eusebius was buried here! I've always imagined that Eusebius's burial site was known to Jerome who may have visited it often while working on the Latin Vulgate. You do know of Jerome's interest in visiting graves," laughed the priest.

"That's quite an image, Father! I can see why you thought that! But what if I really have found the bones of Eusebius? What would the Catholic Church make of that!? Since he's not Jewish, the IAA isn't pressing me to deliver him up to one of their museums. Honestly, I don't know what to do with it. We need to move it out of the present site as we are in the process of a huge archaeological dig, and we do not want to desecrate the skeleton. There doesn't seem to be any Christian graveyard in Caesarea that I know of, so, what do we do?"

Father Abbas was silent for a few minutes, and said, "Let me do some checking. Are you sure it is Eusebius?"

"No, but he does have some sort of ornate early Christian ring on his hand. I've brought a picture of it for you," said Grayson.

Father Abbas pondered the image for some time. "If it is in fact Eusebius, then there could be a squabble among the various Christian groups over his bones. Unfortunately, squabbles over turf seem to be the order of the day around here. So, let me make some phone calls. It's time for Mass in the small chapel. You are most welcome to attend and pray. Then we can talk about other things. Somehow I sense you are troubled."

Grayson smiled and said, "Father, you've always been very perceptive. And I'd be honored to worship with you, though I'm sure you know I am Christian but not Catholic."

"No problem. Sadly, I cannot serve you the Eucharist. Trust me, son, if it were my decision, the Lord's Table would be open to all who love Jesus as Lord and Savior just as you and I do."

CHAPTER FORTY-SIX

PRACTICE SESSIONS

GRACE BROUGHT MELODY, ART, and Marissa over to Menora Arena to watch Jake practice with the Maccabi Elite team. Art decided to hang out with Manny and the coaches. The girls sat in the bleachers.

On the court, Jake was good-naturedly teasing some of the Elite players—performing tricks he had learned from the Harlem Globetrotters who often came to Charlotte for exhibitions. Everyone on the floor was in a light-hearted mood, and the coaches were even laughing. It was obvious that Jake was in his element.

Melody was also enjoying the show; it was a good distraction from her worries about being in the Holy Land in general—until she started getting light-headed again. She sat down, looking rather pale. Marissa quickly noticed.

"Melody, you don't look so good," said Marissa with some concern.

"I'm just feeling a bit light-headed and nauseous," she responded. "I think the events of this week are catching up with me."

"I'll fetch some water and a cold cloth," said Grace. "Be right back!"

Melody reached into her bag and pulled out a power bar. That and the water and cold cloth seemed to calm her down and she felt better.

Marissa whispered in her ear, "How long have you been feeling like this?"

"Off and on for the past couple of weeks. I just chalked it up to nerves—getting ready for the trip was hard enough. And let's not forget what we've been through since we got here! Our car was destroyed! The Temple Mount was bombed! Good grief!" said Melody beginning to get upset again.

"Stay calm, dear. You're right," said Grace chiming in. "That's enough reason to feel a bit off."

"Or it could be something else," hinted Marissa simultaneously staring down at her very pregnant body.

"Oh, my, you don't think . . ." said Melody suddenly imagining herself pregnant.

"It's possible," said Grace smiling. But her smile ended quickly when Marissa doubled over in pain.

"Marissa! What's the matter!" cried Grace.

"Contractions!" said Marissa breathing hard. "I'm having contractions!"

"But you're not due for at least two months!" said Grace.

"It went away," sighed Marissa. "It felt like I was carrying a bowling ball. My stomach just went tight, like a drum, but it passed already."

"Braxton Hicks," said Melody. "It usually happens by the third trimester. Just relax and take deep breaths. If the contractions are very irregular, you don't need to worry. By the way, did you sleep well last night? Did you eat this morning?"

"Not well and not much! And I'm really thirsty," admitted Marissa.

"Dehydration can make it worse," continued Melody.

"I guess I'm the water boy today," said Grace racing off again.

By now, Art was noticing the commotion in the stands, and ran up to check on everyone.

"We think Marissa is having Braxton Hicks," explained Melody whose biology degree was now coming in handy.

"Yeah, I'm having another one—but it's gone already," said Marissa.

"So it's just practice time for the big day—sorta' like the team practicing for the playoffs!" laughed Art with some relief.

Grace Levine's personal gynecologist in Tel Aviv was named Elizabeth Sharon. As a favor to Grace, a longtime friend, she agreed to see both Melody and Marissa Sunday afternoon.

Marissa got a good night's sleep and felt much better. She was still experiencing occasional contractions. Dr. Sharon's brief exam assured her that all was well. "Your baby seems to be normal in size. When you get back home, you can get an ultrasound—around thirty-two weeks is about right."

In her office, she talked to both Art and Marissa. She explained Braxton-Hicks contractions in detail and alerted Marissa to be on the lookout for real complications. But for now there was no reason to think Marissa would deliver anytime soon. "Be safe and don't stray too far from the hospital," was Dr. Sharon's best advice.

Art and Marissa emerged all smiles. "Everything is still fine; just some Braxton Hicks contractions. I'm not going to let that slow me down! Your turn!"

Melody just laughed, and then a nurse poked her head around the admissions counter and said, "Mr. and Mrs. Arafat, the doctor will see you now."

Marissa sat down and sighed. From now on out for the next two months she would need to be careful. Should she go back to the States? Or maybe Izmir where her parents now lived? She and Art looked at each other. The reality of the impending birth was really setting in. Both were thinking, "We need to talk, but not in a waiting room!" Why couldn't life be simpler, she wondered?

Melody's exam included her first ever ultrasound. Jake and Melody held hands as they stared at the monitor.

Dr. Sharon almost whispered, "Look closely. There's a heartbeat! It's faint. Usually we don't see this until at least week six. Congratulations! You are definitely pregnant!"

Jake and Melody were dumbfounded. Jake leaned in and said, "Hi there, I'm your daddy!"

Dr. Sharon cautioned, "I don't know if it's a boy or a girl. That will have to wait until the next trimester—about week twenty."

"Either way," laughed Melody, "I'll bet that little one will be playing basketball in no time!"

After providing Jake and Melody their first ever picture of their first child, Dr. Sharon said, "My nurse will give you some literature on how to handle morning sickness. If it gets really bad, there are safe medications available."

Back in the waiting room, an impromptu celebration broke out, prompting congratulations from the staff and even other waiting patients! Marissa and Melody had been getting along famously, almost like sisters, and now they were both pregnant at the same time.

CHAPTER FORTY-SEVEN

LINE 'EM UP

ON THE ADVICE OF his lawyer, Noah Stein, Menachem wasn't saying anything more to the authorities. Mainly he contemplated his brother's death—a death he had caused. The authorities told him all about El Tigre. Even the name sounded quite ominous to Menachem. Apparently, it was this same El Tigre who turned him in to the police. "So why fight it," thought Menachem. "They know I'm guilty!" Right now, Menachem just wanted to be a hero and admit to everything, but he was just plain scared.

His lawyer reminded the police that they only had an anonymous tip and a grainy security camera picture to link his client to the crime. In other words, the evidence was sketchy. But on this Sunday morning, Menachem was being placed in a line up for the members of the Millennial Dawn Society. An impartial agent, not involved with the investigation, was called in to conduct the lineup.

Stevie Howard was the first to step up to the one-way glass window. Six men shuffled into place and were told, "Face forward," and then "Turn to the left," and then "Turn to the right."

"Do you recognize the man you saw at the Temple Mount on Wednesday night?"

"Absolutely," said Stevie. "It's Number Three."

"Thank you very much, Mr. Howard. "Please wait in the room to the right."

When Graham Forbes came in, the same routine was followed with exactly the same outcome. He pointed out the third man as the guy he saw running across the plaza coming from the Western Wall "like a bullet shot out of a gun."

Once these preliminaries were over, Agents Lentz and Goran took over. They ushered Stevie and Graham into the side room and offered them drinks and chocolate chip cookies. "Thanks so much for your assistance in this matter. Will you both testify at the trial?"

Both men nodded, and Graham said, "Do you know what the Bible says about the testimony of two witnesses?"

"Indeed," said Lentz. "It says the truth of anything must be confirmed by two witnesses. Remember that we are still investigating this crime. Just because you saw a man coming across the plaza does not mean he committed the crime! You are instructed not to talk about this lineup session with anyone! Do you understand!" said Lentz with a menacing look.

"We are members of the Millennial Dawn Society. We have to report what we did today to our leader, Jamison Parkes Law. Since we didn't know the people in the lineup, there shouldn't be a problem. Right?" said Stevie nervously.

"You can report to your leader, but do not under any circumstances talk to the press! We consider that obstruction of justice! Kapish?"

"Got it!" said Stevie, thinking how cool it was to be part of a real crime scene investigation like on TV back in the States.

"Gentlemen, you are free to go for now but we will be in touch in the near future. I hope you don't have plans to leave Israel."

Graham said, "Trust us. We aren't going anywhere unless the Lord returns!" The two witnesses left the police building all smiles. Now they could be part of eschatological history!

CHAPTER FORTY-EIGHT

PRESS CONFERENCE

NORMALLY BENJAMIN NETANYAHU HATED press conferences. There were too many reporters with too many insinuating questions plus too many opportunities to twist his words. This morning, however, he had something to crow about and he was determined to make the most of it. He had arranged for this press conference to take place at nine o'clock in a shaded courtyard at the Knesset. His assistant straightened his tie and tidied his thinning gray hair. Then the Prime Minister strode to the podium, unfolded his text and began.

"I will read a prepared statement, after which I will take questions. Last Thursday, a Jewish suspect by the name of Menachem Sharansky was taken into custody on the basis of an anonymous phone tip and footage from a security camera in the area of the Temple Mount. Yesterday, two eyewitnesses identified the same man running across the plaza in front of the Temple Mount just after the explosions went off. Formal charges have now been filed against him and the man will stand trial.

"In the meantime he will remain in custody for two reasons, the first being for his own safety; his family is also in a safe house. Secondly, he is being accused under the Terrorist Act and therefore we can hold him indefinitely. Jedidiah Waterstone will lead up the team for the prosecution.

"As you are well aware, Israel has exercised capital punishment very rarely in the whole history of its existence. The last time we did so was the execution of Adolph Eichmann, the WWII butcher who was put to death June 1, 1962. The grounds for such an execution are clear enough. In 1954 Israel abolished the death penalty during peacetime; but it is allowed during wartime. And we consider the Arab-Israeli conflict a war. Crimes of genocide, crimes against humanity, war crimes, and crimes against the

Jewish people are reasons for the death penalty. We think this case certainly qualifies on one or more of the grounds just listed and we intend to pursue the death penalty. The attack on the Temple Mount qualifies as a crime against both the Muslim and Jewish people. I have been in close contact with President Abbas and several other world leaders. We are in agreement as to how to legally proceed with this case. I will take your questions now."

Simon Kalman from *Ha'aretz* was recognized first. "Was Mr. Sharansky working alone? If not, do you have anyone else in custody?"

"We do not believe that Mr. Sharansky was part of any formal terrorist group and certainly not Hamas. It appears that he alone detonated the explosions using C4 Wednesday night. However, we have to consider whether anyone else in any way aided or abetted his actions. I can say we are following up on several leads in this regard but no one else is in custody—yet."

"How did Mr. Sharansky gain access to the Temple Mount?" asked Kalman's counterpart at the *Jerusalem Post*.

"Mr. Sharansky was a long-time employee of the IAA with high security level clearance. The details of his actions and motives will not be revealed until the trial."

Kalman jumped back in. "How soon can we expect the trial? Will it be a civil trial or a military one?"

"Good questions," smiled Netanyahu. "It will be a war crimes trial which will begin in one week. Judge Samuel Abramson will preside along with Judges Moshe Landau and Benjamin Halevy. We intend to deal expeditiously with this matter. Justice deferred is justice denied, especially when the crime is as heinous as this one."

A woman reporter from the *New York Times* asked, "Am I correct that only one person, namely Eichmann, has ever been executed previously in Israel under the provisions that might apply to terrorists?"

"That's right," said Israel's leader. "Israel, despite all the negative press, is a much more merciful state than it is given credit for sometimes. And efficient I might add. A press release has been prepared for you. Today's conference is now ended."

On the whole Netanyahu felt confident he had accomplished what he wanted to with that press conference. He was toying with the idea of a public execution, should a guilty verdict be rendered, as a deterrent to future terroristic acts. But he realized there was a down side to such a public spectacle as well.

Now the Prime Minister waited for news of the capture of Malak Al-Zawari, alias El Tigre. Mossad had a lot of questions for that man—the very man his government had traded for Ambassador Reich.

CHAPTER FORTY-NINE

THE BISHOP'S CROZIER

WHEN HIS CELLPHONE RANG, at 7:30 on Monday morning, Grayson was just about to leave his apartment. Picking up the phone he immediately recognized the friendly voice of Father Abbas.

"I wanted to catch you before you went to the dig this morning," the priest said.

"No problem Father, what's your wisdom on this skeleton?"

"My superiors and I propose that we rebury the skeleton in Tel Aviv at Immanuel Church. There is a very pretty graveyard there. Pastor Christian Mortensen will be happy to assist you. He is quite interested in archaeology in general; in fact, he has a minor in archaeology and is very knowledgeable about the history of the Church Fathers in this area. Now he will be happy to rebury the skeleton even if it is not Eusebius, but obviously the idea of having a Church Father in his graveyard is quite exciting!"

"Let's pretend he really is Eusebius," laughed Grayson. "Are you sure you don't want our wandering Church Father to return to St. Catherine's?"

"I have seriously considered that," said Father Abbas. "But I think one saint is enough for us. Jerome is very special to our church here in Bethlehem. Having another Church Father in the area around Jerusalem is just an added bonus—again presuming those bones belong to Eusebius."

"Of course, but I admit I'm starting to call him Eusebius whenever I work at the trench site! It's so tempting! I will call Pastor Mortensen today. We still have more work to do uncovering the skeleton. The Asbury students will return soon to the United States, and several at the IAA have volunteered to help here once they leave."

"The destruction at the Temple Mount didn't scare them off?" asked Father Abbas.

"Apparently not! They have decided to stay awhile despite all that has happened. I admire their guts, although I'm guessing their families are somewhat concerned. Meanwhile, I will keep in touch with you," promised Grayson before he hung up.

Grayson said his morning prayers, hopped into the Jeep, and headed to the dig. When he arrived, his Asbury crew was already at work. Grayson was so proud of them for being diligent, self-motivated and brave in the face of the national crisis.

By mid-morning about half of the skeleton had been uncovered. The students were becoming more and more skilled. Then they became more and more excited! Slowly coming into view was something shiny and gold! Efforts concentrated on a round object that turned out to be none other than the top of a bishop's crozier! The skeleton was holding a crozier, a shepherd's staff, which could only mean one thing—this skeleton really was Eusebius, the Bishop or Shepherd of Caesarea![1]

---

1. This skeleton was found in Cumbria, England on the grounds of Furness Abbey in 2010. It is believed to be that of a twelfth century Abbot. The real crook is decorated with a serpent's head. Some of the wooden staff was also found.

Using gloves, the team gently removed their prize from the gravesite and carried it into the tent. Carefully brushing away the dirt revealed a number of Greek phrases.

Dr. Hall translated the Greek—ισχυρός υπερασπιστής—into English—"mighty defender of the faith." Further cleaning revealed the full inscription: "Bishop of the Church, mighty defender of the faith."

Everyone stood back and admired the golden crook. Grayson broke the silence. "My friends, this is epic. I am now convinced that our skeleton is Bishop Eusebius! The scrolls in the trench scream out, 'Here lies Eusebius who wrote the scrolls'! There's never absolute proof, but this is as good as it gets! Now we have something to tell the media!"

"Really?" said Ashley. "You think we found the Father of Church History right here at our dig site?"

"That's exactly what I think. And you folks were a big part of this and I promise you will all share in the credit!"

"I hope it's worth an A for the course," laughed Anna.

Grayson then called Ada Yardeni, his immediate superior at IAA. He described the find and approached her with the plan to move the body to Immanuel Church.

"That is a very interesting proposal, Grayson. I'm not sure IAA will go along with that, but I can see a lot of merit. How about we both go take a tour of the church and grounds?"

"I would really appreciate that!" said Grayson honestly.

"Set it up then, and let me know ASAP when we can get out there. We do need to move those bones—it worries me that they are so exposed. I think we should beef up the security at the sight. I'll arrange it," ensured Dr. Yardeni.

Grayson's next call was to Art West.

When Art picked up the phone, Grayson seemed quite buoyant.

"Hey, Dr. West! I think we've definitely found the skeleton of Eusebius here! And how do I know that? Because we found a beautiful gold bishop's crozier, a genuine episcopal staff next to the skeleton. And Dr. Hall and I agree the inscription on the staff reads, 'Bishop of the church, mighty defender of the faith'—in Greek of course!"

"That is incredible, Grayson! Way to go! Eusebius was called 'the defender of the faith' in his time, just like Irenaeus before him. I think you've found your man! What does the IAA think?"

"Dr. Yardeni will be over to see the site today. And we are considering moving the skeleton to Immanuel Church in Tel Aviv. That'll give their church quite a boost as a tourist site, I would think."

"I for one would certainly make a visit. We do want to get out to Caesarea again real soon, but things have been a little hectic around here lately. I spent yesterday in the doctor's office with Marissa!"

"What! Is everything okay, Dr. West?" asked Grayson with a frown.

"Yeah, apparently Marissa has been practicing for the big day. They call it Braxton Hicks contractions. And there's more news, but that story is Jake and Melody's to tell. You should have supper with us tonight! We are gathering at the Levine house. I know Grace won't mind. And, by the way, you should call me Art from now on, *Doctor* Johnson," laughed Art.

"That will take some getting used to but I'll give it a go tonight!" promised Grayson.

CHAPTER FIFTY

AND THEN THERE WERE TWO

EL TIGRE DIDN'T MAKE it far into Jordan. After Goran and Lentz notified the Jordanian authorities at GID, they swung into action. All the security footage at Allenby Bridge was examined. A car matching the description of El Tigre's Mazda was spotted although the license plate was different. The photo of the driver, who was identified at the crossing as Kamal Gibran certainly looked different but the general build was the same as El Tigre's. The Jordanian authorities were convinced that it was the same person. A massive manhunt ensued.

After crossing the bridge Friday morning, El Tigre changed the plates once again and began to hit the back roads and small villages in the hopes of ditching his car altogether and stealing another one. But the word was spreading fast. By Monday morning, police everywhere were on the look-out for a man in a Mazda. He pulled into a small town for gas and food. Any stranger would stand out. Soon the local police took notice when the car matched the description they had been given in the Jordanian equivalent of a BOTL (Be On The Lookout!).

El Tigre headed out of town along more back roads alongside a small ditch-like stream that served to irrigate the fields on the far side. Then behind him he saw lights flashing! It was the police! He saw a small but rickety bridge over the stream just ahead. Swerving suddenly, he headed his car over the bridge hoping to escape his pursuers. Too late, he realized the bridge was in shambles. The wooden slats could not hold the weight of the car and began to collapse, sending his Mazda into the water where it lodged in the muddy creek! El Tigre scrambled to get out and make a run for it, but he fell headlong into the muck!

The police arrived quickly. What they found was the most bedraggled cat ever.

"You have no right to arrest me. My name is Kamal Gibran. I'm a legitimate businessman," sputtered El Tigre.

"You are not Kamal Gibran and you sure aren't El Tigre!" laughed the officer. "It's time you owned up to your real name, Malak Al-Zawari, recently released Hamas money-man! It seems you have gotten yourself into a lot of trouble in a very short time! The question is, who's going to prosecute you first—Jordan or Israel? The answer is way above my pay grade! For now, it's off to Amman," explained the GID agent.

Handcuffed, Malak sat silently in the back of the police car. The long ride to Amman was not going to be pleasant. Deep down, he knew he was in deep water. If the Jordanians had indeed linked him to the Temple Mount disaster, he could only imagine what they might do to him. In Jordan, unlike in Egypt and Palestine, he had no real friends and few business contacts, none of whom would admit to knowing him! There were no markers he could call in. He had lots of vital information about terroristic operations in the area. Perhaps he could trade that for some kind of amnesty. Only time would tell. For now, he needed to be as silent as a tomb, unless he wanted to find himself inside of one pretty quickly.

Menachem's defense lawyer, Noah Stein, fought hard to have the case tried as a civil matter but failed. The appointed Judge, Samuel Abramson, knew the State of Israel wanted to prosecute Menachem as a war criminal, and he was in complete agreement.

Staring down at the table, Menachem said to his lawyer, "So what exactly are my options?"

"You could plead guilty by reason of mental insanity. I can ask for a psych evaluation if you want. You can plead not guilty and we can roll the dice at the trial, but remember this will not be trial by a normal jury, but rather by a tribunal with Judge Abramson having a heavy say. That's not a great option either. Of course, you can plead guilty and proceed directly to sentencing. They will surely consider this a war crime in which case, the death penalty is an option."

"But I'm not guilty of any crime against my people. I have made a huge sacrifice for my people. I have given them back the land that is rightly theirs. Now we can rebuild the Temple. God can return and dwell in the

Holy of Holies! God will deliver me!" Menachem was becoming more agitated. And his lawyer was becoming more inclined toward the insanity plea.

"I'm afraid the government doesn't see it that way. You came close to inciting a war—and no one wants war, apparently. The Palestinian and Israeli leaders have joined forces against you. And let's not forget the Jordanians who have lost years of work repairing and managing the Temple Mount."

"But the Jewish people should rise up and take back the Temple Mount!" cried Menachem.

"Yes, they want to rebuild the Temple someday, but not at this price. There will be no war, and the Muslims will rebuild their holy places," said Noah sighing deeply. Even he wished in some way that the land was now part of Israel once again, but he knew there was no present hope of that happening.

Changing the subject, the lawyer continued. "You do know that you secured C4 directly from Hamas, don't you?"

"No!" cried Menachem. "I didn't know he was Hamas! I thought he was Jewish! I told you that the man in the picture promised to help me fulfill my dream of destroying the Dome of the Rock and the Mosque. Why would he do that if he was Hamas."

"Because that man, Malak Al-Zawari, was just a low life businessman who was making money for and off Hamas, that's why! He has no allegiance to anyone! Hamas has denied any knowledge of the bombing! It has not furthered their cause in any way! No, this man had his own motives, and they weren't religious! When we arrest him, and we will arrest him, then maybe we can find out his real motives. But I'm convinced his motives had nothing to do with your dreams of returning the Temple Mount to the Jewish people! Didn't it bother you that he never told you his name! You were used! And that's your best defense if there is one. The jury will never see you as a hardened terrorist."

At this, Menachem broke down and cried. The mystery man would not defend him. His people were turning against him. The government wanted to execute him. His family was ashamed of him.

Then he straightened up and said with new resolve, "I am a good orthodox Jew, whatever others may say or think. I thought I was doing something that would help Israel. I want my son to be proud of me. I will not lie. I am a hero!"

CHAPTER FIFTY-ONE

DINNER FOR TEN

THE WEATHER HAD TURNED unusually cool and fog had rolled in off the Mediterranean. On top of that a few surprise guests were arriving for dinner tonight at the Cohens. Art was bringing Grayson, and Manny was sent to fetch the Arafats, Ruth, and Rachel. Grace was feeling like her old flamboyant self. Thoughts of moving were on her cranial back burner right now, although she realized she had lit a fire under Manny.

Yelena wasn't all that excited about eating with a lot of "old folks" as she reminded her mother.

"Oh, you might enjoy this grownup party more than you think," winked Grace. "Sorry, I'm not letting you hide out in your room. Besides, I really need your help in the kitchen!"

Yelena admitted she liked to cook, but when Grayson strolled into the kitchen, she let out a shriek! "I'm covered in flour; I'm a mess!" she cried out and immediately turned red in embarrassment.

"Well, now you're covered in real flowers!" said Grayson handing his young admirer a special bouquet. Grace grinned; she wisely knew Yelena would eventually grow out of her teenage crush!

Meanwhile, the rest of the guests were arriving, and Grace could hear surprised voices when Jake and Melody saw Ruth and Rachel coming through the door.

Manny found Art and Marissa in the solarium remarking on the foggy weather and discussing last February's unusual sandstorm that whipped across the Mediterranean and up into Turkey. Manny, however, had other things on his mind besides the weather.

"I know a lot of this is going to sound crazy but just let me ramble for a bit. I'm considering taking all of you out of the country on my plane. Let's think of it as an extended vacation—a month or two maybe. You might remember that we had to return early from your wedding in Istanbul; Grace keeps reminding me that we owe each other some down time. We could all stay in Alaçatı. It's a village about forty-five miles west of İzmir near the tip of the Çeşme peninsula. It's one of Turkey's up-and-coming vacation getaway havens. If I'm not mistaken, your friend Levent Oral has a vacation home near there. And Marissa, aren't your parents living in Izmir right now? Have you folks considered having the baby there?"

Marissa's eyes got wide and her jaw dropped. "Wow! That's a lot to think about! We brought a month's worth of clothes, but all the baby stuff is waiting back in North Carolina. Yes, my family is in Izmir now. And truthfully, we have talked about having the baby on this side of the ocean. Of course, my mother would be thrilled," laughed Marissa.

"And my mother will be really bummed," frowned Art.

Manny pressed on. "The point is we all need time to re-center—to get back to a place where we can truly relax. As much as I hate to say it, Israel is not ever going to be normal any time soon, especially with the trial coming up. The Prime Minister's speech this morning said as much."

Art scratched his head and said, "I realize I'm coming to the end of my wandering days. I have to settle down and be a real family man. We think that means North Carolina for us. It's not for me to say what will be right for your family, though selfishly we would be thrilled if you moved to our side of the ocean. Have you and Grace talked about a permanent solution—one that goes beyond just an idyllic vacation?"

"Yes, but such a move involves major career changes—to say nothing of selling a basketball team. Do you know of any potential buyers?" said Manny with a wink.

"Not unless Jake himself wants to move into management—he seemed very interested in Maccabi Elite after his visit with you! But Melody is plenty spooked right now, and I can't blame her. Holy places shouldn't be blowing up on anyone's first visit to the Holy Land," said Art solemnly.

"Let's not forget the car incident also. Yes, I agree it's been tough. She's shown a lot of grace under pressure. But I was actually thinking of Michael Jordan himself—maybe he would want to branch out," suggested Manny.

And with that thought hanging in the air, the three headed to the dining room when the dinner bell rang. The group gathered around the table set for ten. Art and Manny took turns offering grace, each from their own religious perspective. Jake and Melody stood to announce their pregnancy followed by a round of toasts. Ruth and Rachel leapt up to hug Jake and Melody.

Much of the conversation centered on the exciting discoveries at Caesarea which delighted Grayson and fascinated Yelena. Grayson explained that Tel Aviv's own Immanuel Church is his first choice for the final resting place of Eusebius.

"Pastor Mortensen is an archaeology buff and he's agreed to see me. Father Abbas at St. Catherine's said he had a minor in archaeology," remembered Grayson.

"Yes, of course—Christian Mortensen! He took some archaeology classes at the University. We have had lunch from time to time. And, you may be surprised to learn that we've been to his church. But no, we are not considering leaving the Jewish fold! Immanuel has a marvelous music program and we like to attend the classical concerts." Grace was quite happy with this turn of events.

"I have to visit Immanuel tomorrow and I would be glad for any company. Dr. Yardeni will be coming also."

"Count me in," said Grace. "Ada is an old friend and it will be nice to talk to Christian as well." Art and Marissa also wanted to go. Yelena tried to remain "cool" but literally begged to be included. Jake and Melody said they planned to be at the monastery tomorrow. Manny said he was tied up with all the plans to bring Kevin Love to Tel Aviv.

Then the conversation shifted to a bucket list of places everyone wished to visit. Manny and Art kept exchanging glances when Turkey became the most talked about destination.

Grace made a proposal. "How about we all drive up to the Galilee for a few days? I for one love those green, rolling hills. And a pleasant boat ride on the lake sounds so relaxing right now. What do you all think?"

"That's a slam dunk!" laughed Jake.

CHAPTER FIFTY-TWO

TWO COUNTRIES, TWO VILLAINS

JORDAN, THE HASHEMITE KINGDOM, is a constitutional monarchy. Under the reign of the late King Hussein, Jordan developed more and more into a modern democracy. But the reigning monarch, as Head-of-State, appoints the executive branch, including the Prime Minister, the Cabinet of Jordan, the regional governors and the Senate. The House of Representatives is elected. King Abdullah II is also the Commander-in-Chief. In short, he has considerable power.

Once the GID reported that Malak Al-Zawari was in custody, the King emphatically told his general that he wanted the man interrogated "intensely." Specifically, he wanted to know every detail of his involvement with Menachem Sharansky and the explosion on the Temple Mount. He was in no mood to exchange information for a more lenient sentence.

General Yusef followed orders to the letter. King Abdullah wanted justice to be swift and decisive in this case. He did not want a media circus. And he did not want Hamas involvement. King Abdullah made it very clear to both Prime Minister Netanyahu and President Abbas that Malak Al-Zawari, or El Tigre as he was known now in Israel, would be tried on Jordanian soil.

Neither leader on the western side of the Jordan argued with the King. Prime Minister Netanyahu was content to prosecute Menachem Sharansky. Mossad promised to help Jordan's counterpart, GID, in any way possible with their trial.

As for President Abbas he was in no way planning to interfere with the trial of an orthodox Jew, nor was he planning to bail out Malak, especially since he had personally told the man not to do anything stupid. Blowing up the Temple Mount was beyond stupid and jeopardized everything Hamas was working towards. Neither Menachem nor Malak would find a helping hand in Hamas. In fact, Abbas was on the warpath ferreting out anyone in Hamas who had dealings with Malak. Abdul Abdullah was the first to be called on the carpet.

In one sense, the public announcement by Benjamin Netanyahu that the state would be pursuing a case against Menachem Sharansky, an orthodox Jew, for blowing up the Temple Mount, was like a shot heard around the world. The reaction was enormous, and produced protests by the Orthodox community in Jerusalem. Elsewhere in Jewish communities in Europe and America the reaction was one of shock and surprise that Benjamin Netanyahu would do such a thing to an observant Jew.

Netanyahu knew there would be push back on this score, but he was more concerned with the appearance of administering justice after a sacrilege like the bombing had taken place. In his gut, he thought that perhaps this might open the door a crack for better negotiations with President Abbas for a more enduring peace. Maybe the two trials would further marginalize the radicals in the eyes of those living inside or outside Israel. At least this was the hope of the leader of Israel. Time would tell whether his hopes were realistic or not.

Because the trial would be done in military style, each of the lawyers was given only two weeks to prepare. Even less time was to be wasted in Jordan. Al Jazeera had been covering the situation ever since the King himself announced they had Malak in custody. Countless interviews and articles had already brought up the whole history of El Tigre I and Malak's short reign as El Tigre II.

CHAPTER FIFTY-THREE

NORTH TO THE GALILEE

WITH THE RAINY SEASON over, you can count on blue skies in Galilee for any excursion. On this morning Grace was acting the tour guide, cruising up the Yitzhak Rabin Highway (Route 6) on the way to the Galilee. Within two hours they were already at the southeastern end of the Sea of Galilee where the Jordan flows from the lake. Grace parked the van in the town of Yardenit (aka Jardenit, the Little Jordan).

Melody was feeling better; anti-nausea pills had warded off both car and morning sickness. "It's green and beautiful around here, so unlike the deserts of Judea. I'm guessing the locals head to the Galilee for vacation."

"Absolutely right," agreed Grace, "And speaking of cool and refreshing spots, we've just arrived at a popular Christian pilgrimage site—Yardenit. On any one day, there can be hundreds of Christians here. If someone wants to be baptized in the Jordan, this is the best spot. It's only nine o'clock and it's early in the tourist season, so I'm hoping for a relatively quiet visit."

As they walked down the path, Art explained, "The baptism of Jesus is in all four Gospels. Of course the exact site is in question. The favored site was always Beit Abara (House of the Crossing), also known as Kasser Al Yahud near Jericho. According to tradition, this is also where the Israelites crossed over the Jordan River and Elijah the Prophet ascended to heaven. That site was closed for a long time, but I hear it's open now."

Grace added, "John the Baptist may have been there, but I do favor Yardenit. If Jesus went from Nazareth to the Jordan, this would be the closest site for a baptism. Art is right of course; I doubt we'll ever know the exact spot. Regardless, Yardenit is charming!"

"And, in fact, this is where I baptized our friend and favorite tour guide, Meltem," remembered Art.

"And you may not realize that I have never been baptized!" said Marissa smiling at Art.

"Really?" Art responded in true amazement.

"Really!" said Marissa laughing. "So, other than the fact that I'm very pregnant, is there any reason why we can't do this now?" said Marissa, quite amused by everyone's shocked reaction.

While Grace, Yelena, Jake and Melody watched from the shoreline, Art and Marissa made their way into a pool. A minister from the US, Tim Tennent, was asked to help out since Marissa opted for full immersion. After drying off and changing back into their regular clothes, everyone sat along the walls and watched the religious rite of baptism being played out over and over.

Yelena had lots of questions about baptism. Grace explained the Jewish background of ritual purification, and Art explained various Christian interpretations. After an early lunch under the palm trees, the group headed west again along the Sea of Galilee coastline.

Their next stop was the newly built Yigal Allon Museum which houses the famous twenty-seven-foot fishing boat dating to the first century found in the mud of the Sea of Galilee. Two brothers from the local Kibbutz Ginnosar discovered the boat in 1986.

"Wasn't Peter a fisherman? Maybe it's his boat! Maybe Jesus got a ride in it!" exclaimed Yelena.

"There's no way to know any of that!" laughed Grace. "But the two men who found the boat were fisherman which seems appropriate. It took years of work to figure out a way to get the boat out of the mud without destroying it in the process. I first saw it in a shed—now it's the crown jewel of this new museum."

"Boats and fishing and fisherman play a big role in Jesus' ministry, so there's no doubt he rode in a boat on the Sea of Galilee. And I'm hoping Grace planned a nice ride for us as well," hinted Art.

"No trip to the Galilee would be complete without a boat ride! Melody, are you up for this?"

"I'm a North Carolina girl. I grew up around boats!" The group boarded one of the many wooden crafts that take tourists on a one-hour relaxing ride around the Sea of Galilee. At one point, the captain let Melody take the wheel while he talked to the passengers who were all too willing to play tourists.

"I am Captain Ahab. Yes, that is my real name! The so-called Sea of Galilee is the largest freshwater lake in Israel—thirteen miles long and eight miles wide. It's the lowest freshwater lake on Earth and the second-lowest lake overall after the Dead Sea. The lake is fed partly by underground springs although its main source is the Jordan River which flows through it from north to south. We are a bit worried this year. Note the water level is very low around the shore. In fact, the Galilee, like most of Israel, is experiencing drought already. No snow fell on Mount Hermon this year!"

Melody said, "Compared to Judea, it looks great around here."

"Thank you, but Dr. Levine will probably tell you that the hills are not as green as usual."

"The Captain is right—we are having a drought already. Just one more problem for Israel," sighed Grace.

The group stayed overnight in a lovely hotel in Tiberias and enjoyed a buffet dinner filled with chopped salad, humus and tahini, falafel, chicken schnitzel, and St. Peter's fish (a type of tilapia found in the lake but also grown for market in nearby fisheries). After dinner they strolled along the water and were amazed that a full moon was rising over the Golan Heights to the east.

The next morning the group gathered on the patio for a traditional Israeli breakfast—lots of dairy and no meat.

"I presume we are wandering around the lake today," said Melody. "How about Jake and I organize a picnic box lunch? I saw a local kosher deli that would work nicely."

"Fine idea," agreed Grace. "And I know just the place to eat—at the Mount of Beatitudes. But first we will stop at Migdal."

"My colleague, Richard Bauckham, has been sending me e-mails about his studies there. It seems that first century fisherman, like Peter himself, weren't exactly the poor folks some make them out to be. If we have time we should stop at Beth Saida where there's an excavation of a rather elaborate fisherman's house. Anyway, fishing was a big industry around the lake. The fisherman sold the day's catch to the fish factories in Migdal. In fact, Migdal comes from the Aramaic for Fish Tower. Richard will be pleased that I finally made it over here," laughed Art.

"And I'm guessing that Mary of Magdalene came from this town, and I right?" asked Melody.

"You are," said Jake. "When we were young, my mother brought us up here. I remember coming to Migdal before all of the new excavations. Even then there were displays of fishing stuff, like needles and nets and hooks. The pier was closer to the water too. The water really has receded. My mother had a special heart for Mary of Migdala, as she called her."[1]

1. See the article in Ha'aretz on Migdal: http://www.haaretz.com/archaeology/. premium-1.545784

By mid-morning the group was at the traditional site of the Sermon on the Mount. They admired the unique octagonal architecture of the Franciscan chapel built in 1938. After strolling through the gardens, they found a cluster of sitting rocks under the palm trees. During lunch, Jake was asked to read the Sermon on the Mount, a collection of Jesus' sayings found in Matthew 5, 6, and 7.

"One last stop," promised Grace. "This afternoon we are going to Nazareth, the first-century Nazareth. Today it's a city of 80,000. Mary and Joseph would get lost easily! But, since the mid-1990s the University of the Holy Land along with its research arm, The Center for the Study of Early Christianity, has developed an archaeological site into a working first-century replica of biblical Nazareth. And that's a place Mary and Joseph would recognize!

At the visitor's center they enjoyed the new audio/visual touches used by the guide to explain the history of Nazareth Village. Then the group followed their guide along the village trail past the shepherd with his menagerie of goats, sheep, chickens, and donkeys. The wine and olive presses, dating to the first century, were explained in detail. Jake and Art worked together, sweating profusely, to turn the wheel!

Having locals dressed in period clothing brought the village to life. Women demonstrated weaving and herb grinding. Men were working in wood and sewing old goatskin hides for new wineskin flasks.

"How come we haven't been here before?" complained Yelena to her Mom. "To be honest," said Grace. "We just get too busy—I keep forgetting how close these biblical sites are. They seem so far away when you're caught up in all the everyday busyness."

"Let that be a life lesson for us," said Marissa to Art. "This child wants to see the world—let's not get too busy to show it to him—or her."

"Ditto to that," said Melody as Jake imagined showing his own child around his own homeland.

CHAPTER FIFTY-FOUR

ALL YOU NEED IS LOVE

MANNY OPTED OUT OF the trip to the Galilee, but deep down he realized he had missed yet another opportunity to be with his family. "Too much busyness," he mused to himself after sitting at his desk for two days dealing with the details of Kevin Love's visit. The phone rang. It was his legal assistant, Sammy Adelman.

Kevin had landed safely; sailed through security; settled into his hotel suite; and was on the way to the stadium. Maccabi Elite was only two games behind the league-leading Haifa team and Manny believed his boys, with Kevin's help, could catch and pass them.

The phone rang again, and it was Grace. "So what are you up to, man of mine?"

"I'm about to pop the cork on some champagne. Kevin Love has arrived in the building!"

"So, bring him on over for dinner. Everyone here is just relaxing at the beach today. I guess I wore them out on the Galilee trip. Besides, I just got a phone call from Mark Fairchild and Yuliya Karpova. They are in town and I invited them over too. "

"You have become quite the social butterfly! Drinks at five then. Love you."

While Manny Cohen was not a small man by any stretch, when Kevin Love walked through the door of his office, he felt like a dwarf. Looking up, way up, he said, "Welcome to Tel Aviv. Are you ready to play?"

"You know it," smiled Kevin. "Let me on the court and I'll show you what I can do—even with jet lag!"

"The boys are downstairs in the gym practicing," said Manny just as the door opened. "Good timing! Coach Harold here will take you down to the locker room and get you settled. There's a new jersey waiting. I'll be down in a bit for introductions on the court."

"Thanks for giving me this opportunity, Mr. Cohen," said Kevin as he headed to the gym with the coach.

Manny laughed and said, "I suspect I will be thanking you with several green handshakes before long!"

The unsuspecting guests all gathered at five o'clock for wine coolers at the Levine mansion. All sorts of new faces were showing up and Grace was so enjoying the surprised reactions. Yelena nearly yelped when Yuliya walked into the room—a vintage Vakko silk scarf flowing from her neck. Yelena introduced Yuliya to Jake and Melody. Yuliya nearly begged for a tour of St. George's Monastery, long on her bucket list of places to visit.

Art was pleased to see Mark Fairchild, his old traveling buddy. In no time they were sharing adventure stories about off-the-beaten-path archaeological sites they had crawled over in the far reaches of Turkey. "Did I ever tell you about the sandstorm?" began Mark to Grayson and Marissa who had plenty of their own stories to tell.

All eyes turned, however, when Manny came in with Kevin Love who had to watch his head coming through the door. After a moment of stark silence, Manny announced, "Meet Kevin Love. He just flew in this morning, worked out briefly with the team, and I'm sure jet lag is finally catching up with him. This is a short visit!"

Yelena walked up to Kevin and quietly said, "You don't look short to me." That broke the ice.

Over dinner, Mark explained why he was in town. He had already been to the police and confirmed that the man who was killed in Hezekiah's Tunnel was none other than his buddy, Sean Singletary. "A far greater photographer than I am," said Mark. "In fact, he sent me a video that he apparently took in 2004, the year Arafat died. I showed it to the police yesterday. I'm convinced what's on the tape is actually a clue as to how Arafat died. And if that's so, and someone knew about the tape, then it could have something to do with his death. Anyway it's up to the police. I decided to bring it to them personally rather than risk the mail."

"Wise decision," frowned Grace. In some ways, life just seems to go on despite explosions and bombings. But in little ways, life has been disrupted.

Security is certainly tighter. I'm so sorry you lost your friend. I have two of Sean's photos framed in my office; he was truly gifted."

"Let's not scare our guests," said Manny. "I've promised Kevin a safe haven here in Tel Aviv."

"And I appreciate that, but really I want to see as much of this country as possible while I'm here," said Kevin earnestly.

"Well, if you need tour guides, it doesn't get better than Mark and Yuliya," laughed Art. "Both of them work periodically for our friend Levent Oral."

"I'll bank roll that! If you two want temporary jobs, I'm all for it," said Manny in his usual business-like way. "And, yes, I can give Kevin a few days off right now. We've got time to prepare for the playoffs."

Yuliya looked at Mark and both nodded simultaneously. "I have some sites I do want to visit again—for research of course—but I would be glad to take Kevin around the major sites," promised Yuliya as Kevin looked down at the 5'4" woman who seemed oblivious to the difference.

"I'm in," said Mark. "If nothing else, I can provide you with the best ever photo album of your trip!" laughed Mark.

"He's got that right! The only pictures of Mark that I have are pictures of him behind a camera! But don't forget he's a biblical scholar too. Between the two of them you'll get a first class tour of the Holy Land," promised Art.

After dinner, Kevin walked with Yuliya out to the patio. "What's your expertise, Yuliya?" asked Kevin who had certainly noticed that Yuliya was a remarkably beautiful girl.

"Everything from philosophy to art—in Middle Eastern settings. I'm a visiting professor at the Istanbul Museum. Right now, I've been looking at tiles and mosaics of all sorts," explained Yuliya blushing slightly under Kevin's gaze.

At that moment, Grayson swooped in, gently grabbed Yuliya by the elbow and steered her into a conversation beginning with, "Have I told you about the new mosaics at Caesarea Maritima?"

Kevin was amused at being so deftly outmaneuvered, but he realized he was definitely out of his league in more ways than one. Kevin joined Mark and Art.

"Don't feel pressured to act as my tour guide, Mark," said Kevin earnestly. "I'm sure you're pretty shook up over the death of your friend."

Mark quickly added, "But taking you around the Holy Land would be a pleasure, if Manny can really spare you for a few days. And it would take up my time while the police are investigating the tape—I'm hoping they figure out who exactly is in that picture with Arafat!"

CHAPTER FIFTY-FIVE

A DAY OF REST

LAST TUESDAY'S VISIT WITH Rev. Christian Mortensen, vicar of Immanuel Church in Tel Aviv, had gone well. Grayson gave a brief history of the dig site and explained all the facts pointing to the obvious conclusion that the bones belong to Eusebius, Father of Church History. All agreed that the beautifully landscaped cemetery near the church should provide the perfect resting place for the Bishop. The ring and staff, however, would be displayed in Jerusalem, per orders from the IAA.

Then the pastor took his group on a more formal tour of the facilities. Grace, Yelena, Art, Marissa, Grayson, and Ada Yardeni from the IAA were impressed as Christian related the history of the 110-year-old church. He was proud of the fact that the congregation was composed of a wide range of believers in Jesus from many denominations. Frequent fellowship meals, prayer hours, bible study and worship service kept the church full of people throughout the week. Grace reminded everyone that they regularly come to special musical events at the church. The pastor had arranged for the organist to give them a mini-concert. Immanuel's massive organ is considered one of the best in all of Israel.

Today, Sunday, was chosen for the reburial of the saint. Several IAA members came to the eleven o'clock service along with the whole group of Asbury Seminary students who were especially recognized during the service for all their hard work. Grayson spoke to the congregation about the importance of the life and work of Eusebius.

The churchwomen provided a potluck lunch for everyone interested in staying for the reburial. Grayson was asked to speak to the group about the details of finding and removing the bones. The elders of the church were all pleased that such an important church figure would now be resting in their cemetery.

Piles of paperwork were involved to have the skeleton of Eusebius reinterred at Immanuel, but Grayson managed to get this done in just four short days. The IAA fast-tracked the whole project. Reverend Mortensen arranged for a local funeral director to carefully clean the skeleton and place it in a new coffin.

After lunch everyone marched over to the church cemetery. The grave had been dug and alongside it was a new headstone that read:

> Here lies Bishop Eusebius of Caesarea, good shepherd of the sheep,
> defender of the faith, Biblical scholar, leader of the Nicene council,
> aid to the first Christian Emperor, Constantine.

Reverend Mortensen signaled the gathering to make a circle around the grave as he began the liturgy from the 1979 Book of Common Prayer.

"Man, that is born of a woman, has but a short time to live, and is full of misery. He comes up, and is cut down, like a flower; he flees as it were like a shadow, and never continues in one place. In the midst of life we are in death; of whom may we seek for succor, but of thee, O Lord, who for our sins art justly displeased? Yet, O Lord God most holy, O Lord most mighty, O holy and most merciful Savior, deliver us not into the bitter pains of eternal death. You know, Lord, the secrets of our hearts; shut not thy merciful ears to our prayer; but spare us, Lord most holy, O God most mighty, O holy and merciful Savior, thou most worthy Judge eternal, suffer us not, at our last hour, for any pains of death, to fall from thee."

"Oh God whose mercies cannot be numbered, we believe you have already granted the departed, long ago, entrance in the land of light and joy, in the fellowship of the saints through our Lord Jesus Christ. But it is appropriate to gather in this place and honor this great Christian by reinterring him here.

> We now commit his body once more to the ground;
> earth to earth, ashes to ashes, dust to dust:
> in the sure and certain hope of the resurrection to eternal life."

This was followed by several special prayers and the singing of the Doxology. Each one present was given a handful of dirt to throw into the grave.

The service had taken only twenty minutes, but Grayson reflected on the fact that 1700 years had passed since Eusebius lived and worked in this area. As he walked with Art, Grayson said, "Do you feel it? It's like an electric wire stretching back through time. I hope that Eusebius being here will remind people of the long history of church saints."

For the Asbury students, it was a once-in-a-lifetime experience. Never in their wildest dreams did they expect their summer course to end in this cemetery in Tel Aviv. Most students are lucky to dig up a few pots. Today they reburied a true saint.

CHAPTER FIFTY-SIX

THE TRIAL OF
THE CENTURY

THE TRIAL OF MENACHEM Sharansky was not open to the public. The media were carefully screened and the trial would be documented on film. Menachem's wife Rachel was allowed to attend the proceedings with a police escort to ensure her safety. This was the trial of a terrorist whose actions were crimes against humanity. There would be no banter in the courtroom; there would be no light moments. Judge Samuel Abramson's demeanor was grim as death. Menachem's lawyer, Noah Stein, was uncharacteristically somber as he sat with his team. The lead lawyer for the prosecution, Jedidiah Waterstone, was feeling quite confident.

Judge Samuel Abramson opened the proceedings by surprising everyone with a joint statement from the three presiding judges. He delivered an animated outline of the trials and tribulations of the Temple Mount.

"The Temple Mount was captured by Israel in the 1967 Six-Day War but today it is administered by the Jordanian Islamic Waqf. It is arguably the holiest site in all of Judaism. Here, over four thousand years ago, God spared Isaac from the knife of his father Abraham. Here, over three thousand years ago, stood the First Temple of Solomon. Here the Second Herodian Temple was destroyed in AD 70. And following in Jewish footsteps, Christians too revere the site where their Messiah walked.

"It is now one of the holiest sites in the Muslim world. Beginning in the seventh century, the Dome of the Rock and the Al-Aqsa Mosque along with the Dome of the Chain were built. For Muslims this is Haram al-Sharif, the Noble Sanctuary. They believe that Muhammad took a night journey from Mecca to Jerusalem on his winged horse al-Buraq. From here also, he ascended into heaven.

"So who truly owns the Temple Mount? Is it the political State of Israel by decree of war? Is it all Jews no matter how orthodox? Is it all Muslims no matter what their home country? Is it the Jordanians who manage the property? Should the Temple Mount be returned to the Jews who predate Muslim ownership and Jordanian control?

"In more recent times, we have clashed over whether to allow anyone but Muslims on the Temple Mount. Mizrahi-Sephardic rabbis forbid Jews from visiting the site. But religious-Zionist rabbis believe it is our civic and religious right not only to visit but also to pray on the Mount. But we must remember that in December 2013, the two Chief Rabbis of Israel declared again the ban on Jews entering the Temple Mount.

"And we have clashed over how best to protect and preserve Jewish artifacts found there. The IAA maintains a presence under the Mount and works to rescue our heritage.

"Finally, let us remember that in the early 1980s we thwarted a plot within the Jewish Terror Underground to blow up the Dome of the Rock. Thus, the problems facing us today are not new. And extremists on both sides still keep us on edge. Even today, the Temple Mount Faithful headed by Gershon Salomon clearly states that liberating the Temple Mount from Arab occupation is the ultimate goal. And that means for them, removing those pagan shrines. 'Rebuild them in Mecca!' they cry out.

"And what of the future? Jews believe that Messiah will come one day. Will he enter through the Golden Gate? Christians look forward to their Messiah returning. Will he walk again on the Temple Mount? Will changing the Temple Mount today affect religious history tomorrow?

"So today we consider the actions of one man. If guilty, he has taken it upon himself to change the course of history as an instrument of Yahweh. We must determine if he has undeniably broken the laws of the State of Israel despite his religious beliefs. There is no doubt that these events have impacted the lives of everyone who lives in Israel especially Jews, Christians and Muslims. Once again our people are reminded that they do not live in peace; they are fearful for their lives and for the lives of their children! That the Temple Mount is the focus for three religions, and a problem for them as well is well expressed in this poem I found written by a recent American Christian visitor:

CRACKS IN THE WALL

Cracks in the wall,
There by design,
Prayers on plain paper
One of them mine
Rabbis are chanting,
Torah held high,
Sunlight is fading,
In the blue sky.
Guards are watching,
Passing the time,
Nodding acquaintance
With the sublime.

Herod's temple,
All that remains
Limestone platform,
Withstands the strain,
Mosque's gold dome
Shines in the light,
Whose God is honored
By what's in sight?
Prayers of the righteous
Meant to be heard,
But the papers are silent,
Don't speak a word.

"We want messiah"
Yeshiva boy cries,
The irony is thick,
And darkens the skies
Christians with kepas
Stand by the shrine,
Praying to Jesus,
As someone divine.
The wailing wall,

Heard Jesus' lament
That he would have gathered,
If Zion repents.

Cracks in the wall,
Filled up with our prayers,
Perhaps it is this,
Which keeps God right there
Perhaps when Messiah
Comes (once again),
Perhaps then the Spirit
Will descend through the air,
Perhaps then true monotheists
Will kneel at God's feet,
Be filled with his Spirit,
The Father's Son greet.

True children of Abram
Meet at the wall
And confess Trinity,
The One for us all.
Is this a dream—we three could be one?
Just as God is,
Whose plan is not done.
"Something there is
That doesn't like a wall"
But this one unites
The One with us all.

And with that statement, the gavel came down and the Chief Prosecutor was instructed to present the case of the State of Israel versus Menachem Sharansky. Attorney Sam Waterstone had lined up several witnesses beginning with those who identified Menachem at the site on the night in question.

Graham Forbes was excused from the witness stand after his testimony. Stevie Howard was immediately called by Sam Waterstone to present his own version of the story. Meanwhile, Jed's team of prosecuting lawyers scribbled notes. Noah Stein kept glancing at his client to make sure he was maintaining a calm demeanor. His own team was also taking notes. In no time, Sam easily established that both Graham Forbes and now Stevie Howard were near the Wailing Wall on the night of the explosions. Clear evidence was presented that both men picked out Menachem Sharansky from a lineup as the man they saw fleeing the scene.

When Jed finished with Stevie, the Judge said, "Mr. Stein, do you wish to cross examine."

"Yes, your Honor," said Noah, grabbing a pad and heading to the witness stand.

"Mr. Howard, explain why you were at the plaza next to the Western Wall so late at night."

"Me and Graham Forbes were there on watch duty. The Millennial Dawn Society believes that certain events will transpire before Jesus comes back. Then we saw this Jewish guy running across the plaza like a man fleeing a burning building."

"Just answer the specific question, Mr. Howard," said Noah sighing at Stevie's negative spin. Sam Waterstone nearly grinned!

"And exactly what are your beliefs with regard to the Temple Mount and the so-called end times?"

"We believe God will destroy the shrines on top of the Temple Mount."

"Do you believe that the removal of the shrines on the Temple Mount and a belief in a coming messiah are legitimate, acceptable beliefs? After all, some would say that that this is not reasonable! They would say that waiting two thousand years for a dead man to return is unreasonable?"

"They may not seem reasonable to some people. But we truly believe that the Bible is telling us that Jesus will return—and that the pagan monuments on the Temple Mount will be destroyed either before or when that happens."

Judge Landau interrupted Mr. Stein and said, "Is this line of questioning going somewhere counselor?"

"Yes, your Honor. I am trying to establish that many people believe that the buildings on the Temple Mount must be removed."

"Continue, Mr. Stein."

"Mr. Howard, about how long would you say you saw the man who was fleeing across the plaza—thirty seconds, twenty seconds, ten seconds? I mean he was running fast, was he not, and it was quite dark, was it not?"

"It was dark but he ran right by us without even noticing, and he had this panicked look on his face."

"So you think you are sure this was the man you saw, even though it was dark, and even though your glimpse of him was fleeting?"

"Yeah, I'm pretty sure. I picked him out of the line-up didn't I?"

"Sure, or just pretty sure?"

"Pretty certain. I mean there is a slight possibility I'm wrong."

"And for all you know, he was just another man, like you, out walking or watching that night."

"He kept looking behind him toward the Mount, and he was running, running very, very fast—running from something!"

"Thank you, Mr. Howard—that will be all."

Judge Abramson then said, "Mr. Waterstone, you can call your next witness."

"The prosecution calls Joseph Epstein." Menachem, who had been just staring down at the desk in front of him, looked up, surprised.

"Mr. Epstein, could you please tell the court what your occupation is."

"Yes sir, I work for the IAA at the dig underneath the Temple Mount. I'm in charge of security."

"And how long have you been working there?"

"For over two years now."

"And did you know Menachem Sharansky?"

"Yes, he was one of our workers."

"Did you see Mr. Sharansky in the days before the explosion?"

"No sir. He wasn't on site for the two days before the explosions."

"I see. And could you now tell the court what you found under some rubble as you began to clear out the debris from the explosions?"

"I found a backpack, Menachem's IAA backpack, underneath a pile of small stones. This seemed strange considering he hadn't been on the job for the couple of days before the explosions. It had his name badge right on it."

Waterstone smiled and said, "You are excused, Mr. Epstein. We now enter into evidence this backpack. I now call Daniel Goran to the stand."

"Mr. Goran, would you state your occupation?"

"I work for Mossad."

"Can you tell me if this aforementioned backpack has been chemically tested by your agency? If so, what were the results?"

"We found traces of C4." With this Menachem, who was sitting next to Sam Waterstone, laid his head down on the desk and began silently weeping.

"Will you please tell us the name of the man in this picture?" asked the attorney as he handed Daniel the now famous photo of Menachem having lunch with el Tigre.

"Yes sir, my partner, Joshua Lentz, and I along with CIA agent Bob Cunningham identified these two men as Menachem Sharansky and Malak al-Zawari. The latter has an alias, El Tigre, a reference to his brother, a notorious Hamas agent who is now dead. The photo was taken in a restaurant in Jericho."

"Did you interrogate Mr. Sharansky? And did he identify this El Tigre?"

"We did interrogate him. He was not aware that Malak al-Zawari was El Tigre. And he was not aware that the man was Hamas. But he did admit obtaining C4 from this man."

"And is this man in custody?"

"Yes, he was apprehended in Jordan. He is being charged with complicity in the bombings by providing Menachem Sharansky with the C4 used in the explosions."

After several more witnesses were called, Attorney Waterstone said, "The State rests its case."

The Judge then stated that sufficient evidence was presented to support a guilty verdict. "Thus, I will deny any motion by the defense to dismiss the charges at this time."

The next day was taken up with Noah Stein's defense. Only a few character witnesses were called, friends who had known Menachem for a long time. They admitted his Zionist tendencies but vouched for Menachem as a scholar and good Orthodox Jew. Rachel was not asked to testify.

Menachem was called to the stand as the last witness. His lawyer concentrated on his faithfulness to Yahweh and his belief that he was doing God's work. Under cross-examination, however, he broke down and cried. Sam Waterstone would have felt sorry for Menachem but images of the damage done were now displayed on massive easels for all to see. When the prosecuting attorney reminded him that his own brother had died, there was no turning back.

"I killed my own brother," cried Menachem.

Concluding arguments were short. Menachem's attorney suggested temporary insanity, but in a moment of courtroom drama, Menachem jumped up and soundly declared that he was mentally sound!

That being the case, the gavel came done hard yet again. Menachem was declared guilty. The three judges—Abramson, Landau, and Halevy deliberated on Wednesday and signed a joint statement. This was released to the media late Wednesday night. The guilty headline circled the globe with record speed.

CHAPTER FIFTY-SEVEN

CAPITAL PUNISHMENT

JUDGES ABRAMSON, LANDAU, AND Halevy found Menachem Sharansky guilty on all charges and sentenced him "to be hanged from the neck until dead." Capital punishment in Israel has been used only twice since 1948. This would be different, however; this execution would be public—outside the old city walls, near Mt. Zion, across from Jaffa Gate. The media had been alerted as soon as the execution was announced. There would be little time, however, for protestors from afar to arrive. While this was not theater, it was high drama.

At precisely six o'clock Friday morning, Menachem Sharansky, having been allowed to kiss his wife and children goodbye at the jail as he was being escorted away, emerged into the light of day for the last time in his life. With hands cuffed behind his back, and wearing a prison uniform, he looked defeated and thoroughly depressed at having been found guilty by his own fellow Jews. Instead of being a hero, he had become the object of political cartoons and ridicule by even the Orthodox Jews.

Escorted by two men in front and two behind, he walked out through the Jaffa Gate. A rabbi was present and though the surrounding crowd could not hear what was happening, Menachem was saying his prayers, and the rabbi was praying for him.

The crowd was perhaps five deep all the way around the cordoned off area and no one was speaking. It was as if a funeral was already in progress. Just as there is silence in the presence of death, so there was silence in anticipation of death. The gallows had five wooden steps leading up to the platform. The chosen site was not far from Hakeldama, the traditional place where Judas had hanged himself. Menachem would forever be seen as someone who had shamed his own cause.

Standing near the back of the crowd were three well-known figures—one Jewish, one Christian, and one Muslim—Grace Levine, Grayson Johnson, and Hannah el Said. They had not come out of curiosity but out of a sense of history—the execution of justice for someone who had created "an abomination that makes desolation."

Menachem climbed the stairs to where the executioner stood waiting. Judge Abramson said, "On this day Menachem Sharansky shall pay the price for crimes against humanity, crimes that violate the honor of Judaism, Christianity and Islam. Justice should be swift and fair, and we deem it so on this day. Executioner, you may proceed."

The executioner placed the noose around Menachem's head and moments later pulled the lever. Menachem's body dropped below the platform. His neck was instantly broken by the short drop. A gasp went up from the crowd.

Grayson wiped a tear from his eye, and said to Grace and Hannah, "Not far from here a guilty man named Judas hung his head in shame, and then hung himself." At this juncture, Prime Minister Netanyahu, appropriately wearing a black funeral suit, stepped up to a smaller platform with a podium.

"In the ongoing battle with terrorism, it has become increasingly clear that it can have many different faces and show up in many different places. Radicalized religious persons who wish to take bombs in their hands, rather than leaving matters in God's hands when it comes to drastic change, have increasingly been encouraged and have obtained the means by which to do damage even to sacred sites like the Temple Mount. What the case of Menachem Sharansky demonstrates is that terrorism is not the provenance of one particular religion or religious group. A zealous member of almost any religion can be pushed over the edge into sacrilegious behavior. Let me be clear that the Temple Mount is sacred to Judaism, Christianity and Islam.

"The action taken here today is intended as the strongest of deterrents. Terrorists of whatever religion or of no religion are put on notice that with the execution of Menachem Sharansky today there will be zero tolerance for such behavior.

"The function of terrorism is to strike fear into the heart of an enemy. In other words, it is an act of *cowardice,* not bravery. Men and women who have the courage of their convictions and are willing to fight for them do so in moral ways, not by killing innocent men, women and children, and not by destroying sacred religious sites, and then pretending that Yahweh wanted them to commit such acts. I am prepared to say that Yahweh or Allah or God condemns all terrorists and their activities.

"I wish to thank President Abbas and King Abdullah for their help through this difficult time. My hope would be that this event may lead to a future of co-operation against terrorism among Middle Eastern countries. Terrorism against any country, any religion, any person, should be seen as terrorism against all of us. Let the world hear me today as I throw down this gauntlet—let us defeat terrorism together."

There was stunned silence after this ten-minute speech which was delivered slowly and articulately, making sure each word was heard and understood. The crowd began to murmur and some began to shuffle away from the site.

Hannah said, "My father would have approved of Mr. Netanyahu's speech. I would imagine most will applaud this speech, even if they aren't in favor of capital punishment. But even so, I see why he did it."

"To emphasize the extremes that terrorists will go to and why terrorism requires a strong, consistent response," finished Grace. "You have your father's wisdom. I entirely agree with you."

Grayson turned to his Jewish and Muslim friends and said, "As a Christian, I don't agree with capital punishment, but maybe as a lesser of several evils, this one execution might deter future crimes."

"What was it Caiaphas said?" asked Grace. "It is necessary that one man die, so the nation be spared."

"Yeah," said Grayson, frowning, "but he was talking about the execution of an innocent man—Jesus!"

The three friends headed over to Sarah's coffee shop. Back in Tel Aviv, Jake, Melody, Art, Marissa and Manny, with Yelena as well, had watched the execution on television. It was one of those broadcasts where people would later say, "Do you remember where you were when Sharansky died?"

CHAPTER FIFTY-EIGHT

THE AFTERMATH

ON THE SAME FRIDAY morning, just outside Amman, Jordan, Malak Al-Zawari was marched out into the prison courtyard, given a last cigarette, blindfolded, and executed by a firing squad. The details were released the same morning first to Al Jazeera and then to news agencies around the world. His funeral stood in contrast to that of Khalil el Said. No one mourned the loss of Malak Al-Zawari. No relatives appeared to represent him. No friend came to say a few kind words. Even the prayer for the forgiveness of the man's sins, rendered only by the cleric, rang hollow. El Tigre, for the second time, was dead.

Abdul Abdullah had slipped out of Gaza and attended Sharansky's execution. Mossad followed his every movement. Before he could disappear into the crowd, Jacob Marcus suddenly came up behind Abdul, grabbed his right arm and twisted it behind his back. Another Mossad officer slipped on the handcuffs.

"Abdul Abdullah you are under arrest. You have the right to remain silent. Anything you do say can be used against you."

"I want a lawyer!" cried Abdul.

"No problem. You have the right to notify a family member or an acquaintance and a lawyer. In short, you have a right to counsel. But considering we are talking terrorism and treason here, I can't tell you how long you will be held—especially since Mossad is turning you over to the Palestinian authorities!"

Abdul panicked, "Why? What am I being accused of?"

"Murder! We have evidence that you were involved in the murder of none other than Yasser Arafat! And to cover your tracks, the murder of photographer Sean Singletary. We decided to turn the evidence over to the Palestinian authorities. President Abbas himself is looking forward to dealing with you—with dispatch. And I am looking forward to never having to deal with you again!"

That same Friday night, back at the Cohen's guest cottage, the television was on continuously. The major news networks were reporting 24/7 on the events taking place in Israel. At the moment, Art, Marissa, Jake, and Melody were sitting on the couch perusing the late afternoon papers and periodically listening to the news broadcasts.

The response to Netanyahu's once in a lifetime speech was overwhelming. Even the Arab press quoted it approvingly, and Al Jazeera devoted a special program to analyzing its import for Middle Eastern politics.

The *New York Times* had in large bold capital letters on its front page: NETANYAHU THROWS DOWN THE GAUNTLET

The *Jerusalem Post* had in equally bold type on page one: ZERO TOLERANCE FOR TERRORISM

While *Ha'Aretz* took the religious angle: AN ATTACK ON ANY HOLY SITE IS A SACRILEGE

Those who chose to read beyond the headlines were impressed, though some cynics editorialized that this was a publicity stunt by a politician who was working hard to get secular Israelis to vote for him next time around. This made little sense, since at the same time he would be alienating voters among the ultra-Orthodox.

In general, world leaders hailed this speech as an excellent step forward, and Secretary General Ban Ki-moon quoted some of the speech at a UN meeting. Whether there would be long term benefit remained to be seen.

Suddenly everyone was startled when Jake's cell phone started ringing. Jake quickly answered and everyone watched as he crouched forward intensely following the one-sided conversation. When he hung up, he raised his head. Jake was in shock!

Art broke the silence. "Jake, are you okay? Obviously something big is going down."

"Oh yes," said Jake grabbing Melody's hand. "I'm sorry. I'm sure you are thinking the worst! This is actually good news, I think. That was the Jericho police following through on the car bombing. Mossad knows who bombed our car! His name was Malak Al-Zawari. And I do mean 'was'—in the past tense. He's dead! He was executed in Jordan for providing the explosives to Menachem Sharansky!"

"But why did he blow up our car!" exclaimed Melody.

"A good question! It seems he had a nickname. It was El Tigre!"

Art gasped! "But El Tigre is dead! He died a few years ago!"

"True. But this guy was El Tigre's half-brother. He thought he could carry on the legacy of the original El Tigre by using his name. He's been a money-man for Hamas for a long time. I guess he carried a grudge against me for taking down his half-brother."

"So it's over then. There's no real threat to you or Melody anymore?" asked Marissa.

"Mossad doesn't think there's any problem. Apparently, this new and definitely not improved El Tigre was a loner. Even Hamas doesn't want anything to do with him. Blowing up the Temple Mount certainly didn't do Hamas any favors."

"One wonders then why he did it?" mused Melody.

"Fame and glory, I suppose," said Jake as he gazed at Melody. "It can be poisonous. I've seen it in the world of sports. I pray I never fall victim to the venom."

"Don't worry," said Melody brightly lifting the mood. "We'll keep you humble! And maybe this means we don't need our bodyguard anymore! He's been a great chauffeur but I think it's time to say good-bye!"

"And it's time to pack and go home," said Jake.

As for Grace Levine Cohen, she did not believe that one action and one speech would change the dynamics of Middle Eastern politics, and so she was not prepared to change her mind when she came home and Manny immediately asked, "So, can we stay here now?"

"I don't think so, unless you think this speech will make all the terrorists turn in their weapons for fear of what will happen to them."

"Then you think we should start a new life—maybe in the States?"

"I think it's a very real possibility," stated Grace emphatically.

CHAPTER FIFTY-NINE

RUTH AND RACHEL

JAKE AND MELODY ARRANGED a very special trip for Sunday morning. Grace, Manny, Yelena, Mark, Yuliya, and Kevin Love had all been invited to the monastery. Manny borrowed a company van to take them all in one load. Even the trip over proved eventful when Mark's phone started ringing. Everyone sat silently as Mark listened to the phone message from Mossad. When he hung up, everyone turned to look at him with anticipation.

"That was Mossad. They have identified the man in the video I sent to them. And it turns out he's a Hamas leader, Abdul Abdullah. More to the point, he was in the crowd Friday morning—there for the execution. He was arrested! They have him nailed for Sean's murder, and now have implicated him in Yasser Arafat's death. So, stay tuned! I'm sure they'll release this info to the news media eventually. Right now, I'm not supposed to talk to the media about any of this!"

"Wow, that's high-level intrigue!" said Manny. "Who knows where this might lead. Sean was definitely onto something big!"

The rest of the ride was quiet as each pondered Sean's life and death. Ruth and Rachel were there at the gate to St. George's Monastery to greet them and lead the tour. The children, Tamar and Amin, were home from school and dancing around with excitement.

Ruth realized that her son was better off in America, so she resolved in her mind to accept the fact that he would probably never return to Israel to live. She was grateful that Jake's basketball career had provided the resources for Jake and Melody to visit Israel as often as possible. She looked forward to the day when they would bring their first child to visit.

Mark was allowed to take pictures and wandered about the grounds snapping hundreds of shots. He wasn't seen again until it was time to leave.

Yuliya was fascinated with the architecture while Kevin found the mummified remains of the holy corpse of Father John the Romanian which is preserved for all to see in the chapel—"a bit gruesome!"

After lunch in the refectory, everyone wandered outside in order to give Jake and Melody some special time with his family.

"Mother, we both hope that you and Rachel and the children can visit when the baby arrives. You know I can take care of this financially. Surely, the monks can spare you for such an important event!"

"That would be wonderful! Father Demetrios has a servant heart. I'm sure he will be delighted to let us come. Imagine, this would be our second visit to the States."

Melody teased, "You might just grow to like North Carolina so much that you won't want to leave! What do you think Rachel? Can you see our children growing up together?"

Rachel was more subdued. "You are becoming a sister to me—that is true. And I will ponder all these things in my heart. The idea of raising my children in the United States is a bit overwhelming. Prejudice is everywhere."

"Unfortunately, you are right about that. Jake and I know we are subject of, shall we say, not too friendly stares. But you should talk to Grace. She and Manny are seriously considering moving to the Boston area I think."

"That is news," said Ruth. "I would very much like to talk more with your friends, the Cohens." Jake used his cell phone to locate Grace and Manny.

At the time, Grace was getting a first-class lecture from Yuliya on the history of the monastery from an artistic point of view. Kevin was entertaining Yelena, Tamar, and Amin who were beyond delighted with the giant of a man. He had presented the Arafat children with an autographed basketball which he set spinning on his fingertip! With a little help from Manny, they had strung up a net in a tree. Amin was now perched on Kevin's shoulders. The slam dunk was inevitable!

Jake's phone call prompted Manny and Grace to go back inside to join Ruth and Rachel. Grace explained that they were indeed having serious conversations about moving to the United States.

"There are advantages to living in a small land," said Ruth. "It really isn't that far from the Tel Aviv airport to our home here at the monastery. We can fly back and forth to see our son and his family."

"That's true," said Manny. "But the issue is—do you just want to visit on occasion or do you really want to be part of their everyday lives? And what sort of life do you want—the threat of war or some semblance of peace. I think Grace and I wonder if more peace can be found in the States than here in Israel. But we realize we would be leaving behind centuries of family history. It won't be an easy decision."

"May I ask you, Mr. and Mrs. Cohen . . ." began Rachel.

"Please call us Manny and Grace."

Rachel smiled and continued, "Manny and Grace, I would really like to speak with you further about our future in Israel. This will greatly affect the lives of my children and their future."

"Of course! We can come here to the monastery easily enough, but we would be glad to have you visit and even stay with us at the compound in Tel Aviv. A few days at the beach would be nice for the children, don't you think? And we can send a car for you," promised Grace.

"And how would you like to see a basketball game!" beamed Manny. "My Maccabi Elite team is playing in the finals. We've made the second round of the playoffs! You've met my new star, Kevin! The kids would love it!"

"Once a basketball fanatic, always a basketball fanatic! I can promise you front row seats—here and in Charlotte!" laughed Jake.

Manny agreed. "We may have some budding fans outside. Tamar and Amin are enjoying a pick-up game with All-Star and Olympian Kevin Love!"

CHAPTER SIXTY

DINNER WITH GRAYSON

ART, GRACE, AND GRAYSON had planned a short rendezvous at the Caesarea Maritima dig site for late Sunday afternoon. Grace was driving Manny's new BMW; boycotting German cars is a thing of the past. "Here we are!" cried Art as he and Grace peered down into yet another trench. "What's down in the hole?"

"It's a retaining wall of some sort, maybe a household wall. It's lonely here now that the Asbury students are gone. So I'm glad you could meet me this afternoon. I didn't think I would get to properly say goodbye to you before you went home," said Grayson as Art gave him a hand up out of the trench.

"Do you really think I would leave without saying goodbye? Show us around one more time, and then we'll take you out for dinner. We can drop you back here later."

Grayson's smile got wider and wider, and he said, "Really? I am starving. It's a good thing I keep clean clothes on site."

After a quick tour, Grayson headed to the trailer and came back wearing a nice sport shirt and khakis.

"You clean up reasonably well," said Grace.

"For a former hippie dude," added Art.

"Let's have some fun," said Grace, as she cranked up the Tears for Fears road song, "Everybody Wants to Rule the World."

Grace deftly drove south on Highway 2 toward Natanya where she pulled into the parking lot of Aqua Marine, her favorite restaurant, which featured the best in fresh-caught seafood. An amazing jellyfish tank rose up from the center of the restaurant. It was hard not to be mesmerized by the undulating forms.[1]

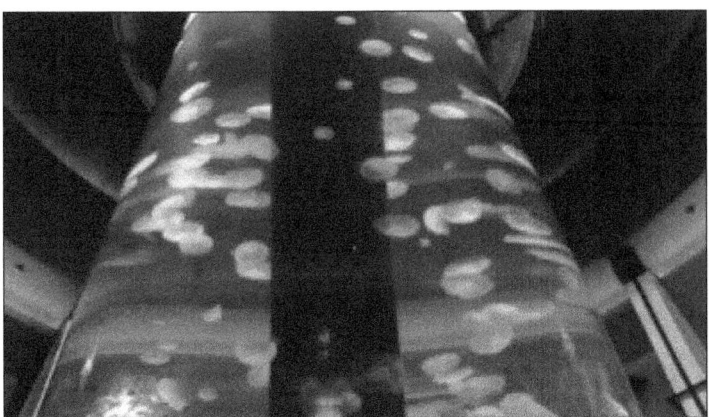

The evening began with toasts to Grayson's archaeological success. They reminisced about good times in Jerusalem, at Caesarea Philippi and elsewhere. There were inside jokes and anecdotes that only the three of them would enjoy, and there was wonderful food. Grayson wolfed down a seafood platter and was having a thoroughly good time.

Finally at the end of the dinner, Art said, "Grayson, I hope you know that Grace and I are very proud of you. You have done so well. So don't get discouraged by recent events in Israel. I think archaeology will go on as usual and I know the IAA is very pleased with your work. What do you see in the future?"

"I'm dreaming of finding the library of Eusebius," laughed Grayson as he saw the surprised faces of Grace and Art. "Really! It could happen! But right now, I want to stay with the IAA. I think I can continue to be a very good dig manager and liaison with international teams that want to work here."

"Works for me!" agreed Art. "But if you're not careful you'll be buried in your work if you get my drift."

Just then the waiters arrived with a cake decorated as an archaeological dig with frosting gridlines, graham cracker walls, trenches cut deep revealing the chocolate cake, and miniature shovels made of marzipan. On the cake was written: "Your Lifework is in Ruins—But Your Life is Not!"

---

1. This jellyfish tank is featured in Coba Cocina, a restaurant in Lexington, KY

Grayson was overwhelmed and said, "I don't know whether to eat it or frame it! As my Momma used to say—'This takes the cake!'"

"Let's eat!" said Grace who had secretly arranged for this special cake. "Art is right—there's more to life than work. Manny and I have both learned this lesson the hard way. For you and your work, the cake says it all!"

"I know I need to make more friends. What do you think of Yuliya?" said Grayson cautiously.

"I thought you were interested in Sarah at Solomon's Porch!" said Grace cocking her head with a slightly confused look. "At Art's wedding last year, I really got the impression you wanted to date her. And Sarah has hinted as much to me."

"We are good friends and I think it will stay that way. But she is Jewish and divorced. We share common geography, but we don't share common interests. And I doubt Sarah is interested in converting to Christianity!"

"Yuliya is a remarkably talented girl, committed to her Christian faith and to her work in antiquities and art. She has been good for Yelena."

"So it's obvious that we share common interests but not common geography. I want both! And for that matter, how did you and Marissa put the two together?" said Grayson putting Art on the hot seat.

"I like to think we are proof that it can be done! But trying to balance our two very different backgrounds has taken a couple of years of hard work. It hasn't been easy. And to be truthful, Marissa is the one who has given up much to become my wife and mother to our future child. Living in the United States—away from Turkey and her family—is a big sacrifice."

"And what about you and Manny?" asked Grayson.

"It was a long road for us too. We certainly shared geography, but our lifestyles couldn't have been more different. Manny has come to enjoy visiting archaeological sites; I've come to love basketball! And now we have Yelena—our new common denominator!"

"So the moral of the story is—keep an open mind and let God [nodding at Art] or Yahweh [nodding at Grace] lead the way!" smiled Grayson.

"Exactly!" said Grace and Art simultaneously.

CHAPTER SIXTY-ONE

ON FURTHER REVIEW

THE PROBLEM WITH ATTEMPTING to find a connection between contemporary events and biblical prophecy is that again and again the attempts prove to be wrong. And the people that make those foolish connections are eventually labeled fools.

Jamison Parkes Law was a true Zionistic but he didn't want to be labeled a fool. He had always supported the US backing of Israel because he believed that Israel had a God-given right to the whole of the Holy Land. And he had always believed that Israel's leaders were spokesmen for Yahweh just as in biblical times. For Parkes, "God Bless America" also meant, "God Bless Israel!"

But doubts were seeping into his organization. Members of his Millennial Dawn Society were beginning to suspect that the current secular state of Israel is not biblical Israel! The recent decision by Prime Minister Netanyahu to publicly execute the Jewish man who blew up the Temple Mount and to help the Muslims rebuild their Islamic shrines made no sense to his followers. How could prophecy be fulfilled by rebuilding the Dome of the Rock? Deep down, the Society members were beginning to come to a disconcerting realization that blind support for Israel's current governmental actions might not be biblical after all.

"I've been reading about *Yesh Din*," said Stevie Howard. "Their people are former high-ranking Israelis who advocate for the rights of Palestinians! They're saying the land in the West Bank was illegally taken from the Palestinians and given to Israelis without compensation. No wonder Hamas can get recruits!"

"I just read Sandy Tolan's *The Lemon Tree*. It's a true story of two families, one Palestinian and one Jewish, who owned the same home. To be honest, it really makes you realize that there are two sides to every story," said Graham Forbes a bit sheepishly.

"I've read the book, too!" said a surprised Smith Davidson with a side glance to his boss. "I guess I didn't want anyone to know I was having doubts about the way the Palestinians are being treated. We've all been to Bethlehem. We've all seen the Separation Wall. How can we turn a blind eye to what's going on around here?"

Parkes Law was amazed. He had no idea that people in his own ranks were beginning to get this uncomfortable with the whole Zionist movement. "Hey, you guys! Don't forget all the Holocaust survivors who immigrated to Israel after World War II. They deserve to be back in their sanctuary, their homeland!"

"Yeah, but what about justice for the Palestinians who were expelled from their land—they've lived here for generations! They've lost land that was legally theirs! And now the Separation Wall! Whole towns of Palestinians are virtually imprisoned behind those walls! Those folks have lost their livelihood—their jobs—everything! Most Palestinians are peaceful people. Many are even Christians like us!" exclaimed Smith.

"To say nothing of the Gaza Strip—that is essentially a giant prison," added Graham Forbes, finally having the courage to jump in.

"Yeah, but they aren't all peaceful. Keep in mind all the bombings by Hamas. The Israelis say they are just protecting themselves by building the wall," said Parkes sternly to his members.

"But what about all the bombings by the Israelis? Lobbing bombs back and forth won't bring peace!" said Graham more boldly.

The whole mood of the society meeting was suddenly changing. Parkes Law felt it was out of control. "Let's keep focused everyone! We're supposed to be about the end-times. We're supposed to be looking forward to Christ's return—in our lifetime!"

"Maybe not that soon," said Taylor solemnly. "Finding signs of the end times is becoming harder and harder. So boss, maybe we are wasting our time in Jerusalem?"

"No, my friends, because I'm convinced when Jesus returns, he will return right here and enter Jerusalem through the Golden Gate. Remember the Creeds: 'He will come again in glory to judge the living and the dead, and his kingdom will have no end! We look for the resurrection of the dead and the life of the world to come!'" said Parkes rallying his troops.

The mood brightened considerably as each pondered the meaning of the words in the Nicene Creed. Smith broke the reverie, however. "But I have to admit that I just don't understand Netanyahu's plan. Why would he publicly shame an orthodox Jew who thought he was furthering the cause? Is he now going to work with the Muslims, especially the Palestinian Muslims? Is the Hawk becoming a Dove? In other words, where is all this going? And what does this mean biblically?"

Parkes suggested, "We all know that no one wants war with the Arab World. They outnumber everyone. The Muslims have control of the Temple Mount for a reason. For all Netanyahu's hawkish ways, even he doesn't want to provoke a war by violently ending Muslim control on their holy hill. But now, he seems more willing to work with the Palestinians. But let's also be clear that he's not going soft on terrorism—the hanging proved that. Radical tactics by Hamas won't be tolerated. But maybe he'll work to improve relations with the Palestinians to avoid terrorism on both sides."

Taylor chimed in at this point. "Whatever else we may say, perhaps the bombing of the Temple Mount and the hanging of Sharansky should teach us not to make absolute pronouncements about the timing of the rapture."

"I reluctantly agree," said Parkes. "I think this also means that we need to redouble our efforts to understand both prophecy and contemporary events. Right now, it does not look like the situation is pointing to an imminent Second Coming. Indeed, it could even be a long way off especially if things get all peaceful around here for some years."

This discussion carried on for some time. Some of the younger members of the Society who had only been in Israel a few weeks began wondering if they should go back home to the States. Maybe the camera pointed at the Golden Gate was not going to show them anything of importance any time soon. Clearly, a crisis of confidence was happening to the Millennial Dawn Society, and it was dawning on them that maybe they had been wrong about how biblical prophecy should be read.

"So, let's plan to start over with a review of the apocalyptic prophecies in Daniel. Let's get out our multi-colored charts, and see if we can figure out where we went wrong in regard to this series of events," said Law.

"Sounds like a plan," said a glum Smith Davidson.

"Sure" said Taylor Bowles without any enthusiasm. Sometime when major events occur, they don't confirm your confident preconceived notions about how God works.

CHAPTER SIXTY-TWO

YELENA'S REQUEST

Yelena was grateful that the Cohen's rescued her from the orphanage, especially now that Ukraine had descended into civil war with pro-Russian zealots. But Grace and Manny Cohen were both Type A personalities—each with life agendas and very strong opinions. So far Yelena had not really been able to get a word in edgewise as far as their future as a family. She was sure that ultimately, she would have little say in the final decision. Yelena knew that her parents loved her, and were trying to include her in "adult" decisions. Still, she was conflicted. She really wasn't sure what she wanted—which is probably true of most teenagers.

Grace had to come into town today for meetings at Hebrew University. Yelena was old enough to be in the city by herself. She roamed through the market and decided to stop by Hannah's antique shop.

The doorbell jingled as always and Yelena felt right at home among the somewhat musty antiquities. Hannah was delighted to see her.

"Yelena! Come on in and visit a moment with Samuel!" Over cookies and milk in the back kitchen, Yelena played quietly with Samuel but Hannah knew she had something deep on her mind.

Finally, Hannah asked, "Is everything all right? How are your folks?"

"They're fine. You were with my Mom at the hanging weren't you? Was it horrible? Why did you go?"

"Well, I think we went because deep down I knew it was such an historic event. It's hard to explain, but when you live in the shadow of the Temple Mount as I do, it becomes a part of your soul. Losing it was like losing a loved one—like losing my father. Seeing that man die was closure—like seeing my father buried. It's complicated really. Have you talked to your mother or Grayson? I'm sure they have a different perspective."

"No, Mom doesn't seem to want to talk about the hanging right now. Plus, Mom and Dad are in a tizzy about whether to stay here in Israel or move. Now that your father is dead, what are you going to do—stay or leave?"

"I've been mulling this over for a long time. I'm staying. I love my life here and I know I can carry on with the shop. I've been keeping the books for years. Financially, I'm set. But there's more to life than money. I want to do something with a purpose. So I'm keeping the shop and hiring assistants. But I will probably get a place to live outside the city. Samuel needs fresh air and sunshine and green plants to grow and appreciate the world Allah has given us."

"That sounds good to me. If we leave, I would miss you—even if you are Muslim!"

"Thanks, Yelena. I understand what you're trying to say. We all get along because we respect each other's beliefs. I want Samuel to learn that."

"Thanks for the cookies and milk. I'm supposed to go to Solomon's Porch and wait there for Mom to pick me up."

Yelena continued her wandering until she arrived on Ben Yehuda Street. By lunchtime, Solomon's Porch was filling up with customers. She watched them come and go for a while and wondered if any of them were even affected by the bombing and hanging. It didn't seem like they were—life just went on. She slipped into a free booth inside the deli and gave her caramel macchiato order to Martha the waitress. Within minutes, the sweet drink was brought to her by Sarah who instantly noticed that Yelena was not smiling.

"Hi, Yelena. Your Mom said you would be coming by. Why so pensive?"

"Everyone is just eating lunch like nothing ever happened. Will things change here at all?"

"Deep questions for this time of day," smiled Sarah as she slipped into the seat across from Hannah. "It may seem on the outside that nothing has changed, but I can assure you it has. You see I go from table to table—I talk to people—many have known me for years. They talk to me—like a patron to a bartender. And people are talking about what happened. And they are asking about how it will affect their lives. And, more importantly, they are talking about being more tolerant of other people's views.

They are starting to realize that you can't force people to accept beliefs. Sharansky believed that bombing the Temple Mount would force everyone to reclaim the Mount solely for Judaism. That didn't happen. In fact, our

Prime Minister is seriously reconsidering his rigid positions and beginning to realize that we all have to work together to solve our problems. I'm optimistic. I think things will change for the better!"

"Then we can stay!" announced Yelena.

"Oh, I get it. You think your parents want to leave because they believe nothing will change—or maybe things will just get worse. Well, it's possible. They worry more about you. I don't have children, so maybe it's different for me."

"Hannah has a son, and she is staying at the shop. I just came from there. She's not running away!"

"And your folks wouldn't be 'running away' either. I don't think they make decisions that are fear-based. For you and your family, maybe moving would be a good idea—a great opportunity! But again, it's different for everyone."

"Right now, Mom just seems to be afraid of life here in Israel. Dad seems to be calmer about everything."

"Maybe he's just being patient," suggested Sarah.

"You're staying, right?"

"Yes, I'm happy here. I have my friends and my Jewish community. As you know, I'm divorced. My husband was a soldier and becoming very radical in his thinking. He scared me! Actually, I am going to talk to him soon about how recent events have affected him. If he has softened his anti-Palestinian views . . ." Sarah's voice trailed off. Her divorce still saddened her.

A group of musicians set up their instruments outside the coffee shop. Sarah waved to them. "What do you think of our *klezmer* music, Yelena" asked Sarah, changing the subject.

"I'm not too sure what it is. But it sounds like some of the Ukrainian folk music I heard as a child."

"That makes sense. It's Ashkenazi Jewish music. The Ashkenazi are Jews who settled in Europe, especially Germany and France, centuries ago. They eventually spread into the Slavic lands. They speak Yiddish which is written in Hebrew but isn't the same as modern-day Hebrew. Anyway, *klezmer* means 'instrument of song' and refers as much to the musician as to the music itself. Anyway, people seem to love it and it's good for business!"

"Yeah, it's kind of toe-tapping music!" laughed Yelena for the first time since she came into the shop. Then she got quiet again. "I wonder where we will end up. I mean they are talking about Boston! Really! Boston! Isn't that where the bombing was? At the Boston Marathon! How can that be better than living in the Promised Land? Nope, I've got to convince Mom and Dad that I want to stay here."

Sarah smiled. "So, what you really want to know is how to talk to your folks so that they not merely listen but seriously consider your request to stay here."

"Right! I just knew you would understand—totally, completely—that's what I want. I want my voice to be heard!"

"Okay, the lunch crowd should clear out soon, and your Mom should be here around two o'clock. So I'll make sure you have a quiet spot on the second floor to talk. Just remember one thing. You can have a say, but you can never have the final vote. That right comes with adulthood and parenthood. Those are the ground rules. Got it?"

"Got it! But I will make my case," promised Yelena.

"Meanwhile, just chill out here with your iced macchiato." Yelena headed upstairs to enjoy her drink and read a magazine. She looked out on the street below, teaming as it was with Jewish life—robust, effervescent, fun, loud, vigorous. She longed to be a part of this, a part of the only country where Jews had their own land. It would not be the same in America. She watched the orthodox Jews walking down the street and looking askance at McDonalds. There used to be regular protests there until a Kosher option menu became available. After what seemed only minutes, Grace appeared with drink in hand and set down her briefcase of papers on the seat next to her.

"I trust you've had a busy day, "said Grace.

Yelena smiled and said, "I've been busy talking to Hannah and Sarah, and now I want to talk to you! I've been doing some thinking."

"Always a good thing," said Grace.

"I've been thinking I really do not want to move to the United States!"

There was silence. Dead silence. Grace was contemplating this pronouncement and gauging how to respond. "And why would that be? You'd be safer there."

"Maybe, but they have bombings and shootings and . . . But anyway that's not the main issue. I think we should make decisions for positive reasons, and my positive reasons for wanting to stay are that not only do I like it here, but as a Jew, I feel like I belong here. I want to grow up here. Whatever the problems in this land, it is the Promised Land, and we have a right to be here. We shouldn't make fear-based decisions. So, let me grow up in a truly Jewish environment! I promise I will work extra hard in school and attend synagogue with you, and all the usual stuff."

Grace was again silent. She rehearsed in her mind all the bad things she had seen happen in Israel, and knew that a choice to stay would be a calculated risk. But then, if her daughter could be brave, so could she, and besides Manny didn't really want to give up his home and basketball team. And, at least at the moment, Jerusalem was quiet—or at least stunned into silence.

Finally, after a deep breath Grace said, "Honey, I love you, and I realize there will be danger wherever we live. It seems like that is often true for Jews. So, I will take your wishes into consideration. Tonight we will have a heart-to-heart with your father. I think I can tell you that he's on your side. Your wish is not my command, you understand, but your speech has certainly swayed me. I'm proud of you! Of course, if war breaks out, we are outta here!"

"Gotcha! Sounds like a plan to me."

Right then Sarah showed up and quickly sized up the situation. She chimed in, "Where would I be if I lost two of my best customers here at Solomon's Porch?"

Grace just laughed and said, "You'd be just fine, judging from the line downstairs."

"It's been steady and busy today. But girlfriends, I would sure miss the two of you!"

"You can relax," said Yelena. "I don't think we are going anywhere anytime soon!"

CHAPTER SIXTY-THREE

HOME AND FAMILY

GOODBYES ARE HARD, ESPECIALLY when they mean, "I will not see you for a very long time." So it was with considerable sadness that Yelena, Grace, and Manny were helping Art and Marissa, Jake and Melody pack for the flight home. This time they were all on the same flight—first class no less.

Manny was reminding everyone about his big plan to take everyone to Turkey. "Are you all sure you can't spare another week?!"

"It still sounds like an idyllic vacation," said Marissa. "But I've got a baby to deliver—and it's going to be in North Carolina for sure."

"We'll take that trip someday!" promised Manny.

Grace was still rehearsing in her mind the long conversation she, Manny, and Yelena had last night. With reluctance, Grace had to agree with Yelena and Manny that Israel would remain their home for now.

Art came over and gave Grace a big hug. "Why so glum, chum?"

"Well, I haven't told you that Yelena has convinced us to stay here, at least for now. So we will not be moving to the other side of the pond, unless war breaks out. Deep down, I know it's what Yelena and Manny both want, so I'm taking one for the team."

Just then Marissa came up and gave Grace a sideways hug. "Baby's making a racket today. Another two months of this and I'll be worn out."

Yelena suddenly said, "Hey, Mom, you keep saying you want to go to the States. How about you and I visiting after the baby arrives!"

Marissa answered, "That's a good idea! Before school starts next fall you should come on over. Yelena has never been to the States, and I'll bet you'll find North Carolina a bit quieter than the northeast."

"Amen to that," said Melody while dragging a suitcase into the living room. "Can someone explain why my suitcase seems so much heavier than it was before?"

"It's all those packs of Ahava cream you bought for your family. And I know you have other surprise gifts for them," said Jake, as he tickled Melody, making her jump and yelp.

"The biggest surprise gift will be our baby news! I haven't told them yet!"

"It's true folks. Melody wanted to tell everyone face-to-face," explained Jake.

Manny opened the front door. "Our driver is here with the big van. Let's load up!"

After another round of hugs and promises of reunions, the four travelers headed to the Tel Aviv Airport for their flights back to New York and then Charlotte. Yelena disappeared into her room to text her friends.

Manny and Grace stood looking out the door long after the van had disappeared up the road.

"Somehow, I think we'll see those folks again," said Grace with tearful sigh.

≈ ≈ ≈

Two Months Later

"I'm coming honey, I'm coming," said Art, running around his new house in Chapel Hill. It was sunrise in late July and the birds were chirping in the pine trees around the house. Art and Marissa's cat, Archie (as in archaeology), was howling for breakfast. Marissa's water had broken an hour ago.

Art ran upstairs to grab the small suitcase that had been packed for the last two weeks. When he flew out the front door, Marissa was already wedging herself into the seat sideways.

Art arrived at the driver's side of his Carolina blue Toyota Camry hybrid only to discover that he forgot his keys. Marissa just smiled and sighed.

Back in a flash, Art revved up the engine and headed down Rosemary Street straight to the Medical Center.

"My baby's having a baby!" Art shouted out the window to nobody in particular.

"Close the windows!" ordered Marissa. "My hair is getting all mussed up."

Marissa got checked in and escorted to the birthing center.

Six hours later, the head of the baby crowned, and with a little help from the midwife, Art delivered his one and only first child.

"It's a girl with lots of dark curly hair," shouted Art.

The baby was gently laid on Marissa's now much flatter stomach and Art was allowed to cut the cord.

Then the baby was swept away to be checked, washed, and swaddled while the midwife tended to Marissa. Soon, the baby was brought back and Marissa was allowed to nurse her for the first time.

Finally, the midwife asked, "And what is the name of this little dark-haired beauty?"

Marissa said quietly, "Her name is Joy—just Joy."

Art chimed in. "That's right! Pure Joy. Nothing but Joy. I never thought I'd have a child this late in my life. God is so good!"

"And now I get to call the grandparents," said Art.

"Hello, Mom, guess what? We have a baby girl! And her name is Joy!"

THE END

AUTHORS' FINAL NOTES

1. Our family and friends play prominently in all the novels, albeit with name changes. So far no one has complained! They are the good guys! We don't know any bad guys!

2. The grave of Eusebius has not been found. But it is certainly possible. Excavations continue in and around Caesarea Maritima.

3. We have never been inside the Monastery of St. George although visitors are allowed. We, like most, have only sat and viewed the amazing complex from across the deep valley.

4. The discussions about Muslim burials, Israel's use of capital punishment, the building and effects of the current Separation Wall, and archaeological problems related to the Temple Mount are factual to the best of our knowledge.

5. All sites described in the novel are ones that we have personally visited and enjoyed. This includes the Nazareth Village and other areas in the Galilee, Jericho and Bethlehem, the Allenby Bridge, Caesarea Maritima, and Jerusalem. In 2014, our group wound its way through Hezekiah's Tunnel. Ben has the T-shirt to prove it!

6. Maccabi Tel Aviv (aka Maccabi Electra) is a professional basketball club based in Tel Aviv, Israel. The team also plays in the Euroleague. Kevin Love is a well-known American basketball player—but we doubt he's ever been offered a chance to play with Maccabi Tel Aviv!

7. In truth, Israel's Mossad and Jordan's GID were used in the story in name only—we did not try to represent their normal operating procedures. This is also true for the Israeli Court System. To move the

story line along, Sharanky's trial took three days. Adolf Eichmann's trial lasted at least a year.

8. Finally, threats to the Temple Mount are very real. The following excerpts are from a *Haaretz* article published July 24, 2004. http://www.haaretz.com/news/yatom-jews-nearly-succeeded-in-1984-temple-mt-bomb-plot-1.129418

"Likud MK Ehud Yatom, who as a former Shin Bet official was one of the commanders of the operation to seize the members of the 'Jewish Underground' terror group, said Sunday that the group was 'very close' to carrying out a planned multiple bombing against Muslim holy sites on the Temple Mount in 1984. Yatom was responding to a statement by Public Security Minister Tzachi Hanegbi, who confirmed Saturday that the security establishment had identified rising intent among current right-wing extremists to carry out a Temple Mount attack to derail Israel's planned withdrawal from the Gaza Strip. Security sources have said possible actions included an attempt to crash a drone packed with explosives on the Temple Mount, or a manned suicide attack with a light aircraft during mass Muslim worship on the Mount. Other possibilities include an attempt by right-wing extremists to assassinate a prominent Temple Mount Muslim leader, perhaps from the Waqf Islamic trust. . . . Speaking on the Channel Two 'Meet the Press' program Saturday, Hanegbi said: 'There is no information about specific individuals, because the Shin Bet and police would not let them continue [with their plot]. But there are troubling indications of purposeful thinking, and not detached philosophy. . . . There is a danger that [extremists] would make use of the most explosive site, in the hope that a chain reaction would bring about the destruction of the peace process. Yatom, a member of the hawkish wing of the Likud and a strong opponent of the disengagement plan, said that in the wake of warnings by Hanegbi and the Shin Bet of potential Jewish extremist activity, 'I am indeed fearful, and I do not wish to return to those terrible, tense days of 1980–84 in which the Jewish Underground was active with its wicked plans, may the Almighty protest us from them.' Had an attack succeeded twenty years ago or in the current period, the effect would have been similar, and 'horrible, terrible,' he said. 'It would have meant the entire Muslim world against the state of Israel and against the Western world, a war of religions,' Yatom said. 'With all of their pain and suffering, today's terrorist attacks would be nothing compared to what could happen—even World War III.' . . . According to Hanegbi, 'We sense that the level of threat to the Temple Mount from the standpoint of extreme and fanatic Jewish elements carrying out a terrorist attack in order to reshuffle the cards, to serve as a catalyst to a change in the entire political initiative—this level has risen in recent months and more so in recent weeks, more than at any time in the past. Saturday's disclosures about possible Temple Mount terror plans were preceded in recent months by a number of troubling indications. Nine months ago a suspect in a Jewish underground terror group affair, Shahar Dvir-Zeliger, told authorities a prominent West Bank settler activist had planned a Temple Mount attack. Zeliger cited two other names of West Bank settlers, suggesting the two were involved in the Temple Mount attack conspiracy. Last Thursday, the Temple Mount Faithful group petitioned the High Court, asking to be given clearance to go up to the Holy Site for prayers later this week for Tisha B'Av.'"

9. The Society of the Millennial Dawn is fictitious but there are plenty of groups especially in the United States that espouse Zionism and search the scriptures and news reports for signs of the end times. We do not support their agendas.